Truths and Lies

Truths and Lies

Willow Hill Book 3

Bretta Elaine

Paperback: 979-8-9887720-8-8

Ebook: 979-8-9887720-7-1

Edited and Proofread by Brooklyn, Brazen Heart Books

Cover Design by Acacia of Ever After Cover Design

Bloomburgh

Anger Management
Now or Never (coming soon)

Willow Hill

Cherry
The Relationship Bargain

Before You Read

Content Warning

Truths and Lies is a steamy contemporary romance that features the death of a parent (off page), family secrets that include adoption, strong language, mental health disorders such as anxiety and bipolar disorder, strong language, and explicit sexual content.

For modification or steamy spoilers please see the *dick-tionary* located in the back of the book.

To anyone who is brave enough to dip their <u>toes</u> into unknown waters.

IYKYK…If you don't you will soon.

Chapter One

Griffin

B ile burns the back of my throat as I splash water on my face, trying and failing to ignore the searing pain in the middle of my chest. The cool water trickles down my neck as my nausea subsides.

I can't fucking believe I'm here again.

Bloodshot eyes stare back at me from the dimly lit bathroom mirror as I grip the cool porcelain sink.

I can do this. I *have* to do this.

Standing up straight, I run my fingers through my hair, brushing it back behind my ears before straightening my tie.

With one last deep breath, I open the door and walk out.

My brother Brenden is leaning up against the wall directly across from the bathroom.

Sadness radiates from his usually mischievous eyes as he lifts a brow. "Ready?"

"Does it matter?" I ask, not bothering to hide how I would rather be anywhere else than here.

Pinning me with a blank stare, he claps me on the back. "That's the spirit."

We amble down the hall just in time to find people trickling in. Their black clothing harmoniously blending with the somber music echoing from the front of the church.

Five days ago, my life changed. My mom, the woman who raised me into the man I am, passed away after her long battle with kidney disease.

And today is the day my brother and I will put her into the grave beside our father.

In black suits and ties, Brenden and I match perfectly. The sad expressions on our faces are identical too. The picture of sons in mourning.

We made it to the church early, per Bren's request.

If I had my way, we would've arrived at the last minute and been the first people out of here.

But no, apparently, when you lose one of the most important—if not *the* most important—people in your life, society forces you to console others. Letting them touch you and tell you they're sorry, all to make themselves feel better.

I practically begged Bren to let me skip, but as the new leader of our family of now two, he refused to let me out of it.

So I play the part of the dutiful son and brother. I do it for our mother, but also for him. If he needs me to go along with this bullshit, I will. I'll do anything for him.

We stand at the front of the room, shaking hand after hand. Sympathetic smiles and sorrow-filled eyes all blend as I thank person after person until my mother's favorite pastor, Ethan, signals that he's ready to begin. It's weird that my mother, a nonreligious woman, would have a favorite pastor or even a funeral in a church, but Ethan is the son of her hairdresser she had gone to since he was a baby, so even in death, she wanted to support the man she had watched grow.

In my front-row seat of the crowded pews, I fight the urge to flee as Pastor Ethan's voice raises over the sniffles. "Today, we are gathered to celebrate the life of Leslie Henderson, a wife, mother, and friend..."

He drones about humanity and the loss of life, but I try to drown it out.

I don't want to think about this anymore or cry in a room full of people waiting to see me break. Little do they know, I've spent the last five days crying more tears than I probably have in the past twenty years. And the only person to witness that breakdown was Bren himself, whose emotions mirrored mine.

If they came for a show, they were going to be disappointed.

Because today, we both sit stone-faced. The loss might be shown by our lack of usually smiling faces. But other than that, we let nothing pass.

My eyes burn as I will the tears not to come. With a glance at my brother, I'm shocked to find he's struggling far more than I am. His jaw quivers before he locks it, taking a deep breath.

Reaching out, I capture his forearm and give it a quick squeeze. *You okay?* I mouth.

With a glance, he gives me a look that's a mixture of annoyance and hurt that screams "What the fuck do you think?"

I snort, turning back to Ethan as he rattles on about life and death. I try to focus on him, on his words, but my gaze strays to the one place I don't want it to go.

The casket. The flowers strewn across it making the symbol of death look beautiful.

The mahogany shines in the church's light like it isn't a beacon for Bren's and my sadness and heartbreak.

It's a twin to our father's. His death wasn't long and drawn-out like Mom's. It was a car accident that broke us three years ago. I don't know which is worse, having someone you love be taken from you suddenly or watching them suffer for months on end, knowing what was coming.

I don't want to think about my mother's body lying in the dark locked box adorned for everyone to gawk at.

I don't want to think about how my biggest champion is being put into the ground today.

I don't want to think about the shell of a son she left behind.

Snapping my eyes shut, I squeeze them as hard as possible to bury the emotions threatening to spill out.

Not here. Not now.

Later. I can give in to the pain later.

My body trembles as I hold back the war of emotions fighting to break free from me. Brenden clamps his hand down on my mine, gripping me until I relax.

I expect my brother to pull away, but he holds my hand, giving me a gentle, reassuring squeeze every few minutes.

His hand and presence are the only things keeping me here at this point. If it weren't for Bren, I would be out the fucking door. Mom wouldn't have cared for her kids' grief on display.

By the end of the service, my hand is practically numb from Bren's iron grip.

The two of us are quickly ushered to stand at the massive oak door at the front of the church. Once again, people—the majority strangers to my brother and me—form a line, readying themselves to shake hands and offer their love for our mother.

Person after person steps up to us.

With every handshake, I count down until I can leave.

There are only a few people left, thank fuck. Between the two of us, it should only take a couple more minutes.

I look up to find Bren stuck speaking with the pastor.

Fuck, so it's all on me.

I continue doing my torturous duty until I hit the last of the sympathy wishers: two women. One around my age, who is stunning, and if we weren't at my mom's funeral, I would probably make a move. The other woman is probably in her late forties and must have been a friend of my mom's. The younger of the two steps up, giving me the same sad smile I've gotten all day. "I'm sorry for your loss." Her voice is warm and comforting, like honey.

"Thank you," I say, turning to the other woman. Her gaze is already locked on me, traveling up and down my face like she's studying it.

Ten seconds pass without a word. The woman merely stares at me.

I shift on my feet, looking at the younger woman again. Her eyebrows narrow as she stares at the other woman. "Bel," she scolds.

"Oh, I'm sorry," the woman says, blinking at me.

"It's okay," I say, trying to calm the nervousness radiating off her in droves.

"You're just like I always imagined you would be." She reaches out to grab my hand.

"I'm sorry, what?"

Her lips lift in a big smile. "I'm your mother, Griffin. Not Leslie."

An icy chill rolls down my spine as confusion assaults me, and I peel my hand away from her. "Excuse me?"

"It's okay. It will all be better now."

Is this some sort of joke?

No one would be so cruel as to prank someone on the day of their mother's funeral, would they?

My lips part as I look at this woman, who is clearly having some sort of psychotic break in front of me.

Her smile falters. "I'm your real mother," the woman says again, as if she thinks I didn't hear her the first time. She reaches to grab me again, and I twist out of her way.

Her chin trembles as she glances from me to her friend, as if waiting for someone to back her up. But silence is all she gets. Then, without another word, she flees out the door.

Stunned, I stand there silently.

Apparently, her friend is as well because she just stands beside me, staring at the entrance where her friend had fled.

She looks at me, eyes wide. "I'm so sorry. I—I had no idea she was going to do this." She rushes away, turning back one more time. The shock and horror mimicking what I feel as she repeats, "I'm so sorry."

Her chestnut curls flow behind her as she speeds out the door and down the church's steps.

It takes me a few moments before I start after them. I'm not sure why I follow, but I do. The idea of speaking to that lunatic ever again has my heart pounding and sends a sick, sinking feeling rippling through my stomach. But I can't let this go.

Chapter Two

Audra

Shit. Shit. Shit.

That's all I can think while I watch this delicious man's face fall. His already somber expression turns into one of confusion and pain. This should not be happening right now. It's not the time or the place. And I definitely shouldn't be objectifying someone at a funeral.

Shit.

"I'm your real mother," Belinda repeats as he leans back, eyes widening as if she physically struck him.

What in the actual fuck is happening?

There is no way my best friend of five years thought this was a good plan.

There is no way my best friend of five years has an adult son and didn't tell me.

Apparently, his lack of words and body language don't clue my Bel in that this is not going well, because Belinda being, well, *Belinda*—aka the worst person at reading the room—she reaches out to touch him.

With a swift yank of his arm away from her, she stops. Her hand shakes as she retracts it back to her side. Her mouth opens, only to close as her lips purse for a moment before her chin quivers.

She looks at me, eyelids rimming with tears, before she spins around, running out the door, leaving me and the stranger to watch her leave in horror.

We stay like that for a moment. Eyes plastered on the door Belinda just made her escape from.

Slowly, I lift my gaze to his face.

His heartbroken expression is leaking every emotion possible. Shock, horror, sorrow...

"I'm so sorry. I—I had no idea she was going to do this," I say, unsure of how to make this better besides leaving. Nearly tripping over my feet, I hurry to the door before turning back to him. "I'm so sorry."

I'm not sure my feet have ever moved as quickly as they do to get me out of that funeral. My hair whips in front of my face, making me miss my old pixie cut. *Fuck these responsible, give-me-a-business-loan brown locks.* I haul ass to my little black Camry, parked catty-corner to the church. Thankful that Belinda is in the passenger seat already.

"What the fuck, Bel?" I ask, hopping in the car.

Her face is pale, almost green, as she stares at her hands fidgeting in her lap.

"Belinda." My voice is harsh, but at the moment, I don't care about being gentle with her. "What did you just do?"

She glares at me with tears in her eyes before bringing her gaze back to her hands. "What I had to... I just wanted to see him. Make sure he was okay."

"Well, he isn't. And now he probably never will be," I say, not caring that my best friend is breaking in front of me. What she just did goes beyond friendship, understanding, and support.

"I know," she sobs. "I just couldn't help it. I had to tell him."

"At a funeral? His *mother's* funeral?"

"She wasn't his mother... I am," she says in a hushed tone.

"No you're not. That woman he is about to put in the ground was his mother. And you just hurt him, most likely beyond repair."

My words cause her to cry uncontrollably. And a pang of guilt stabs my heart for being so harsh.

I scrub a hand down my face before starting my car, looking around the street to see if I'm clear to pull out. And that's when I see him. His eyes latch on to mine, and the sorrow is overwhelming. I mouth yet another apology to him before driving away.

"Fuck, Bel, I wish you would have talked with me about this beforehand."

She wipes her hand under her nose. "I knew you would try to talk me out of it."

"You're damn straight, I would have."

"I just—I had to tell him."

I sigh, braking at a stop sign. "I understand that... But you fucked up."

With another whimper, she sobs again. I feel for her, I do. But I feel more for the man whose life and memories she just ruined.

I pull up in front of her house and cut the engine. "Do you want me to stay? We could get some ice cream or maybe wash the day away with whiskey?"

She sniffles. "I think I just want to be alone right now."

"You sure?"

"Yeah," she says, opening the car door. "I'll call you later."

I wait for her to enter her house, still unsure if leaving is the right move. But she said she wanted to be alone. And I get it, I really do.

I can't imagine how she's feeling. Embarrassed? Hurt? Probably both.

But I'm still not sure what she was expecting from the situation. Hell, I'm still in shock about every single part of it. From the fact that Bel has a son—a drop-dead gorgeous *adult* son—to the fact that she released the bio-mom bomb at his mother's funeral.

Belinda has been one of my closest friends for going on five years. Five. *Years*. I knew she had a past she didn't talk about, but I never thought it was anything like this.

There are so many questions I want and need answers to. But I know now is not the time.

Now is the time to get a shot of something strong to help purge my brain of this day. And the fact that Bel knows every dark secret about me, but she doesn't trust me enough to tell me she had a kid when she was—fuck, based on his looks, I would place him at anywhere between twenty-eight and thirty-three. Bel must have been a child herself when she had him.

I park my car at my apartment, then grab my purse and trek a few streets over to my favorite bar. The warm air and scent of stale beer and greasy onion rings blast away the icy chill from outside as I slink out of my coat and wave at the bartender, Wyatt, a handsome middle-aged man who I'm pretty sure owns this hidden gem. Ordering a shot of tequila, I slide onto a barstool, then down the glass before signaling for another.

Wyatt gives me a look of concern but says nothing as I shake my head. He nods, walking off to leave me to replay the earlier nightmare over and over in my head.

How did I miss the signs of what was going to happen?

Bel had been fidgety all morning before the funeral, but I figured it was her way of dealing with her own mortality and all the other heavy thoughts death can bring around. I never thought it was a secret-child bomb about to detonate.

I think back to how she fixated on how she looked, changing three times and reapplying her lipstick just as many. It should have been an eye-opener that she was nervous, not sad. But I was so wrapped up in thoughts of the most recent string of texts from my ex, Nick—or Dr. Bubble Butt, as Bel and I refer to him any time we are in public.

Nick

I've been thinking about you lately.

I miss you.

Want to get coffee and talk about us?

Nick and I have been an on-again, off-again thing for the past nine months, but two months ago, I called it off. For good this time. Not needing his pompous, perfect ass in my life anymore.

We met at a local university event that my family's florist shop was working. Nick was a charming PhD with a body that looked like it was built for sin. And trust me, it was. We'd hit it off right away, and I fell quick for his charm.

But I wasn't the only one who had. He'd been dating two other women, claiming we never had the exclusivity talk. Needless to say, we broke up. Well, for the first time. After about a week, he came back, saying he ended it with the others, and I was the only one for him. And I took him back like the dumbass I am.

One day, months and a few breakups later, I was giving him the most intense blow job of his life when he marked me with his *seed*, as his haughty ass would say.

He didn't do the decent thing and ask me if it was okay.

He didn't direct his aim toward my chest.

No, the motherfucker shot his load all over my face, including my eye. Yeah, that burned like a bitch. I was pissed, so I did what any rational, classy woman would do. I yelled at him until my lungs gave out. That breakup lasted about a month before we found ourselves back together.

But of course, in my usual messed-up relationship fashion, I was thrown yet another curve ball. I started having vision problems in my left eye. After a few doctor visits, some steroids and tests later, come to find out I had chlamydia... of the eye.

Of the freaking eye.

Chlamydia... in my precious eye.

Yeah, I was embarrassed beyond words. But I found them when I saw Nick later that week after my antibiotic treatment had finished and my precious eyeball was one hundred percent normal again.

That was the end. The last straw.

Especially after he tried to accuse me of being the one to give it to him.

Yeah, so at the funeral, all I could think about was how I could've gone blind because of that dickhole and if chlamydia could kill someone. If so, how fast? Could Nick have been my cause of death? I was still mulling it over when Bel went up to the deceased's son and dropped the most world-shattering secret into his lap.

Chapter Three

Griffin

What in the fuck just happened? After the woman claiming to be my "real" mother bolted and her just-as-stunned accomplice apologized, I couldn't help but watch them drive away in confusion.

Well, confusion and anger.

How dare this woman walk into my mother's funeral and spit out claims like that?

The day I bury my mother should have been about her.

About her beautiful life ending too soon.

About the painful hole her absence is going to leave in everyone's hearts.

But instead, I'm thinking about this crazy woman and how it cannot be true.

My mother was amazing. She was everything a child could hope for. Hell, she put TV moms to shame. She was always there for me. Even as I became an adult, her job didn't end. It just shifted. No longer was she trying to rear me into a good man. She knew she had done that. So she became a confidant. Someone to help guide me further in my goal. A shoulder for me to cry on at times. Without her, I'm going to be lost. She was my compass, always helping me find my way.

But now, instead of cherishing every memory I have of her, I'm replaying them, wondering if it's true. Is it possible that she wasn't my biological mother? All my life, I had heard how we looked just alike. With our dark brown, gold-flecked eyes and hair to match. And I saw it too. I was her twin in so many ways. And to think that might not be the truth is heart-wrenching.

If she wasn't my biological mother, why wouldn't she tell me? She was always open and honest about everything. Sometimes to the point it was unbearable. So why wouldn't she tell me this?

I must have been standing outside of the church for a while because I startle as a warm hand clasps on my shoulder.

"What the fuck are you doing out here?" Brenden asks, blowing into his hands. "I feel my balls already receding into my body as we speak."

Blinking away the shock, I swallow down the lump in my throat. "I—There was a woman—"

"There's always gonna be a woman, but right now, it's time," he says, his voice falling into a somber tone I'm not used to hearing from him.

I nod, following him to the limo parked around the corner, ready for us to begin the funeral procession to the cemetery to lay our mother to rest.

We don't speak to each other for the rest of the funeral, only responding when someone talks to us, wishing us condolences or offering their support. Other than that, we stay side by side in silence. Both knowing what the other is thinking or feeling.

Well, not exactly. On top of my pain for my mother is a new confusion and weariness surrounding the crazy woman's words from the church.

"What the fuck are you doing?" Brenden asks, scaring the shit out of me.

I've spent the past two days scouring my mom and dad's photos and files, hoping I won't find anything that gives that woman's claims any truth. And I haven't.

I should be thankful for that, but I have this nagging feeling like I'm missing something. Like a seed of doubt has been planted that I can't shake.

I glance up from my spot on the floor of my parents' office to find Bren leaning against the doorframe, and I feel like I've been taken back in time. From this angle, Bren looks like a giant—though he practically is one. I sit at a pretty six feet tall, while Bren is a whopping six foot five. The man is enormous and has a way of shrinking me back down to his scrawny little brother in an instant. "Just organizing Mom's files, making sure we didn't miss anything important," I say, refusing to look him in the eye.

"Really?" His tone drips with skepticism.

"Yep."

"'Cause from here, it looks like you are searching for something and making a gigantic mess while doing it."

When I don't respond, he steps into the room, crouching beside me. "Griff, what the hell is going on?"

I scrub my hands over my face. Not wanting to tell him. Not wanting to give this crazy idea life.

"Please," he begs, his voice soft with concern.

"At Mom's funeral, a woman approached me..."

"Okay... A lot of women approached us. She had a shit ton of friends. You are going to have to give me more than that."

I take a deep breath. "The woman said she was my mother. Not Mom."

I expect him to laugh or deny it. But he doesn't do either.

Instead, he falls silent, his face paling.

"No," I whisper.

"Griff, I—"

"Stop. I need a minute."

He nods and leaves the room with a hand covering his mouth.

Saliva fills my mouth as nausea hits with the force of a semitruck. I bolt to the bathroom and empty my stomach into the toilet as my entire body shakes. My breathing becomes erratic. Wiping my mouth, I brace myself against the tub. With my head in my hands, I try to stop my racing heart.

Fuck.

Everything is falling apart around me.

I inhale a deep, long breath through my nose, holding it in my expanded lungs for a few seconds before exhaling, then repeat until the muscle pounding in my chest is back to a normal rhythm. The trembling that was racking my body is now only present in my hands.

As much as I hate to admit it, I need to know more.

It takes me twenty minutes before I work up the nerve to talk with him. I find him in the living room, sitting on the couch with his hands clasped together in front of his face, almost as if he's praying. It's an odd sight to see. My big brother, a solid rock of man, rattled.

Brenden has always been a strong shoulder to lean on. No problem is too much for him. His composure is something I'm used to and admire. So seeing him like this has the hair on my arms standing up and anxiety coursing through my veins.

I take a seat beside him, not saying a single word.

He inhales sharply, waiting a beat before saying, "I was never supposed to be the one to tell you." His head tilts, and he looks at me. "This was Mom and Dad's job. And trust me, if I could, I would kill them both for keeping this from you."

"So, it's true... Mom wasn't my biological mother?" Even though his previous reaction and shaky breaths have already answered the question, I'm nervous for him to say it. I don't want it to be true. I don't want my whole life to be built on a lie. Not just a small lie, either; a part of my identity isn't true.

He nods, and a tear slips down my cheek. I didn't even realize I was on the verge of crying or that my emotions were that obvious. His hands find mine, and I look him in the eye. They shine with brown and gold specks—just like mine.

"Did Dad cheat on Mom with that woman?" I ask, not waiting for his response before I ask the other question burning in my mind. "Is Dad my—"

He shakes his head.

"What the fuck, Bren."

"I know, I know. I'm sorry. It changes nothing, though. You are still my baby brother, and we had the best mom and dad anyone could have asked for."

When I don't respond, his knee knocks into mine. "Okay?"

"Yeah, I know. I really do, but I'm so confused. Who are my birth parents?"

"All I know is that your father was Dad's younger brother, James."

"James? I thought he died right after high school." Knowing that my biological father is dead should have my stomach twisting with grief for what could have been, but instead, I feel nothing. Maybe it's because the two people who raised me—my *real* parents—are dead, and I only have so much grief to give. And their passing has taken it all.

"Yeah, well, right before he died, he had gotten his girlfriend pregnant, and she left you on our doorstep before running away the day after you were born."

"She left me on the doorstep? Like, legit left a baby outside, alone?"

"Yeah." He grimaces. "Or at least that's what I remember. I don't know a lot of the details. I was only, like, five when you were born. But from that first day, you were my brother."

I let out a breath. "I don't even know what to say."

"It's a lot to take in." He stands, heading toward the bookshelf along the wall. Reaching up to the fifth row, he pulls out a bottle of whiskey from behind the books. He twists the cap off, then takes a large swig before walking back to me with the bottle outstretched.

The moment the warm amber liquid touches the back of my throat, I have to fight off a choke from the burning. But I do, and then I take another drink.

"This is so fucked up," he says, taking the bottle back from me.

"You think?" I look up at him, wondering what in the hell else he knows.

"Are you mad?" He winces, closing his eyes while he waits for what he thinks is going to be my blowup.

"At you? Nah. At Mom and Dad? Yeah, I'm pissed they kept this from me. That they let me be blindsided by that woman." I want to yell at him in place of them, to take all my aggression toward them out on him. But I can't. He is all I have left. We are our only family now.

"Please, please don't let this change the way you think about them. Or your memory of them. Please, Griffin, don't let this take away from how great your life is."

I give him a curt nod, and he joins me on the couch again, where we spend the rest of the night discussing everything he knows regarding my birth parents and my adoption.

Chapter Four

Audra

"Bel, I swear if your stupid ass doesn't call me back in the next five minutes, I'm gonna—I'm gonna—" My mind blanks on threats. I've already used them all in my million other voicemails. So what's the point. "—I'm gonna call you again," I say truthfully before hanging up the phone.

It's been five days since I've heard from Belinda. The first couple of days, I wasn't concerned. It isn't unusual for Bel to disappear for a day or two when she gets into her feelings. But once I hit day three, my anxiety about the whole situation flared, and it continues to get worse every day she doesn't respond.

We both have a shift starting in thirty minutes at my parents' floral shop, and she will clock in, even if I have to drag her by her hair to make it happen.

The outside of her small yellow cottage is welcoming with her perfectly manicured grass and bushes. You'd think she takes great care and pride in her home, but that's not it. She's too scatterbrained to pay this much attention to detail. No, Bel isn't the brain or the brawn behind this lawn. This was all Jerry, her on- and off-again man friend.

Jerry is very persistent in his pursuit of Belinda. He's head over heels in love with her and has been since the day he saw her in the bank he works at. Bel was making a deposit, and the rest is history. Now he takes care of anything and everything she doesn't want to do, while Bel provides him with her fabulous company. Which seems like a very one-sided relationship, but who am I to judge.

Walking up the sidewalk and onto her porch, I brace myself for what I might find inside. She could be curled up in a ball of misery. Or passed out drunk on her floor. Anything could lie behind this door. And that... that scares me. The unknown of what could be going on with her. The unknown of how to fix this for her.

Steeling myself, I lift a fist and knock three times before waiting for the door to open. But it never does. After knocking again, I'm met with silence on the other end. I yell through the door but get nothing in response. My hands tremble as I search my purse for my spare key to her house. My fingers grasp around it as I yell out one more time.

"Belinda, I'm coming in."

Unlocking the door, I open it up, finding the house dark and spotless, not her usual whimsy of messy-things-strung-about-every-where style.

"Bel?" I call out to the silence. It feels wrong, all wrong. The house is normally full of a chaotic mixture of candle flames crackling and the mariachi music that Bel says reminds her of the time she lived in Mexico.

A wave of panic hits me as I continue to search the house, not finding her. In her bedroom, her dresser drawers are wide open, with clothes missing. Her bathroom is the same. Both her toothbrush and signature Russian red lipstick are missing as well.

Where did she go? I pull out my phone, trying to call her again. It rings two times before heading straight for voicemail.

"You've reached Bel's phone. I'm probably off on my next adventure or on my next glass of wine. Either way, leave me a message."

"Bel, where are you? I'm at your house. It's freaky clean and some of your things are gone. It's making me really worried. I—I know that stuff the other day had you shaken up, but you can talk to me. My reaction doesn't mean you can't talk to me. Please, Bel, let me know you are okay."

Lifting the phone from my face, I drop onto her bed. This is my fault. I was a shitty friend when she clearly needed me, and now she's run off without a word. And I can't blame her. I was mean when she was hurting. I didn't try hard enough to be there for her. She would have gone to the ends of the earth to be there for me, no matter what the situation was. No matter what she felt about it.

And me... I let her down.

Any other time, I would agree and say I deserve the cold shoulder, but this is more than that. Leaving without a word... this is giving me frostbite.

I don't know how long she's been gone or how long she plans to stay away, which isn't helping to prevent my concern from rising higher and higher.

Glancing at the clock, I grimace. *Shit.* I have ten minutes to make it to work and open up, or my mom will have my head.

Neon light illuminates the window as I flick the open sign from off to on, then unlock the door for customers. Behind the counter, I find a list of orders ready to be fulfilled. I get to work pulling the flowers from the fridge and arranging them to perfection. Order after order, I can't get Bel out of my mind, and it isn't because I'm doing the work of two people since she's MIA.

After three hours of nonstop arrangements, I finally take a break. And by break, I mean I go through my emails. One of which is a list of documents Bel and I need to bring to the bank for our meeting about a potential business loan. I check the list, noting I have all the items already gathered thanks to Cooper, my brother's best friend and my secret financial advisor. I just need to make sure Bel has everything ready as well.

Once I'm done making a note in my phone about gathering her documents with mine, I try Bel again with no luck. Fine, if she wants to be that way, I guess I'll have to go a different route. I scroll through my contacts, searching until I find a number I've never bothered to use before.

"Hello?" Jerry answers after one ring. Who only lets the phone ring once? Hell, I can't even find my phone until it rings at least three times. Not like I would answer it for a strange number, anyway.

"Hey, it's Audra."

"Audra? What's up?"

"Um, nothing. I was just wondering if you have spoken to Bel today?"

"Today, no. Why? What's wrong?"

"Nothing, I hope. I just haven't seen or spoken to her in a few days after we went to—" Suddenly, it hits me. I don't know how much Jerry knows about that day. About Belinda. "—the funeral."

"Ah, yeah, I talked to her that next day. She was pretty upset, which is normal when you lose someone."

"Yeah..." I pause, unsure if I should even ask, but screw it. This is important. *Bel* is important. "Did she say anything about taking a trip when you talked with her?"

"Belinda is an adult. She can go a few days without seeing or talking to a friend," he says, sounding more annoyed than anything.

"Yes, Jerry. I'm aware of that." I grit my teeth together. "But this isn't like her, and I'm concerned."

"Well, don't be. She is okay, nothing to worry about."

"Listen, I'm her best friend, and I know something is wrong."

"She's good. She wants space. So give it to her. Leave it alone, Audra," he says before hanging up on me.

I'm in shock and awe that Jerry, the nice guy who once rescued a turtle from being run over in the middle of traffic, would not only tell me what to do but also hang up on me.

And not only did I learn that Bel has skipped town, but that she also lied to Jerry about how she is, because there is zero fucking way that a woman who was just rejected by her adult biological child the first time she meets him would be okay. It's impossible, especially for Belinda.

Chapter Five

Griffin

Brenden and I spent more time together in the past two weeks than I think we have in the past six months. But I guess that's what happens when you go through a major life change. Mom's death still doesn't feel real. Not for me. And not for Brenden.

I think the only thing keeping us from completely breaking down is the fact that we have thrown ourselves into my biological history.

Our investigation serves two purposes. One is to find out more about who my biological parents are—who that woman is. And two, to take our minds off how we no longer have any parents. Our future children will never grow up knowing them. Knowing how our mom would sing us her favorite Prince songs when it would storm, not caring how inappropriate they might be. Or how our dad could tell us everything we could ever want to know about cars and how to fix them but couldn't stand teaching me or Bren to do it ourselves.

We don't acknowledge that we're doing this, but it hangs between us every day, with the threat of collapsing the walls we've created to protect us from our grief.

"Over here, Griff. I think I found something," Bren shouts from across the attic. We started going through all Mom and Dad's junk up here yesterday in hopes of not only finding a sliver of the truth about my parentage but also reminding us of the two people who raised us.

I find him kneeling on the floor, hands buried in a cardboard box labeled *Ray's high school shit.* I can't help but chuckle at it. It is completely and totally something our mom would do. She was always busting Dad's chops about his "glory days."

"What did you find?" I crouch beside him as he hands me a hardcover book. "Old yearbooks? I'm pretty sure looking at Dad in his prime isn't going to help us."

He scowls. "Look at the years, you little shit."

I glance down to find the years 1992–1993 in my hands. "Dad graduated in 1989."

"Damn, you are lucky you're pretty." He slaps me across the face with a chuckle. "Those aren't Dad's, they're Uncle James's."

My eyes widen as I open one up to find handwritten personal messages addressed to James inside. "No way."

"I bet you can find something about both him and the bio—lady in there."

We both agreed earlier this week not to use the term *mom* or *mother* regarding the funeral crasher. I didn't want to disrespect my mom like that, and Bren, being the brilliant, supportive brother that he is, agreed to follow my lead on the whole situation without question.

Downstairs, we set ourselves up with a couple beers and the yearbooks, because there is no way in hell we can do this sober.

Page after page, I find references to BJ, which I can only hope is Belinda and James's couple nickname and not a sexual thing.

"Hmm," Bren mumbles mid-sip of his beer. "Look at this pic right here."

I glance to where he's pointing, only to find a picture of a couple labeled *Senior class cutest couple, Belinda Peterson and James Henderson.*

It's her.

Funeral woman is Belinda Peterson.

They both look so young and happy, with their arms pulled tightly around each other as they are all smiles for the camera.

I used to think I looked just like my mom and dad, and in a way, I did. But looking at this picture of Belinda and James, I'm struck by how much of myself I see in both of them.

I have James's hair and nose, the same as his brother—my dad. But the dimples on Belinda's cheeks match mine. *I have her fucking dimples.* My heart speeds up with every similarity between us. It's beating so fast it hurts.

I rub the ache in my chest, trying to force the pain away.

"You look just like them." Bren's voice is quiet with hints of regret. "I'm sorry, Griff."

I swallow the lump in my throat with some beer. "It's okay. I guess we should have realized I would."

"Yeah, I guess. It's just that you've always been mini clones of our parents."

I laugh. "Apparently, we both saw what we wanted to."

"You okay?"

I shake my head. "No. I'm really not."

"You want to stop looking? You don't have to do any of this."

I scoff, "Sure I do."

"I'm serious. We can pretend this shitstorm never blew into our lives. It's up to you. I will follow your lead. Okay?"

"I don't know."

"Think about it. I just hate seeing you in so much pain."

I sniffle, using the back of my hand as a tissue.

"Shit, man, you're gonna make me cry again." He presses his fingers into his eyes as he gets up, walking up the stairs to his childhood bedroom.

I sit there looking at that picture of the two people I never knew about for the rest of the night, wondering what else of mine might be from them.

I think of all the things my mom and dad shared with me, talents and loves that I assumed were from them. But maybe they were from these other two strangers.

Fuck, it's weird knowing that every part of me is in question. From genetics to my taste in food.

I hate this. I hate wondering who I am. Who I come from. Especially since, until last week, I knew exactly how to answer those questions. And today I'm confused, without a fucking clue.

A pain in my side startles me awake to the sight of Brenden's hulking body standing above me, his left foot lifted, ready to strike.

"Did you fucking kick me?" I rub at my now sore ribs.

He crosses his arms over his chest. "Better question: did you really get so drunk last night you fell asleep on the floor in front of the stairs?"

"I don't know what you are talking about, asshole." I scrub my hand over my face, sitting up to find I'm indeed at the bottom of the staircase, next to what I can only hope is a puddle of beer on the floor.

"Yeah, want to try that again?"

My head pounds as I stand. "Can you take it down a few notches, *Dad*?"

"You best be glad I'm not Dad, because he would have whooped your ass and mine for letting you get so drunk you couldn't make it up the stairs."

"Yeah, yeah." I climb the stairs while fighting the urge to throw up.

By the time I make it to my childhood bedroom, I have a full case of the beer sweats and have no choice but to shower it off.

After toweling off and throwing on a fresh pair of sweats, I find Bren downstairs with a cup of coffee in one hand and his phone in the other. I fill up a cup for myself, taking a seat across from him at the kitchen table.

"There are biscuits in the oven if you want something to soak up all that alcohol." He gestures without taking his eyes off his phone.

I look to the oven, then back at him; the man is a mother hen even on his worst days. He is the best parts of our mother and father, and the more I study him, the more I see them in him. The spitting image of Dad when he was his age. And with all his kindness and nurturing, he is most definitely our mother's son.

He must sense my staring because he glances up, frowning. "What?"

"Nothing, it's just you are definitely their son."

He smiles for a moment before letting it fall. "Griff, so are you."

My head shakes. "Not like you. You are—"

"Stop. I can't stand this anymore, especially after finding you this morning."

Blow landed. I'm definitely on the verge of an identity crisis.

Fine. Not on the verge... I'm one thousand percent in the middle of a crisis, but I don't know what the man expects. It's a lot to take in normally. But finding out at your mother's funeral adds an extra layer of trauma that I can't brush off with a laugh. "Brenden, what do you want me to do? I can't just stop thinking about it 'cause you or I want it."

He sighs. "I know that. Which is why I think you need to face the problem."

"Huh? I thought that's what we've been doing?"

His face falls even further. "No, I mean, I think you should confront the source."

"You don't mean...?"

He nods. "Belinda. I think until you speak with her and get the truth, you are going to continue to be this mess of a human being that is mourning not only his mother's death but the death of who you thought you were."

I swallow. "I'm not sure I can do it."

"You can, trust me. You're stronger than you think."

"How do you know?"

The corner of his mouth curls into a smile. "Because you were raised by Mom and Dad."

"I don't even know how to find her."

"I can handle that for you." He shakes his head. "You always forget that I'm no longer a beat cop, don't you? Finding stuff out is what I do for a living."

"It's not that." That's not completely true. I forget he is a detective pretty much all the time, but in all fairness, he isn't the type of person you'd think would be a cop. "If you could have just detectived the information this whole time, why haven't you?"

"Detectived the information?" He laughs. "Because it wasn't my place to do so without your permission."

I raise my eyebrows in question.

"It would have violated your privacy."

This time, it's my turn to laugh. "Since when do you give two shits about privacy, especially mine? I seem to remember you showing everyone my browser history in high school to embarrass the shit out of me."

"In my defense, it's not my fault you googled some hilarious stuff like *What age does my penis stop growing?* And that was different. *This* is different. We are all we have left. I won't ever do anything to ruin our relationship."

"Damn it, Bren." I sniffle. "Stop with the heartfelt speeches."

"Whatever. You want me to do it or not?"

I hesitate for a moment. "Do it."

Chapter Six

It's been almost two weeks without a word from Bel. My nerves are fried with worry for her. I keep switching back and forth from feeling apologetic to pissed every time I think of her.

How could she do this? Disappear and worry me like this without a single word. Leaving our business plans hanging in the balance. It is infuriating.

During the first week of her absence, even though I was seething, I covered for her with our boss, aka my mom.

"Belinda is grieving the loss of a family member" is what I told her the first week, and she accepted the answer but was still upset that Belinda hadn't bothered to call in herself.

This week, though, is a different story.

"Audra, where is she?" my mom asks as she struts from the office into the front of the shop where I'm arranging a bouquet to be delivered to a very lucky woman that I now call my sister-in-law. She really won the lottery when it comes to partners. My brother Nate is absolutely obsessed with her and showing his love. The man sends her a new bouquet every week just because.

"Who?" I ask, playing dumb as I rethink the color scheme Nate gave. I mean, yellows and blues only? Come on, man, way to stifle a sister's creativity.

"Don't play dumb, dear. It's unbecoming," she says, stopping directly in front of my worktable.

"Unbecoming," I repeat in my impression of a hoity-toity, rich woman's voice. "Heaven forbid."

She crosses her arms, signaling she isn't in the mood for my shit today.

"She's sick, Mom. So overwhelmed by her grief that she let her guard down, and now a stomach bug has taken root inside her intestines, making her wish she was dead herself." I internally cringe at my insensitivity to the recently deceased.

But apparently, that answer doesn't fly.

"Cut the shit, Audra. I was already over Belinda's antics, but this—this is the final straw. Since she can't be bothered to call me herself, you can inform her the next time you speak with her, she is no longer employed at Fisher Floral."

Delia Fisher is no fool.

I want to argue for Bel, but it's useless.

My mom isn't her biggest fan.

She did this to herself.

She did this to *me*... How am I supposed to count on her as a friend and as a business partner—if she is ghosting me as well?

For the millionth time since she took off, I can't help but think about how this is going to affect our plans. We were so fucking close to hitting our goal.

We have been saving for years now, hoping to open up our own floral preservation store.

But with Bel up and disappearing, so did my dreams.

Sighing, I set the flowers down, my self-pity making it hard to create something beautiful that will brighten another's day. "I understand."

"I'm sorry. I know she's your best friend, but we can't keep an unreliable employee." She steps around the table to give me a one-arm hug. "Is this the arrangement Nate ordered for Vivian?"

I wince. "Ugly, isn't it?"

She hisses her agreement. "You'd think such a creative man would have a better eye for color."

"I think he's choosing sentimentality over beauty with this one."

She snaps a quick picture to text my dad to make fun of my brother before leaving me to finish the monstrosity.

I try to admire my work, snapping a picture for my brother to ask if they are what he envisioned, but as I pull up my pictures to add it to our thread, I see the picture I had taken a few days before the funeral. Bel and I thrifting new clubbing outfits with the aim of making them granny chic. Hers featured a hand-embroidered school-themed vest with no top under it. Mine was a little girl's Sunday school dress with a lace collar that barely hit my thighs. We had the time of our lives. My chest aches as I let myself miss her.

After sending the picture to my brother, I get a quick thumbs-up of his approval before exiting the thread and trying Bel's number again.

The bitch sends me straight to voicemail, which is nothing new. Every time I've tried to reach her this week, it's been the same. Either her phone is off, or she's a backstabber who has blocked my number. I assume it's the latter, but I'm not willing to rule out anything at this moment.

So I try Jerry again.

Audra

Any news?

Jerry

Just leave her alone, Audra. She clearly doesn't want to talk.

Audra

Could you at least tell her I'm sorry? And that I'm getting worried?

Jerry

I would, but she isn't taking my calls.

Audra

WHAT?!

Jerry

Calm down. She told me she was turning off her phone the moment she made it to the coziest place in the north, so no need to panic.

But I do panic. I can't help it as it slices through me as the realization hits. Bel skipped town. I have no clue where she is, and we have a meeting for a business loan coming up in a few weeks.

Holy shit.

If she doesn't come back soon, we're screwed.

This only solidifies my need to find her. I need to figure out what the hell is going through that mind of hers.

In between customers, I spend the next few hours trying to research where she might have gone. With "coziest place in the north" in my search engine, I have a list of options that won't stop growing.

"Welcome to Fisher Floral," I call out after the bell above the door chimes.

I don't bother looking up, my eyes glued to my list of potential places.

"Hi, I'm looking for a Belinda Peterson," a deep voice says from behind me.

I lift my head, only to come face-to-face with a mouthwatering man. I check him out for a good ten seconds before I realize who he is: funeral guy. The man whose life Bel threw a bomb into.

My mind short-circuits as I search for something to say.

No longer dressed in a dark suit of mourning, he has my brain glitching on just how ridiculously handsome he is. Sure, he was noticeably attractive in his black suit and tie, but that was a funeral, not a time to ogle. But today, in jeans and a thick coat, is a different story, and damn, he's mouthwatering.

The kindness fades from his face as the recognition hits him. "You."

"Me?" I squeak out.

His jaw tics as he looks me over with disdain. Uncomfortable under his scrutiny, I fidget with my apron pockets.

"Where is she?" he asks.

My heart speeds up as he stares me down with his fists flexing at his sides. Crossing my arms over my chest, I say, "She isn't here."

"Where is she?" he repeats.

"Why?" I ask, the need to defend her stirring in the pit of my stomach because I can't imagine he has come to embrace his long-lost mother.

"I don't have time for this. Do you know where she is or not?" he asks through clenched teeth. He clearly doesn't like me. I can't blame him, though. I was with her that day, so I'm sure he has me lumped into that horrible moment with her forever etched in his mind.

"I'm not telling you anything when you look like you're going to hurt her."

He blinks as if my words offend him. Uncurling his hands, he relaxes his body. "I'm not going to hurt her. I just need to speak with her," he says in a softer, reassuring tone.

I take a step closer to the counter between us. "Again, I ask why? What she did was wrong. So why would you want to see her or even speak to her after that?"

"That's none of your business."

"Well, you see, I kind of think it is, since I have been involved in this shit show somehow."

"Look, I don't want to talk about this with you. Fuck, I don't even want to talk to her, but I need to. Okay? So can you please just tell me where I can find her?"

"What's your name?" I ask, stepping up to the counter.

He lets out a huff of air before answering, "Griffin. Griffin Henderson."

I jut out my hand at him. "Audra Fisher. Daughter of Miles and Delia Fisher, sister to Nate Fisher, and auntie to the cutest Fisher of us all, Evelyn."

He reluctantly places his hand in mine. The warmth from his skin radiates up my arm as the rough edges of his fingers graze my palm.

With a shiver, I realize his hand is still in mine after what feels like an awkward and inappropriate amount of time. I let go, dropping his hand and bringing mine back to my side to wipe my now sweaty palm on my apron.

"Okay, Audra, now that you know my name and I know your entire family tree, are you going to help me or not?"

I shake my head. "I don't know where she is. Haven't seen or spoken to her since the fu—" I stop myself from finishing, not wanting to poke the bear. "Well, since that day."

His jaw tics again. "I thought she worked here."

I give him a small smile. "Emphasis on the word *worked*. She hasn't shown up or called in, in two weeks."

He lets out a growl of frustration. "Great, just fucking great," he says, turning back toward the door.

"Look, I'm sure you have your reasons for wanting to talk to her as much as I do. I mean, Belinda is my best friend, and this whole situation was nothing I ever saw coming." I take a note card from the jar and jot down my phone number. "Will you call me if you find her? I'm really worried."

He sighs, looking at my hand and back at me. "I don't think I'm going to be much help to you. All the information I was given was this place and her home address."

"Well then, why don't you give me your number so I can call you if I find anything out?"

His eyebrows draw together. "Why would you do that?"

"Because I can only imagine what you're going through... And if talking to Bel is what you need right now... Then I will do what I can to help."

He stands there staring at me for a few moments before nodding and taking the outstretched paper from my hands. Pocketing my number, he grabs the pen from in front of me and a card from the jar, writing his number. He slides it across the counter without another word before stalking over to the door and leaving.

The moment he is out the door, my body hums with relief and excitement.

Griffin Henderson.

I can't believe Bel has a son.

I mean, I knew this.

I learned all this two weeks ago.

But to have him come here in search of her is something else. It makes it all real.

And might I just say *damn*!

He is something else.

Something hot as hell, but also a little dark.

If this were any other situation, I would want to climb him like a tree, wrapping my legs around him tightly until I could feel every part of him against me.

But no, this is not the time.

For one, I have sworn off men ever since Nick and his lying-bastard ways.

And two, this person came out of my best friend.

He came out of her.

The fruit of her loins.

I can't. I couldn't. I *wouldn't*. But maybe... No, I won't touch the attractive man with mommy issues.

A shiver runs up my spine at the thought. It doesn't seem possible. I mean, Bel is so young, and he is so, so... delicious.

Stop it, Audra. You are being horny. You need to be concerned about your best friend's safety, not about your best friend's mouthwateringly hot son.

The day dwindles as customers come in every so often, asking for an arrangement for their loved ones and significant others, while I can't help thinking about Bel and Griffin. Wondering how I'm going to find her. If I should share what I know with him—if Bel would want me to.

Needing to get out of my head, I escape to Brew It, my favorite dive bar, to see my favorite bartender.

Should I be frequenting a bar so much that I have a favorite bartender? Eh, that's questionable. But let's just say that life has been more than a little boring without my crazy bestie by my side. So boozy, regrettably, is the new Audra until further notice.

With my ass hugging the barstool, Wyatt slides me what I can only assume is whiskey based on the noxious smell coming from the glass.

I raise my eyebrows in question.

"You need it. Trust your friendly neighborhood bartender. We know everything," he says, giving me a quick smirk while he wipes the counters clean.

I take a swig, only to immediately regret it when the burn causes me to cough. "Damn it, Wyatt." I pound on my chest. "Why did I trust you?"

"Fuck if I know. I'm just your bartender, not your mother."

My eyes water while I wait for the burning to subside. "Wyatt, I don't know what to do."

"About?"

"I can't say... Well, I could, but it isn't for me to tell. You know?"

He opens his mouth and blinks. "How on motherfucking earth would anyone know what you meant?"

A laugh slips from my lips. "Ugh," I groan. "Everything is a mess, and I'm afraid I'm just going to make it worse."

"Take another drink."

"I can honestly say that I don't think alcohol is the answer to my problems."

He shrugs. "Probably not, but at least you will feel better for a while."

With a snort, I smile at my glass. "Bottoms up," I say to no one in particular as I swallow the rest of the amber liquid in one gulp. This time, the whiskey melts down my throat with no complaint.

Overplayed dad rock streams through the speakers, and I catch myself bobbing along to the beat as Wyatt pours glass after glass for the other customers. He laughs and jokes with everyone as if he knows them. Maybe he does. Either way, it doesn't matter. What matters is that it makes me feel a mixture of jealousy and sadness.

I have other friends. There's my brother, Viv, Sutton, and Cooper. Sure, those people are technically family, but that counts. Sort of.

I have loads of friends... I just can't think of them all right now.

Hell, Wyatt counts as a friend. Okay, perhaps I only see or talk to him when I'm paying, but we still gab like two teenage girls in the bathroom between classes, so I consider that a tally in the friend collum.

But Bel's disappearance and the guilt from the last time I spoke with her has left a gaping hole in my chest.

And the need to make it right is driving me crazy.

I know what I need to do—find Bel and apologize. But most of all, I need to bring her the one thing—the one person—who might be able to help.

Griffin.

Chapter Seven

Griffin

I don't know what I was expecting when I went to the flower shop Belinda worked at. Or hell, when I went to her home.

Both times, I found myself relieved and disappointed that she wasn't there.

I don't know what I would have said or done if she had been. Bren and I rehearsed a speech, writing everything I wanted to say and know. Going over and over the information until I had it memorized. But the moment I got to her house or the shop, I blanked. And thankfully, she wasn't there to witness my epic fumble.

What I didn't expect was to see the pretty brunette again.

Or for her to be apologetic.

That day at Mom's funeral, she seemed just as shocked as I was by her friend's outburst, but she was still with her. She's obviously close with the woman who claims to have given me life, and that alone makes her someone to be wary of in my book.

But she shared my desperation to find her. Which means we have a common goal. And maybe we can help each other.

I'm considering asking Brenden to do a little more detective work for me, but I feel like that would be pushing it. He already did a basic background check for me. Nothing that would break the rules, but I feel like asking him to get her cell phone records would be a little too much.

So I wait. And wait.

And fucking *wait*.

Even though it's only been a couple of days, I had hoped that Audra would have called me by now with some sort of update. But with every passing hour that I don't hear from her, I fall deeper into a pit of despair.

I need to stop my pity party and try to be productive. Use all these bottled-up emotions for something good.

I head to my studio first thing in the morning. That's a lie. The first thing I did was fuel up on caffeine. I would be useless without it.

Nervous energy surges through me, or maybe it's the giant Monster energy drink; either way, my keys tremble in my hands as I unlock the doors. It's been weeks since I've stepped foot in my sanctuary.

The moment we found out Mom was in her final days, I dropped everything, and the smell wafting from within tells me that includes some now-rotten food.

Flicking on the lights, I find the source of the smell, a half-eaten breakfast burrito from my favorite food truck. I tear through the space, picking up any other lingering food and drinks, then take out the trash before lighting a scented candle to help cover up the stench freshly ingrained in my nostrils.

With my mess gone, I'm ready to let the music heal me. Ready to let my favorite thing, my passion, and career help me forget about the misery that has been my life.

I wait for inspiration to strike, my fingers poised over the strings of my guitar.

But nothing happens.

Not a flicker of notes or lyrics to be found in my officially useless brain.

Even recording the instrumental tracks I had previously prepared doesn't bring me the sliver of joy I had hoped for.

No, my mind continues to think of my mom and the woman who has made me question everything I knew.

Days pass like this. Me sitting in my studio, the place that is normally my sanctuary, feeling so lost. Bren pops in and out during the day. Bringing me lunch and my favorite fountain drink from the gas station by the police precinct because he knows their carbonation hits the spot like no other.

It's Wednesday night, and I'm busy staring at the small crack in the exposed-brick wall on one side of my studio, wondering if time had created that crack or if it was man-made. Or maybe the stone has always been slightly damaged like that?

I'm about to google if one should repair cracks in brick walls when my phone lights up with an unknown number.

I debate answering or letting it go to voicemail.

In the end, my mind can't handle the itching curiosity.

"Hello."

"Griffin? Hey, it's Audra from—well, you know."

"I sure do," I seethe, even though her voice is full of nerves. It's an asshole move to treat her like this, but she's friends with Belinda—a woman who ruined my mom's funeral. If you can be friends with someone like that, chances are, you're most likely just like that too.

So yeah, I think I'll stick with the dick act. It's the best way to get the whole situation done and over with.

A pause of silence stretches on the line before she continues, "Okay, well, I was wondering if you would be willing to meet up and discuss some information I might have on Bel."

"Or you can just tell me now."

"I'd rather speak in person."

"Well, I'd rather not speak at all, but here we are."

She huffs. "You know what, never mind." And then the line goes dead.

Fuck. Fuck. Fuck.

I toss my phone on the couch. I can't believe she hung up on me. The *nerve* of that woman.

Ugh, as if I was just going to meet up with her. What does she take me for, some kind of desperate fool?

But I *am* a desperate fool. Desperate to finish this damn Belinda business ASAP.

I tug at the hair on my scalp.

"Fuck. Fuck. Fuck," I mutter to myself while picking up my phone to call her back.

"What?" she asks after only letting the phone ring once.

"I'll do it. Where do you want to meet?" I grit my teeth, attempting to keep my anger at bay.

"Brew It, downtown. Be there in thirty if you want the information. Or don't, I don't care."

"Fine." That's all I manage to get out before she hangs up again.

When I arrive at the run-down hole-in-the-wall bar, I'm surprised to see so many people there... On a Wednesday night.

Honestly, to see this many people here in general.

The moment I walk in, the stale aroma of beer, cigarettes, and body odor hits me. The place looks and smells like it's been open for thirty years and subsequently hasn't been properly cleaned in that long.

I don't even have to scan the crowd to find her. My eyes immediately shoot to her. As if on instinct, I just knew exactly where she was.

Alone in the back of the room, with her back pressed against a small booth, she's twirling a glass between her hands. Her shoulder-length hair twisted into a knot at the top of her skull, flopping with every head tilt. She looks like a perfectly nice woman. From this distance, you would never know that she's besties with a soul-sucking hag.

I stop by the bar before going to her because the only way I'll be able to handle any of this is with the help of alcohol.

With a beer in my hand, I slide into the booth across from her. She instantly smiles with warmth before turning her face into a scowl.

"I forgot I'm mad at you," Audra says, folding her arms across her chest.

I fight the urge to smile at the crinkles on her forehead.

"Look," I say, leaning my forearms on the table. "I was a jerk on the phone earlier, and I'm sorry."

"I think *jerk* is putting it lightly." She snorts, refusing to look at me.

"Okay, fine, I was an asshole."

"A giant one."

I nod. "Okay, now that—"

She cuts me off, leaning into the table. "Oh, I'm not done. You are a giant, gaping asshole of a person who just ate a ton of Taco Bell."

I frown at her, my jaw grinding with annoyance. "That seems like an extreme and unnecessary visual. Are you done now?"

"Yes." She smiles. "Yes, I am—for now."

"Okay, good. So, Belinda…"

She circles a finger around the rim of her glass, then tilts her head to the side and sighs. "I still haven't heard from her—"

"Then why am I here?"

"If you would listen for more than a second, I would tell you."

I toss my hands up in surrender. "The floor is yours, Fisher."

"It's Audra."

Fighting to keep my anger in check, I suck in air through my teeth. "Well, I like Fisher better."

She groans, taking a sip of the clear liquid in front of her. I assume it's water, but who knows? She might be into drinking hard in the middle of the week. No judgment—to each their own—but still, it would be pretty crazy for her to be drinking a glass of vodka.

"Well, I prefer Audra, and it's my name, so." She recrosses her arms, leaning back into the booth. "Anyway, the last time her sort-of boyfriend, Jerry, spoke with her, she said she was 'almost to the coziest place in the north.'"

A throbbing pressure forms behind my eyes. *Great. Just great.* This conversation is giving me a tension headache.

Lightly massaging my temples, I ask, "Okay, how does that beyond-vague answer help us?"

"I don't think it was vague. I think it was a slogan for wherever she was heading."

"A slogan?" I pull out my phone, typing *The coziest place in the north* into the search engine. Dozens upon dozens of results pop up. "This is no help. There are too many places."

"See, I thought that same thing. Then I took my knowledge of Bel and used it to narrow it down to these three places."

I'm skeptical, and by the smug look on her face, she knows it. "You narrowed it down that much just by knowing her? I don't get it."

"You bet your tight ass I did. I used everything I know about her likes and dislikes, narrowing it to these three. I'm pretty confident we will find her in one of these places."

I'm going to pretend I didn't hear that tight-ass comment because now is not the time for my ego to preen for a pretty woman.

"What do you mean 'we will find her'?"

She tilts her head to the side, then gestures between us. "I mean me and you teaming up to find her."

"No, no. No. That's not happening."

"Why not? You want to find her. I want to find her. We might as well do it together."

"There is no way in hell I'm going on a road trip with a complete stranger to find the woman who is claiming to be my biological mother. That shit isn't happening."

"Fine. Well, good luck finding her without me. I'm sure you know all about what kind of place she would stay at, the fake names she would use, or anything else that might be helpful."

I scrub my hand over my jaw. Shit. She has me there. I know nothing about this woman other than she likes to pop into funerals and tell secrets that should have been buried with the dead. "I'll think about it."

She smiles. "Okay, when do you want to go?"

"I just said I would think about it. Not yes, let's plan it out."

She rolls her eyes, scooting out of the booth to stand. "Well, I have already informed my employer that I'm sick with the flu as of today and won't be in until I'm one hundred percent. So get to thinking."

I watch her walk away as I drink the rest of the contents from my bottle.

Am I really going to do this?

Go on a road trip with a stranger to find another fucking stranger?

My life is turning into one big joke.

Bone-chilling night air whips my hair around my face with each passing mile I drive back to my parents' house. The fresh winter air helping to clear my head as I go back and forth on what the hell I should do. Could I actually do it? Join a complete stranger on a road trip in search of a crazy woman?

I don't bother with music. There's no point. Ever since Mom's funeral, it all falls flat. My inspiration is shot. When I sit down and try to write or play, nothing happens. It's like all the creativity has been sucked from my soul, dying the moment my world was turned upside down. And it's all her fault.

Belinda.

By the time I put my Tahoe in park in my parents' driveway, all the heat has been leached from my body, leaving my skin with an ice-cold burning sensation, but my mind is made up.

I'm going to do it.

Not only to get the answers I so desperately need and deserve, but to get my creativity back.

Inside the house, I take the stairs two at a time up to my room, the one my mother had kept the same since I was in college. I can't help but to stop and stare at the pictures on the wall of us as a family.

Everyone smiling and hugging, a picture-perfect family.

A lie.

I hate that my mind is falling into that dark path of resentment.

The questions that keep popping up, the memories that are now tainted.

The uncertainty weighs on me, every day growing a little heavier than before. And I'm not sure how much strength I have left in me.

Lying down in my bed, I look at my shelves of action figures. I count them repeatedly, trying to clear my thoughts, or at least shift from my parents' lie. But I can't; no matter how many times I count them, I still find myself wrapped up in the whys of it all.

Why did Belinda tell me?

Why at my mother's funeral?

Why did she give me up?

Why didn't my parents ever tell me?

My eyes grow heavy, and I know what I have to do—what I'm going to do. Now the only question is, will this make or break me?

I roll over, grab my phone off my nightstand, and send one text. Two words.

Griffin

I'm in.

Chapter Eight

Audra

I may have walked out of the bar looking confident in the ultimatum I had thrown at Griffin. But in reality, I was shaking with anxiety that I hoped didn't show.

So I did what any rational woman would do when her emotions were spilling out of her: I drank my feelings and had a dance party of one.

Dancing around my apartment at two in the morning might seem weird to the average onlooker, but to me, dance is cathartic, fun, and, most importantly, a distraction.

Spin after spin, the anxiety flees my body, leaving behind a trail of sweat in its wake.

My phone buzzes, the incoming text interrupting the sweet musical styling of the cast of *Chicago*—the movie soundtrack, not the Broadway production. What can I say, I'm a sucker for both feminine rage and Catherine Zeta.

Picking up my phone, I'm cautious, knowing that at this time of night, a text could only be one of two things: a booty call or an emergency.

I'm in.

I squeal in delight, clutching my phone to my chest as I pirouette across my living room.

Fuck yes, I did the impossible. I got the hot, moody man to agree to my half-assed plan. Take that, BuzzFeed. Apparently, I'm a natural-born leader.

I text him back quickly before he has the chance to change his mind.

We leave tomorrow at 10.

Then I send him my address, followed by the gate code to my apartment complex.

Maybe I shouldn't have sent that information to a practical stranger.

Eh, I'll be fine. It's not like he's a psychopath or anything.

Well, he *could* be. How does one know if someone is a psycho?

Pulling up Google, I type in *How to tell if a hot stranger is a psycho?*

I'm soon so deep in a rabbit hole, I fear I may never look at anyone the same.

Well, after tomorrow, he won't be a stranger anymore, will he? Whether he likes it or not, we're a team in this.

But just to be on the safe side, maybe I should do a little research while packing my bag.

With Google by my side, I can do anything—even bond with a man who seems to hate me.

How to bond on a road trip?

What he and I need to do is build some sort of trust before we find Bel. Because even though we will work together to find her, I don't trust his intentions.

Yes, the man has every right to want to speak with his birth mother, especially after she contacted him. But that doesn't mean he won't hurt her. In fact, it gives him a reason to. Not that I think he would physically harm her, but emotionally, he could destroy her.

People forget physical bruises fade, but emotional cuts can last a lifetime.

I need to protect my friend and make things better not only for our friendship but also for whatever pain she is going through.

So by going with him, I can keep a close eye on him.

Watch for any signs or red flags looming near him.

That, and I also hate solo road trips. There is nothing worse than being stuck behind the wheel for hours upon hours, with nothing but your thoughts to keep you company.

My phone buzzes with another text notification, and logically, I know it must be him responding, but my heart hopes that maybe it's Bel finally answering one of my hundreds of messages.

Griffin

Fine. But make it 11 a.m.

I'm disappointed and excited at the same time.

Disappointed that my best friend is still shutting me out to the point it hurts.

And excited that I get to go on what is basically a super complex game of hide and seek. It's been forever since I've had an adventure, and this one is already shaping up to be... interesting, to say the least.

With only eight hours till we leave, I rush around my house, trying to get my bags packed as quickly as possible so I can get a couple hours of sleep before we head out. It's moments like these I'm thankful that my parents instilled in me a need to always have the laundry done. It's a struggle to zip my bags up, but I do it. I have warm clothes and some that are lighter, depending on where we end up. Needless to say, I'm prepared.

Audra

You ready for an adventure?

Griffin

No. I'll be there in ten minutes.

Audra

Perfect. When you get here, you can put your stuff in my car. It's the Camry parked directly in front of my apartment.

Griffin

I've seen that death trap you drive… We're taking my car.

Okaaay, rude. Someone is a control freak. Got it. Not that I have a problem with it. My old girl has seen better days, and her tires aren't the best, but what she lacks in safety, she makes up for in personality.

Audra

I laugh to myself at my lie, hoping he always thinks of penises when he hears that phrase.

Staring out my dining-room window, I pick at my cuticles that are in desperate need of oil and trimming, but that will have to wait for another day because, any second now, he is going to pull in. A stranger. A hot stranger that I'm about to be stuck in a car with for hours, maybe even days.

What on earth am I thinking?

I shake off questioning my sanity as a black Tahoe parks by the curb, and my stomach flutters with nerves at the sight of him climbing out.

Thank the lord for the legroom.

Running around my apartment, I check that every light is off and that no candles are lit for the second time in twenty minutes before I place my bags on my front step and lock my door.

I spin around, knocking into a solid wall that has never been there before.

"Ouch," I say, my hand rubbing my sore shoulder as I look up to find Griffin standing there with a scowl on his far-too-pretty face and one of my two bags in his hands.

"You know, the polite thing to say when you bump into somebody is excuse me," he says, gesturing his head to where he parked his big black vehicle.

I scoff, reaching to grab the last bag. "I got it," he says, leaning down to pick it up. "You just open up the back, please."

With a salute, I jog ahead to do as he asks before stepping aside and waiting. Griffin trails up, carrying my luggage with such ease that I can't look away from him—from the way his gray Henley is showing every sculpted muscle of his arms to the tight fabric expanding across his broad chest.

A small sigh slips past my lips at the sight of him as he bends to put my bags in the back next to his. His thick thighs and tight ass cause the denim to stretch so deliciously around him.

He peeks over his shoulder. "What was that?"

"Hmm?"

"Did you say something? Because I heard a noise." He closes the hatch.

My cheeks heat. "Nope, no noise here. You should get your ears checked," I say, scrambling to the front passenger door.

With a deep breath, I open it and climb in without another word. Immediately, I'm hit with a woodsy aroma. The scent causes a buzz of energy to flow through me—as if I wasn't already on edge around this man. Now my body is betraying me by flushing and tingling because of his hot, manly scent.

"Where are we heading first?" Griffin asks, his hands braced on the steering wheel and his gaze dead ahead in the parking lot.

"Um, I figured we would try the closest place first and work our way further out as we go."

He presses his lips together and gestures for me to put the address into the GPS.

Sheesh, someone forgot their coffee this morning. As soon as the navigation is set, he starts the car and pulls out of his parking space and onto the open road without another word.

I send up a silent prayer: *Please don't be a murderer.*

We drive in silence for longer than anyone ever should on a good old-fashioned road trip. At first, I tried to keep myself entertained by looking up available commercial space in Willow Hill. If I found a place, maybe the newly unemployed Bel could spend her time prepping while I sweet-talked my mother into understanding my need to branch out from the family business.

Every once in a while, I sneak a look at Griffin, and every time, it's the same. His stony face staring out at the road, jaw clenched the entire time. I wonder how much pain that man can take. Because I tried to clench my jaw to copy him, and two minutes in, I was done for.

"Want to play the alphabet game?" I ask, swiveling in my seat to get a better view of him.

"No."

His clipped response does nothing to stop my determination to bond with him.

"Okay, how about the license plate game?"

"No, thanks."

"Ooh, I know. We could play I Spy or Never Have I Ever."

"Jesus Christ, it's like you found a list of the most annoying road trip games and decided to torture me with them."

"They aren't the most annoying... they're fun and a wonderful bonding experience."

He rubs his brow.

"Do you have a headache? I have ibuprofen somewhere in my bag. If you pull over, I can—"

"What I need is for you to shut up," he snaps.

"That wasn't very nice." I lift my chin and glare at his stupidly defined jaw that won't stop flexing.

And we're back to playing the silent game.

What kind of person does a road trip in silence? A fucking psycho, that's who.

We are on hour three of this mute-off when I cave.

"Dear God, I can't stand this anymore. I need noise, conversation—some sort of stimulation." I throw my hands up in the air.

But Griffin doesn't respond; he just continues to watch the road like the responsible driver he is.

So freaking annoying.

The only inkling I get that he's even heard a word I've said is the twitch of the muscle in his fucking jaw.

I almost groan at the sight.

"Are you trying to make this a miserable experience?"

His eyes flick in my direction, *final-fucking-ly*. "How could this be anything but a miserable experience?"

"I just told you. Conversation or music? You know what music is, don't you?"

An eyebrow quirks at that. "Yes, Fisher. I do indeed know what music is and the entertainment it can provide. But this isn't fun for me. This isn't meant to be fun."

"So, because you want to throw yourself a pity party, I have to suffer too?"

"Guess so." He shrugs.

I turn away from him to face the window. Trees roll across the gloomy haze of January. The route we're taking is the quickest one listed. It also happens to be the scenic route, so win-win.

Once again, we drift into the mind-numbing silence. Instead of letting Griffin and his sourpuss ways get to me, I make a list of things to tell Bel when I see her.

First, I will start with a sorry. I will grovel if I have to. All I know is she is the best friend I've ever had, and even though she kept a tremendous secret from me, it doesn't change a thing. Then, after she has accepted my apology, I plan to yell at her for scaring me like this. I will also go into great detail about Jerry being a dick to me for her and how she should either put a ring on that man or cut him loose.

I know I want to talk to her about the whole secret-son thing, but not while his broody ass is standing beside me.

Soon, with each tree we pass, my eyelids grow heavier and heavier until I can't fight it anymore.

Chapter Nine

udra has been asleep for maybe thirty seconds before the snoring starts. Every breath grating on my nerves. How can such a loud, obnoxious noise come from such a small person?

I try to ignore her, going over my speech again in my head, as if I'm somehow going to find something new or witty to say.

No, the damn speech hasn't changed since Bren and I carefully and methodically came up with it a week ago.

It only takes thirty minutes of her snoring before I cave, turning on the radio to drown out the noises coming from her open mouth.

With my car connected to my Spotify account, I select my favorite playlist. I watch Audra like a hawk as I turn up the volume little by little, taking care not to wake her.

I strum my fingers along to the beat but still can't connect with the music like I'm used to. Instead of feeling the beat—the rhythm—I just listen, unaffected by the sounds that normally move me.

Stealing a glance at Audra, her hands folded under her cheek as she faces me, I frown. With her asleep and the snoring tuned out, I can actually admire her. It surprises me how beautiful she looks, even with her hair thrown up in the most unattractive ponytail there ever was.

A shiver runs over her, and I can't help myself. I reach into the back seat and pull out the blanket I packed, a fleece quilt my mom made me a couple of years ago that is mixed with all my old high school shirts. With one hand, I not so gracefully cover her up. I'm half tempted to cover her face to help cut out the sudden distraction she has caused, but I refrain. Barely.

Bren would have my head if I embarrassed him by accidentally suffocating a woman.

I turn back to the road, only stealing glances over at her every once in a while. For the next couple of hours, I continue to drive, only stopping for gas and a bathroom break, at which point I'm forced to wake up the snoring sleeping beauty.

"Fisher," I say murmur while brushing my hand over her shoulder. "We're at a gas station."

Her eyes flutter open, and she gives me a small smile before looking around.

"Get out, stretch your legs, use the bathroom, and whatever else you might need to do. We still have a shit ton of road to cover."

With a nod, she stretches her hands above her head and yawns, causing the blanket to fall into her lap and her shirt to rise up her stomach, exposing a sliver of flesh.

That minor flash of skin has arousal stirring in me. *Not the time, place, or person,* I berate my junk as I get out of the car and head inside.

The cashier greets me with the dip of his chin, and I mimic the movement before prowling through the rows of snacks until I reach the restroom. Immediately, I'm blasted with the overwhelming scent of fermenting urine, but that doesn't stop my desperate need to take a piss. Breathing only through my mouth, I march over to the urinal, with its sad excuse for a puck that is long overdue to be changed, and unzip my jeans.

The relief that washes through me is instant, and I quickly finish up, only gagging once before leaving to grab a shit ton of snacks and drinks.

When I reach the Tahoe, I find Audra standing by the pump. She swipes her card before turning to me. "Unleaded? Or do you like the fancy stuff?"

"You don't have to do that. I can get it."

"Sure you can, big boy, but I'm doing it anyway. So unleaded or the other thing?" she asks again.

"Unleaded," I say, placing my snacks in the back seat before climbing behind the wheel.

After she finishes filling up the tank, she goes inside the store, only to return five minutes later with a larger-than-life energy drink in one hand and a candy bar in the other.

"What?" she asks, buckling her seat belt as I continue to stare at her insane snack choices. "Seriously, what?"

"Nothing." I pull back out onto the road. Again, there is silence, only being broken by the munching of food. I look over at her to ask the question that's been burning in my mind since she said it. "Did you call me big boy?"

Her lips quirk up. "Maybe."

Eyes widening, I open my mouth to respond but can't think of a damn word to say.

A laugh bursts out of her, filling the car. My mouth is still gaping as she flings one hand up to her chest and the other to stifle the sound.

"Okay, I heard you wrong. That's all you had to say." Heat fills my cheeks.

She reaches over and squeezes my forearm. "You didn't mishear anything." She pulls the blanket up from where it rests across her lap, finding the tag in the corner. "'To Griffin, my baby boy, who is now a big boy. —Mom.'"

"Oh." My embarrassment is at an all-time high. Not only because of the cheesy message on the homemade tag, which I love, but also because I honestly thought she meant something else.

"I'm sorry. I wasn't trying to make fun of it. In fact, I think it's very sweet. Did she make this?"

I nod.

"What are all these?"

I look over to find her glancing at the different patches all over it. "It's all my old high school T-shirts. Well, not all, just the ones from important events or times."

Her voice is soft as she says, "You must really miss her."

I clear my throat. "We should get there by around 9 p.m."

Audra stares at me for a second before taking the hint to change the subject. "Awesome. You want me to drive while you rest?"

The blank expression on my face tells her everything she needs to know.

She lifts her hands up. "Okay, okay. It was just a thought. And if you want to take me up on it at any point, just let me know."

"I won't."

"Why? I'm a great driver. I've never gotten a ticket or into any accidents."

"That's not it."

"Then why?"

Pain radiates through my jaw as I grit my teeth together. "Just drop it."

"Not until you tell me why."

"Fine. Since you want to know so fucking bad. It's because you're friends with her. I can't trust you."

Her face falls. She turns to face the front and folds the blanket before placing it on top of the console between us.

I scrub my hand over my mouth. *Why the fuck did I just do that?* The defeated, hurt look on her face tells me I fucked up. "Audra—you don't have to do that. You're cold. Use the blanket."

"No, I wouldn't want my untrustworthy hands all over something that means so much to you."

Her words are sharp and hit me square in the chest. I'm an asshole, and now she's going to shiver out of spite.

"Audra."

"Stop. Just stop," she whispers, leaving me full of regret.

By the time we arrive at the first destination—and hopefully the last—it's already dark. The clock on the dash reads a little past nine as I park the car and gaze up at the idealistic and very busy inn.

"Are you sure this is it?" I ask.

Her glare cuts into me. "Yes, but I'm not sure you can trust that I'm telling the truth."

I groan just as she hops out of the car.

"Audra, stop," I beg, jogging to catch up with her. I grab her arm, spinning her to face me. "I'm sorry."

She holds my gaze for a moment before rolling her eyes to stare behind me. "Sorry you said it, or sorry 'cause it's true."

I study the tightness of her features as she refuses to look at me.

"That's what I thought," she scoffs. With a quick tug, she pulls her arm from my grip and walks toward the inn.

I'm not sure what I was expecting. But it wasn't this.

The Ashford Inn is a larger-than-life white three-story building with windows everywhere, surrounded by a light dusting of snow. It's everything I imagine a Hallmark movie looks for when location scouting. But none of that is strange. Its lawn decor, though...

The grass and bushes are lit up with string lights, illuminating a cluster of pineapples. Pineapples with smiles, pineapple hats, pineapples that are upside down.

"Someone sure loves the hell out of some tropical plants," I say, with my eyes still roaming over the fruit-infested lawn.

"I think it's cute and whimsical," she says with a snarky smile as she stomps off. "And it's something that Belinda would love."

I follow her inside to the desk that sits unattended. A faint sound of music trills from down the hall. But there's not a soul in sight.

"Hello," I call out while dinging the bell. "You made a reservation, right?"

"Yes, Griffin. I made the reservation first thing this morning," she snaps.

"Sorry." I toss my hands up. "But can you blame me for asking? It looks like this place is having some sort of private party."

Her nostrils flare. "I made the *damn* reservation."

"Did I hear reservation?" a voice calls from the hallway right as a man in a shirt that states *fineapple* comes into view.

"Yes, hi. My name is Audra. I called bright and early this morning about the rooms."

He smiles. "Oh, yes, Audra. I've got you down for two rooms."

She turns back to me with a shit-eating grin. "See, told you."

"What's that, honey?" he asks.

"I said I love the decor outside. It's so fun," she tells him.

"Yeah, fun," I mutter, which earns me a jab in the ribs from Audra. "Ow." I rub at the site.

Is big boy okay? she mouths at me.

Unaware of the tension between us, the man whose name tag says *Trevor* hands us our room keys. "Oh, if you like that, you should join the party tonight." His eyes roam over her body. "Anyway, it looks like you will be on the top floor, Audra. And you, sir, will be on floor two."

"Thanks." I turn to go back to the car to get our bags but am stopped by Audra.

"Wait, Trevor."

"Yes?" His grin grows even larger every second he looks at her.

"We're looking for someone."

"Of course you are." He waves his hand. "Say no more. Follow me, and we'll find the person you two desire."

"Thank you," Audra says as she turns and walks behind him. But I reach out and grab her wrist, forcing her to a stop.

"I don't trust him."

"You also don't trust me, so."

"I'm serious. Something about this feels off, not to mention he was checking you out the entire time."

"Whatever, Griffin, no he wasn't. He was just being polite. And besides, didn't you see the ring on his finger?"

"Rings don't mean shit to some men."

Brushing off my hold, she spins on her heels to follow him through the doorway. "Besides, it doesn't matter if he was checking me out, anyway. I'm still going to look for Belinda." She walks off, hollering over her shoulder, "Are you coming or not?"

I groan but still chase after her into a large room full of people, booze, and loud music.

The entire room is dressed in the same tropical theme as the outside of the inn, heavy on the pineapples.

"Roam around, mingle, and maybe you two will find the right person." Trevor winks before turning to join a group of couples.

"Well, this is fun," she says, her shoulders shimmying to the music.

"Again, not the word I would give it."

We push through the crowd to the bar for a better view of our surroundings. I scan the room three times before giving up and ordering a beer. "I don't see her."

With a sigh, she plops onto the barstool beside me. "Me either."

The sad expression on her face has me reaching out to comfort her. "We'll find her."

"Excuse me," a smooth-as-silk voice drawls from behind us. We both swivel to face the attractive woman wearing a halter summer dress. "I couldn't help but overhear you two are looking for a woman."

Audra perks up. "Yes, yes, we are."

The woman grins, taking a step between the two of us. "Well then, maybe I can be of some assistance." Her hands trail up both of our thighs. My eyes dart to find Audra's wide on me.

I lift her hand from Audra's thigh first, then from my own. "I'm sorry, I didn't catch your name."

"Oh," she purrs, "call me Kitty. And you two are?"

"Confused," Audra says.

"I'm sure you are." She winks at her. "Like I said, I can help with that."

Chapter Ten

My mind goes blank at her words. She can't possibly be suggesting what I think she is.

I glance at Griffin, whose face gives nothing away. He almost looks bored at the exchange happening between us.

Kitty takes my silence as shyness instead of the pure shock that it is. She trails her fingers up and down my arm. Out of the corner of my eye, I catch the glint of a wedding band on her finger.

"Where is your spouse?" I ask.

"Oh, Dean is over there with Paula." She points toward the back of the room to a not-so-dark corner where a woman's straddling a man's lap as they go at it. "He's going to be busy with her for a while, but if you would like, I can invite them to join us."

Griffin tosses his beer back, his Adam's apple bobbing as he swallows every last drop. "We need a few to discuss some things—privately, okay?"

"Absolutely," she purrs, batting her eyelashes. "Just find me when you're ready for the ride of your lives."

As she walks away, I look around the space, noticing couple after couple kissing and dancing.

Griffin stands and grabs my hand to lead me away from the bar and into a dark, unoccupied corner.

"You know what this is, right?" he asks.

"Some weird tropical party with a very assertive, sexually advanced woman?"

"No, I think we're at a swingers party."

"No…" I let out a nervous laugh. "That's crazy."

He shakes his head. "I'm serious."

"Just because a woman hit on us and her husband is hooking up with a woman in the same room doesn't make them—oh. Oh, I see it now. You don't think they *do it* in public, do you?"

She was hitting on me. *Me.* The girl with rumpled clothes and greasy hair that's a few days past its wash day.

I would flip said oily hair over my shoulder if it wasn't piled on top of my head and weighed down with previously mentioned oil.

His eyes dart around the room as if to ensure no one is, in fact, fucking right now. "I think we should bathe in hand sanitizer to be on the safe side."

"That sounds like a solid idea." Across the room, Kitty stares us down while she licks the rim of her shot glass before wrapping her lips around the opening and shooting it back, drinking every drop in one gulp. All the while never once breaking eye contact with us.

"Holy shit," I whisper, gripping Griffin's wrist. "I'm terrified and turned on all at the same time."

"Yeah." He clears his throat, and I can tell he's having the same conflicting emotions as me. "I think it's time we get our bags and call it a night."

"Agreed, that's probably for the best." I laugh, taking one last look around the room at the groups of people who are far more adventurous than I could ever imagine. "You know, Bel would love this place."

Griffin shudders, and I laugh again at his discomfort.

Halfway to the exit, Mrs. Assertive spots us trying to flee. "Heading out already?" she pouts.

I'm struck with awkwardness, unsure of what to say or how to get out of this situation as painlessly as possible. I look to Griffin for help, only to find him glancing back down at me.

He sighs, "Long day."

"I bet I could help you both relax." She flutters her lashes at him.

"I'm sure you could," I mutter under my breath, just as Griffin replies, "We'll be back down after we freshen up."

A lust-filled, sultry smile breaks across her face. "Looking forward to it."

"You aren't serious, are you?" I ask as we walk away.

He glares at me. "Shut up and move faster."

Griffin and I stick together as we race back to the Tahoe. He grabs both of our bags, hoisting them over his shoulders.

"You don't have to do that," I tell him as he closes the hatch.

"Let me be the gentleman my mother raised me to be, please."

I toss my hands up, allowing him to walk past me. "Okay, I was just going to say you didn't have to grab all three bags. The medium one has everything I'll need for tonight."

"Oh," he says, his steps stopping as he glances back to the Tahoe in silent debate. "Should I... put it back?"

I chuckle. "It's fine. Thank you, Griffin."

He leads me up to my room on the third floor, monitoring our surroundings the entire time. At the door, he looks around again as if he's paranoid.

"What?" I ask.

"Nothing." He straightens, waiting for me to open it.

I place the rustic key into the lock and turn the knob to find a small and cozy room full of charm and frills. The pink lace and ruffles are more than a little overdone, but I can't help but grin. I hop onto the large queen bed and sink into the fluffy pillows.

"Oh my God, this bed is heaven," I groan.

"This room looks like it belongs to my nana," he says, setting my bags by the entryway table.

I laugh because that is precisely what I was thinking too. The thought brings me comfort. My grandma was a spitfire, and I strive to be that type of woman every day.

Griffin is still standing near the door, shuffling back and forth on his feet uncomfortably.

"Thanks for bringing my bags up. I'll see you in the morning." I roll out of the bed, walking toward him to lead him out. But he doesn't move. "Earth to Griffin. This is where you go to your room."

He rubs the back of his neck. "I know, it's just—I'm not comfortable leaving you here. *Alone.*"

"That is the lamest line I have ever heard. Get out, you aren't getting lucky tonight. And if you were thinking somehow you were, think back to how you've treated me."

He opens his mouth, speechless for a moment. "I wasn't coming on to you."

"Sure you weren't," I say in a mocking tone.

A moment later, a bang rattles the door. We both freeze as it shakes again when someone knocks against the wood.

"Pretty lady," the raspy male voice calls through the door. "I thought you might want some company tonight."

My eyes widen as Griffin gives me a pointed look and gestures to the entrance.

"That proves nothing," I whisper yell at him.

"Are you joking?"

"Pretty lady," the man calls out again. "I've been told I'm a generous lover."

I smirk at Griffin. "That means he likes to eat puss—"

Griffin's hand slaps over my mouth. "Stop it. I know what it means. And this is why I'm staying here tonight."

I shove his warm, albeit clean-smelling, hand away.

"I can handle myself," I say, just as the doorknob jiggles. I freeze.

"Come on, baby, open the door and I promise you won't regret it."

Griffin steps closer to me, wrapping his hand around mine to pull me out of the doorway and around the corner.

He ducks to meet me at my eye level. "Audra, it's okay. I'm going to take care of it."

With one last squeeze of my hand, he stalks to the door, unlocking it and opening it with a yank.

"What the—"

"Look, man, as much as I would love my pussy licked, I think my dick gets in the way, so take your creepy advances elsewhere."

"Whoa, no need to get pissy, man. I thought that sweet little piece was in here."

Griffin goes quiet for a second before his voice drops to a deep growl, sending shivers up my spine. "So you thought you would yell at the door and try to break in? What about that is okay in any way?"

"It was an honest mistake."

"Sure it was. Now get the fuck out of here."

There's an inaudible grumble and then the sound of the door shutting, followed by the *click* of the lock sliding into place.

I turn the corner to find Griffin running a hand through his hair. His eyes meet mine. "You okay?"

I nod. "Just a little freaked out, is all."

"Yeah, me too." He steps closer to me. "I'm going to stay here tonight, okay?"

"Okay." I grab my bag and head to the bathroom to get ready for bed.

After changing into my pj's, which consist of an oversized shirt from an ex-boyfriend—honestly, I can't even remember which one—and a pair of shorts, I climb into the bed as Griffin moves into the bathroom, only to come out two minutes later in nothing but a pair of pajama pants. My eyes trail up his toned chest, then back to where his pants sling low on his hips, revealing every woman's kryptonite—the deep V.

Holy fucking hottie.

I have to bite my lip to suppress the groan threatening to escape my mouth as he crosses the room to sit in the pink-and-white striped wingback chair in the far corner.

Of course he looks like that. It's so unfair that he not only has a gorgeous face but also a mouthwatering body. It's just not fair. I need something to be wrong with him. Well, besides his piss-poor attitude toward me.

"What are you doing?" I ask as he pulls a small throw blanket over his body.

"Trying to get comfortable."

"I see that. But why over there?"

A smirk plays on his lips. "Why, do you want me in the bed... with you?"

I yank the covers up over my head. "Never mind, Griffin. I hope your back suffers all night."

He chuckles, and a moment later, the bed dips. My heart pounds so hard I'm sure he can hear it as my body and mind both realize that he's lying next to me with no shirt and his ridiculously low pants that show off way too much pleasantly tempting skin.

Peeking out from under the blanket, I find Griffin's muscular back facing me as he lies on top of the comforter with the small throw blanket barely covering up his torso.

"Goodnight, Griffin."

"Goodnight, Audra."

Warmth settles in my chest as I realize he's stopped calling me Fisher.

Sunlight streams through the pink lace curtains as the soft, rhythmic noises of breathing wake me from sleep. Slowly, I blink one eye open to see that Griffin's sound asleep beside me.

But that's not all. His hand is wrapped around mine, nestled between our bodies. Carefully, I uncurl my fingers from his and slip out of the bed.

I stand there, merely admiring him in his unconscious state. From the sleep-mussed hair to the peaceful look on his face, I take in every inch of him while I can. The temptation to pull the blanket down so I can admire more of him is strong. *So damn strong.*

Just as my hand inches closer to him, his phone rings on the nightstand. Griffin groans, tossing a pillow at the ringing when it doesn't stop. He turns toward the noise, and I scurry away to the bathroom as fast as I can without making a peep.

The ringing stops right as I close the bathroom door.

"Hello?" Griffin's sleep-laced voice fills the room.

I press my ear against the door, wanting to hear more like the eavesdropping nosy Nancy I am.

"Whoa, Bren, it's way too early for this interrogation," he grumbles. "Look, I can't talk right now."

The cold wood of the door that is in desperate need of a sanding or some oil scratches my cheek as I press my face against it harder, not wanting to miss a word.

"No, I'm not alone."

Quickly, I start the shower, giving him the illusion of privacy, before tiptoeing back to the door.

"It's not like that. Ugh, seriously, I know you're upset, but can I call you back after I have some coffee in me?" There's a pause before he mutters, "Yeah, yeah. I love you too."

The sound of his footsteps draws closer, and I rip off my shorts and shirt, then scurry into the shower.

"Shit," I squeal as the bone-chilling cold water rains down on my body. With a glance at the faucet, I realize that, in my mad dash to snoop, I didn't turn on the hot water.

Shivering, I crank the heat as I press my body into the wall and out of the stream.

I moan as the steam from the water fills the air around me. My body sinks under the flow, and I bask in the warmth.

I finish up in the shower, using what's in here instead of my shampoo and soap, which I had packed but am too much of a little dick to go out and get or even shout for Griffin to bring them to me. So I now smell strongly of roses.

The soap, the shampoo—everything in this room is rose-themed, and for some reason, it only just hits me. I think I was in such a haze of being creeped out and nervous to have Griffin so close that I didn't notice it last night.

Once I'm dried off with, you guessed it, a rose-patterned towel wrapped around my hair and body, I walk back into the room to find Griffin gone and the bed made. I dress quickly, not wanting to waste any more time here.

With my hair still damp, I go downstairs to look for Griffin, running straight into Mr. Front Desk from yesterday instead.

"Hey, Audra, right?" he asks, his warm smile still present, but now it's tainted with the swinger knowledge. The gold name tag adorning his shirt glints in the light as he drags his gaze across my body in a perusing manner that causes a shiver of disgust to roll down my spine.

"Yep." I smile politely. "Have you seen the tall, very attractive, broody man I came with yesterday?"

"Honey, I'm not sure who got you to come yesterday, but I'm sure you can find another if that's what you're wanting." He winks, and I have to fight the stomach-churning urge to vomit on his face.

"Audra," Griffin yells as he jogs over, wrapping an arm around my shoulders while looking Trevor the perv up and down with a glare. "You ready to head out?"

"Yep."

He ushers me in the opposite direction.

"Oh no, not already." Trevor jumps in front of us, blocking our escape route. "You two have to stay for night two. It's when everyone really lets loose."

"Look, *Travis*," Griffin sneers. "As much as we enjoy the unwelcome sexual advances and harassment at every turn, we are leaving. So, if you'll excuse us." He pushes us past the now slack-jawed Trevor, who looks both confused and offended.

When we're far enough out of hearing range, I let out a small laugh. "I kind of feel bad for the guy."

"Don't. He was the one who was cunnilingus happy last night."

I stop in my tracks. "Shut up, that was him? Mr. Generous Lover?"

"Yeah." He nods.

A shudder runs down my arms. And just like that, my pity for Trevor is replaced with repulsion. "Ew."

A smile breaks out across his lips as we continue to walk back to the room to grab our bags. "I'm glad I read that situation, right?"

"What, were you concerned I was into him?"

His nose crinkles as he cringes. "A little."

"Gross." I shove him. "I like to think my standards are slightly higher than that."

"Just slightly?"

"Well, I don't have the best man picker. My last boyfriend was a total tool. Cheated and broke up with me constantly."

He places the bag in the back with a "Hmph." Without another sound, he climbs into the driver's seat and hands me his phone to pull up the directions to our next destination.

After twenty minutes of driving, he ends our silence. "Then why?"

"Why what?" I pop a chip into my mouth.

His eyes stay glued to the road, as usual. "The ex, then why were you with him?"

I mull over his question. "Because it was safe?"

"Safe?" He gives me a questioning look. "How is being broken up with and cheated on safe?"

"It was safe in the sense that I wasn't going to get attached and let down... He is who he is, and that was comforting."

He's quiet for a few moments before he reaches over to squeeze my hand. "That's sad, Audra, and nobody deserves that kind of relationship."

He pulls his hand back as quickly as it came. "Eh, it's all good."

"It's not if you think that is in any way healthy."

"Oh, I never said it was healthy. But it just was what it was." I shrug. "Tell me about your last relationship since you seem to be such an expert."

"Nothing to tell. It ended about a year and a half ago."

"Why?"

"Why did it end?"

"Yeah, what happened?"

"Nothing happened—we just grew apart."

"How long were you two together?"

"Around three years."

"Three *years*?" I screech past my tightening throat. "How are you so calm about that?"

"I don't know. It's been over a while now. And besides, it was on and off."

"So! It must still hurt. Three years of feelings don't just disappear."

He laughs. "You sound just like Brenden. He said the same thing at first when we broke up."

"Yeah, 'cause he isn't an idiot."

"Me and her, we were just complacent. It took us a while to see that our relationship was based on friendship and not love. So, when it ended, it just made sense."

"Did you cry?"

"What kind of question is that?"

"The kind to see if you are a sociopath or not?"

"When it officially ended, no. But a year earlier, when I felt the distance between us, yeah."

"You knew it was over a year before you guys broke up? Holy shit, Griff. That is insane." I look at him with wonder. "Why didn't you end it then?"

He swallows. "I don't know. I think I stayed because we still cared for each other and showed each other respect."

"That's sad, but also feels like a happy ending." To this, I get a small smile as his eyes focus back on the road.

Chapter Eleven

Griffin

"**P**lease!"

I shake my head, ignoring her pleading that's been going on nonstop for the past five minutes.

"We are about to stop. It would be the perfect time, and you know it," she says again, for the third time.

"Audra, why on earth do you want to drive so badly?" I ask, eyeing her with suspicion.

"How many times do I have to tell you? To give you a damn break," she groans, tossing her hands up in exasperation. "It's getting late, and you've been driving for hours. Let me take over before you fall asleep at the wheel and kill us both."

"I told you, I'm fine." That's a lie. The truth is, I'm exhausted. I could use a break from driving. Maybe a nap. But I can't tell her that. Audra would be all over that with an I told you so.

There is also the fact that I don't know this woman. Yes, we shared a bed last night, but it was innocent. I was just being a gentleman, not wanting her to be alone in that swingers' sex den. That didn't automatically make me forget that she was still a stranger. A sexy stranger that I continuously had to tell myself to be wary of.

But that didn't stop my body from reacting to her. Every accidental graze of her arm to mine was like an electrical current running through me, awakening every hidden desire inside me. I crave more and more of her every minute.

Hell, the only thing stopping me from staring at her lips is my relentless compulsion for safety, which has my eyes glued to the road.

Driving has been my saving grace. Without it, I'm afraid I might say *fuck it* and make a move. So giving up my distraction from her is a horrible idea that I'm completely, one thousand percent against.

As I pull into the next gas station, her pout is impossible to miss as it's directed straight at me. The hair from her thick bun on top of her head falling to the side as she angles her head closer, her eyes widening into enormous emerald seas that beg me to reconsider.

"Fuck," I mutter, slamming the car door before stomping off into the store to take a piss and buy a drink. With two Cokes in my hand, I stop in front of my car, finding Audra sitting in the driver's seat, adjusting the mirrors to her liking and pulling the seat up far too close to the steering wheel to be safe.

It's like my entire body is full of energy as I let the realization of what this means wash over me.

Well, shit.

Without a word, I toss the drinks into the back seat and fill the tank.

Placing the hose back on the pump, I consider how I'm going to handle this. My skin crawling with the anticipation of being able to look at her with all my concentration. Of what it will mean. What if she catches me being a creep with her? It will make this whole situation fifty times more uncomfortable than it already is.

My finger grazes over the door handle, allowing me one last moment to collect myself. I pull the door open and take my seat, looking anywhere but at her or where she's preparing to drive my car.

"You ready to be lulled to sleep by my smooth driving skills?" she asks with a smirk playing on her lips, the same lips that I'm now wondering what they feel like.

Off in the distance, the sun is setting, the sky turning pretty shades of pink and orange that light up her face.

"Do I have a choice?"

"That's the spirit, Griffy!" She shifts the vehicle into drive, looking around the parking lot before pulling onto the street.

"Please don't call me that?"

Her brows furrow as she glances over at me, then back at the road. "Griffy? Why? It's cute, and you know it."

"It sounds like something you would call a dog," I say matter-of-factly.

She reaches over, patting the top of my head. "There, there, Griffy. Be a good boy for Audra, and maybe she will let you out for a run at our next stop."

I glare at her stupid, beautiful profile, my face giving away nothing. Definitely not how I want to lean into her touch and sigh. That I want more than anything to have her run her fingers through my hair and caress my scalp. Nope. Instead, I remain solid and indifferent as I scowl at her out of the corner of my eye.

"You're the worst. Do you know that?" I ask with all seriousness because it's true—she is the worst. The way she keeps stirring up my desire for her is becoming insanely difficult to ignore, and it's awful.

And I need it to stop. I need her to stop touching me, to stop smiling at me, and to stop looking at me with those beautiful eyes.

"Don't be rude. Besides, you know you like me." She wags her eyebrows.

My spine stiffens. I know she's teasing, but it hits a nerve... because damn it, I do. I really *fucking* do like her.

Instead of responding, I put some music on. It's my safety blanket right now, the only line I have to hold on to while my mind tries its hardest to let me drown in this sensual stranger next to me.

We continue to drive in silence. The only thing filling the car—well, besides the tension—is the music playing. As the sky changes from a pinkish orange to a deep blue purple, with a flurry of snowflakes visible in the headlights, I let my eyes drift closed, wanting sleep to take me but knowing it will be impossible, at least with her beside me, driving my fucking car.

I keep my eyes closed, listening as she sings along under her breath, as well as mumbles to herself repeatedly about Belinda. It feels like eavesdropping, but she's doing it right in front of me, so I can't help but hear.

She talks herself through multiple different speeches and approaches that she plans to use when she sees her friend again. But that all stops when the car jerks to the right, then the left. A panic-laced "shit" bursts out of her mouth.

My eyes pop open as we slide sideways on the road. Audra grips the wheel, trying to correct us. It works for a second, but then another patch of ice catches us again, and we veer off the road. I reach out with my arm to cage her to her seat like a soccer mom as we crash into a snowy embankment.

Snow crunches beneath my boots as I hang up the phone, walking back to the Tahoe. Closing the door behind me, I let the heat soak into my chilly bones before I turn to find Audra huddled up in the driver's seat, with her legs pulled up to her chest and my blanket draped across her shoulders.

"The tow truck said it's going to be at least four hours until he can get to us."

"Four *hours*?" she shouts, running her hands through her dark hair.

"At least," I correct her. "There are six other vehicles in front of us."

"Oh my God, Griffin," she says in a rush. "We are going to freeze to death, and it's all my fault." Her hands are shaking, and tears line her eyes again.

"We are going to be okay. You didn't do anything wrong—the roads are icy. It happens."

"How can you be so calm when I ran your car off the road and now we're going to be popsicles?"

I glance out the window to where the hood is buried in a snowy ditch. It sucks, but I'm not going to tell her that, especially when she's hanging on by a damn thread. "First, we aren't going to die. And two, it's just a car. It's not important, we are."

"We're going to freeze to death before he gets here." Panic laces her voice.

"I promise you, we aren't," I say, climbing into the back to push the seats down and make us a large area to lie down. "Come on back here. It will help to be farther away from the snow-covered windshield."

She swallows, then climbs over the console to sit on the now-flat back seat.

"Let's play a game," I say, trying to get her mind off our situation.

She shakes her head, eyes still wide with panic. "I don't want to play. I want to get out of here."

"Humor me."

She sighs, her knee bouncing. "What game?"

"A secret for a secret. I'll even go first." Unable to take it anymore, I place my hand over her knee. "I cry every time I hear the song 'Let It Go.'"

"Like, from *Frozen*?"

"That's the one."

A small laugh breaks past her lips. "Why?"

I smile. "Because it's heartbreaking and beautiful all at the same time."

"You're a sensitive guy, aren't you?"

I shrug and nudge her with my shoulder. "Your turn."

She takes a deep breath, then rushes out the words. "Sometimes I don't wear socks."

"What?" I choke out, forcing my jaw not to drop.

"Okay, that's a lie—I rarely wear them, and only with certain shoes."

"That is just gross, and you know it. Wait, are you wearing socks right now?" I look at her boots, reaching, but she smacks my hand away. "Let me see."

"No, you perv. Look at someone else's feet." She laughs as I try to pull off her boots.

"Griffin," she squeals as I get her left one off.

I frown at the fuzzy baby-pink sock gracing her foot. "Did you lie about your secret?"

"No." She chokes down yet another giggle. "It's winter, and I don't want any frostbite. I like my toes where they are."

"You should think about those piggies all the time, not just in freezing weather."

"Why are you *so* concerned about my toes?" she asks, giving me a wary look before she snaps her fingers. "I've got it. You got some sort of foot fetish, don't you?"

"I don't have a foot fetish," I grumble, but it's too late; she's already looking at me like she knows my deepest, darkest secret. Lying on my back, I grab the blanket from the front seat and pull it over my body before throwing out another secret to veer the conversation back into safe territory. "I kissed my brother's high school girlfriend at a bar a couple years ago—and cried during said kiss."

She throws her head back in laughter. "You cried? Like, mid make out?"

Aha, victory. The subject change worked. No more fetish talk.

"Not just cried, sobbed. Like, full-on snotty mess."

"Did your brother find out?"

Her smile is infectious. Grinning, I tell her, "I'm pretty sure he figured it out when she called him to come get me from the bar, and I was still crying over being a shit brother."

"Was he mad?"

"Oh yeah. But he laughed and said my emotional breakdown was good enough for him."

"He sounds like a cool brother." She slides her other boot off and pulls the socks up higher to cover her exposed ankles.

"He is." I roll to face her. "What about you, any siblings?"

"Just the one. Which I'm fairly certain I told you about when I officially introduced myself to you." Her eyes cut a sharp glare in my direction. "I can't believe you already forgot. It was practically yesterday."

"To be honest, I was only half listening to the words coming out of your mouth when we met."

She scoffs and rolls her eyes. "Rude. Just for that, I'm going to talk your ear off for the rest of the road trip."

"Isn't that what you've already been doing?"

She smacks my arm in fake offense but beams brightly as she continues to tell me about her family. "Anyway, my brother, Nate, is the fucking best. Cool as shit, actually. The man writes and illustrates children's books." She chuckles. "He's annoyingly great. The little asshole took the leap of leaving the family business to focus on his art before I had the chance to jump ship for my own dreams, and now I'm stuck and resenting his stupid ass."

"Why does his leaving the family business affect you following your dreams?"

She sighs. "Because now all my parents' hopes and dreams are on me alone. I have to take over at some point."

"I'm not seeing the problem. The flower shop was beautiful as hell and appeared to be a success. They are practically handing you success on a platter."

"The problem is, I have my own business idea. Well, Bel and I do. We have a plan set and ready to go. I mean, it *was* ready to go, until Bel up and had a breakdown, fleeing town."

I push down the anger that boils under my skin at the mention of Belinda. "And you don't think your parents will support this plan?"

She laughs. "I know they won't. I brought my floral preservation ideas to them multiple times over the years, and each time, they've shot me down, refusing to hear me out."

A mixture of emotions runs through me: empathy for her having a close-knit family but not having them support her goals. But also jealousy and anger over Belinda choosing to be close to this random woman but not her own son.

I know it's irrational to be pissed, but I am.

Do I want Belinda to be part of my family? Fuck no.

I would never do that to my parents' memory. But something about it all still causes an ache in my chest.

I close my eyes, trying to push out all the negativity flooding my senses. Opening them up, I glance over to where Audra sits shivering. Lifting the edge of the blanket, I gesture for her to join me.

"You want me to lie under there... with you?"

I drop my arm. "I know. I'm such a troll. How will you survive being so close to something so hideous?" I deadpan, lifting the blanket again. "Do you want the body heat or not?"

She bites her lip, and for a moment, I think she's going to say she would rather freeze than be next to me. But she moves closer, scooting under the blanket, leaving a few inches between us.

A shiver runs through her body again, and I can't stand that she's being so stubborn and causing herself more problems instead of touching me.

"Fuck this." I wrap my arm around her waist, dragging her until her back is flush against me. Encasing her in my arms, I press her closer, and she stiffens to an unnatural stillness, like she's trying her damnedest not to breathe.

"What the hell, Griffin? You can't just spoon people."

"Audra, I'm not going to let you shiver all night because you don't like me. So yes, I'm going to spoon the shit out of you to help keep both of us warm."

She doesn't respond right away, but after ten minutes, her shoulders relax, followed by the rest of her body. She whispers, "Thank you, Griffin."

I try not to think all the dirty thoughts that are running through my mind with every microscopic move she makes.

God, she feels so good in my arms.

Her body touching mine is like heaven and hell combined. The promised pleasure, just the barest of touches, but the utter pain of not being able to act on it.

We aren't a thing.

She is here for the same reasons I am, and that is not to feel each other up. I keep telling myself this over and over until my eyes grow heavy and the sound of her soft snores lulls me to sleep.

A sharp knock on the frost-covered back window startles me awake. Already, I wish I was still asleep, with Audra's body keeping me warm and her pert ass nestling against my crotch.

I peer out of one eye into a thick mess of brown hair, my face buried deep in it, the smell of roses filling my nostrils. I could lie here all day—wrapped around Audra, with nothing but the quiet surrounding us.

The knock sounds again, only this time, it's accompanied by a loud, gruff voice. "Hello? I'm here to pull you out of the ditch."

Leaning up on my elbow, I scrub my hand over my face. "Yeah, we're in here. Just a minute." I look to where Audra has curled even closer to me, turning to wrap her arm around my middle.

I give myself one more minute of this peace. Of being able to enjoy her company, her warmth, before waking her up and going back to the way things were. Back to bickering and glares. Back to her being the best friend of the woman who has torn my world apart.

With one last glance, I bring my hand to her face, pushing her long locks out of her eyes. "Audra," I whisper. "The tow truck is here to get us out."

She mumbles something incoherent but doesn't wake.

"Audra, you need to wake up."

"No," she groans, pulling the blanket up over her head.

I chuckle, tearing the blanket off her. "Come on, we need to let the nice man pull us out of the ditch." She frowns up at me, her lips pulling into a large pout.

"Do we have to?" she asks with her green eyes swimming with sleep.

"Yes. Or we just might actually freeze at some point." I pull away, glancing at the watch on my left wrist. Three in the morning. I groan, finding my shoes and coat before climbing out of the back hatch and into the dark of night.

The frigged air hits me, and I instantly regret leaving the warmth of Audra's embrace under the blanket.

"Holy fuck," she shrieks as the stiff wind hits her inside. Quickly, she pulls on her boots and coat, then jumps out after me.

We stand across the road, watching from behind the tow truck's spotlight as the man hooks the wench up to the back of my Tahoe and pulls us out of our snowy ditch.

I walk around to the front, using my phone for light to inspect the damage with a shivering Audra beside me. The front bumper took the brunt of the impact and only suffered a few dents. It could've been worse—hell, I've done worse just bumping into a curb.

"I'm sorry." Her voice is much quieter than usual.

"It's fine," I say, turning to find tears welling up in her eyes. "Hey, don't cry. It's okay, remember? Just a car, not important."

She nods, but the tears still fall.

"Shit," I mutter, moving beside her to gather her in my arms. I rub my hands up and down her back, trying to soothe her the best I can.

Her arms wrap around me inside my jacket, just as her forehead rests on my chest. Tears continue to fall, soaking through my shirt. I let her cry it out while we wait for the man to finish and give me the bill.

With a paper in hand, he walks back over to us. "You two got lucky there. The couple I went to before you guys totaled their car."

I take the bill from him, then walk Audra back to the passenger side door, opening it for her. Once she's in the seat, I quickly shut her in and run around the car as fast as I can without falling on the ice.

The car door slams shut behind me.

Sniffling and wiping at her nose, she mumbles, "I'm so sorry. I'll pay for it all, I promise."

"Audra." I push a strand of hair behind her ear so I can look at her face. "Can you stop it? Do I look like I'm going to hold it against you?"

Her head shakes, but her jaw trembles, telling me she doesn't believe me.

"Will you please stop beating yourself up about it?"

Another tear falls, and she quickly swipes it away. "I'll try."

"Thank you." I blast the heat, letting us warm up for another moment before getting back on the road.

"Can we listen to some music for distraction?" Her eyes are enormous, shining with the remaining tears as she waits for my response.

"Yeah." I fish my phone out of my pocket, pulling up my music. "Have at it."

A shy smile forms on her lips as she reaches over, her fingers brushing mine as she takes it from my hands. She scrolls through, glancing back at me. "This is a shit ton of music, Griffin."

"Well, yeah, it comes with the job."

"The job? Wait, are you a musician?"

I nod. "Yeah."

"Really?"

"Yeah." I laugh. "Why, you can't see it?"

"Oh, no, I totally can. You've got this whole broody thing that works perfectly with a tortured musician."

I snort.

"So are you, like, in a band?"

"No."

"Solo, eh? Hmm. I wouldn't have pictured that."

I laugh. "Wrong again."

"Orchestra." She nods.

"Nope, not in the orchestra."

"Okay, I don't get it."

"I'm a studio musician."

She stares at me blankly.

"It means I write and record songs for other artists to use."

"Oh, so you are the background noise. Got it."

"No, not background noise… I play instruments that make up the music you hear, along with vocals."

"Lame," she says with a laugh, and I can't help but smile along because she's not crying anymore. "Do you have anything of yours on here?"

"Why? Are you going to make fun of me some more?"

"Maybe. Is it really bad? Or worse, *cheesy*?"

I cringe.

"Oh my God, it is, isn't it? I have to listen to it." She bounces in her seat to face me. "Please, please, please, Griffin."

Sighing, I play her the most recent track I was working on. It's solely instrumental. I expect her to be bored or not into it. But she closes her eyes, letting her fingers drum along her knees to the beat of the music.

When the song finishes, she studies me. Eyes searching my face. "That was really nice."

"Nice?" I side-eye her.

"Yeah, it was nice."

I clutch my chest. "Oh, that hurts."

"What, why?"

"*Nice* isn't the word anyone wants to hear their music described as." I sigh. "Nice is how you describe the handmade sweater with angels and cows embroidered on it from your grandmother."

Her infectious laughter fills the car. "Please tell me that is a real sweater that you own."

I nod. "I can confirm that it is, and my brother has a matching one that we wear every Christmas."

Chapter Twelve

I'm a piece of shit.

I wrecked his car...

His fucking car that I forced him to let me drive.

And to make matters worse, he didn't yell or cuss at me. Hell, he didn't even appear mad at all. Not even a slight raise of his voice.

Nada.

No, instead of blaming me, he comforts me.

That son of a bitch—please forgive me, Belinda and recently deceased momma—actually told me it was fine and that *our lives* were more important than his expensive car.

Like, what the hell is he getting at?

I need him to stop torturing me and just yell.

No one can be this calm and kind in a situation like this. The fact that he's talking to me about random things like ugly sweaters and playing his music to make me feel better has my chest aching.

We spend the rest of the night and the next day like this. Him driving and talking to me about anything and everything. Only stopping a few times for food, gas, and the bathroom, but never once do I offer to drive again.

Last night might have scared me off driving forever. Maybe I'll take up cycling.

Yeah, that's what I'll do.

I'll sell my car to pay for Griffin's repairs and then buy a bike.

But it's a long way to peddle to work from my apartment. And how would I buy groceries? I guess I can only buy enough to last me, like, two days, and only if they can fit in a backpack. Sweat beads along my hairline. I can already feel the ulcer forming in my gut from the stress of having to plan my grocery trips.

We turn off onto a small dirt road that seems to stretch on and on forever. Surrounded by trees, it seems to never end.

"Maybe we made a wrong turn?" I glance over at Griffin to find his brow pinched, as if he's as confused as I am. "You don't think we're—"

He holds up his hand. "Don't say it. If you say it, it will jinx us."

"You cannot be that superstitious, can you?"

"I sure as shit can. Time after time, the universe has proven these things to be fact," he says in all seriousness.

I cackle so hard my stomach aches in pain, making me groan. Griffin laughs, probably at my pain.

"You sound just like Bel." And just like that, his smile falls, disappearing as if it was never there.

Silence takes over again as he turns his attention back to the road without another word.

I want to backtrack, to rewind to before I said it. He had been letting me in, joking and sharing things with me, and I went and ruined it all by bringing up the person who, coincidently, is the only reason we even know each other.

I don't know what I was thinking, saying he reminds me of her. Well, I do know; I wasn't. It was just what I felt at that moment.

But his reaction stings. He was hurt by me. And I hate it.

It's only like this for a few more minutes, though. Because, around one last turn, we finally see it, our destination.

Both of our jaws go slack at the sight.

Hidden behind pine trees and the long, winding road is a giant log cabin with red shutters on every window, highlighting them in a quaint and inviting way that warms the coldness that had been settling between us.

"It's so—"

"Idyllic," Griffin says, finishing my sentence.

"Exactly." I nod, every tense muscle in my body relaxing now that he's speaking to me again.

As we park, I think of what I'm going to say to him, how I'm going to apologize for comparing him to a person I respect. The entire situation is giving me a headache.

He unbuckles his seat belt, moving his hand to open his door, but I grab his forearm to stop him. Shocked dark-brown eyes dart to where my hand is holding on to him. "Griffin—I'm sorry. I didn't mean to upset you. I didn't think before I spoke, and I'm sorry."

Still looking at where my hand is lying, he doesn't respond. The only reason I even know he's listening is because of the way his throat bobs as I speak.

Guilt weighs me down once more, and I move to pull my hand back, but he stops me, holding his hand over mine. That familiar electrical jolt that seems to always happen when he touches me shocks my system.

"Thank you."

The warmth of him disappears abruptly as he releases me so fast I almost question if it actually happened.

Griffin leaves the car so quickly that I'm left wondering what the hell just happened.

Confusion ripples through me at his abruptness, but I shake it off and follow his lead, hopping out of the car.

The frigid air hits, and I let out a hiss as I wrap my coat tightly around my chest. Snow crunches beneath our feet as we walk side by side up to the cabin's front door. As usual, Griffin holds it open for me, his gentlemanliness making my heart skip a beat and my core throb with desire for him.

Fuck, who knew I was so into chivalry?

I sure as shit didn't.

Maybe it's because all the men I know—besides my family—are pieces of garbage and only care for themselves. Which is fine most of the time.

Hell, I prefer it.

I like knowing where people stand. And douches tend to be pretty transparent and not expect too much from me in return.

Beside me, Griffin's arm brushes against mine as he drifts closer and closer to me while we approach the older man sitting at a large round wooden desk in the center of the lobby.

Fires roar in multiple fireplaces around the room, and the guests lounge in oversized chairs with drinks in their hands, laughing and kissing.

"Hello, welcome to Winding Wolf's Lodge," he says with a smile that lifts his long beard. "Checking in?"

"Yes." I smile. "We have a reservation under Fisher, Audra Fisher."

He types away on his computer. "Ah, there you are, Ms. Fisher. Just one moment, and I will get you the keys to your cabin."

I look at Griffin. His face is stony as he observes the man. My brows furrow in confusion. *What?* I mouth to him.

He glances my way for a second before training his gaze on the old man, who is bent over, looking for the keys to our cabin.

"Found it," the man calls out as his head pops out from under the desk. "Cabin seven."

Griffin reaches out, taking the key from him without so much as a smile or thank-you. I elbow him at that, giving him a stern look.

"Thank you," I tell the man.

He waves off Griffin's inappropriate behavior without a word, just smiling instead as he gives us directions to our cabin.

"If you need anything, don't hesitate to ask."

"Actually," Griffin says. "We are looking for someone. Any chance a Belinda Peterson checked in?"

He frowns. "I'm sorry, guys, I can't tell you any guest information."

Griffin nods, and my body shrinks with disappointment as I turn around.

"I might not be able to tell you if she is here, but you can always come to breakfast in the morning and see if she shows up," he calls out to us.

I look over my shoulder, giving him a small wave of appreciation.

After a short walk from the main building in the frigid wind, we find our cabin. Griffin sets our bags on the porch in front of the door before taking the key from my hand. His calloused fingers grazing along my skin, sending heat up my arm and down to my toes. It's so intense, I almost sigh, only stopping myself by biting the inside of my cheeks.

He unlocks the door, pushing it wide so I can step in before him. My eyes widen the moment I flip the lights on.

The cabin is nothing more than a king-sized bed with two small tables on each side and a bathroom off to the side. I knew we would have to share a room and bed again, but this feels more intimate than the times we've slept together before.

In the swingers' inn, the bed was smaller, but the room was filled with extra seating that didn't limit us to the bed. And the time in the car, well, that was pure survival, or so I keep telling myself.

That being said, it's fantastic. I've never been somewhere so cozy before. It's glamping at its finest, and I'm beyond excited.

Above the bed is a massive skylight. I plop on the mattress, not bothering to tour the rest of the room. The moment my head touches the pillow, I'm in heaven. The soft flannel sheets are inviting and warm as I run my hands up and down them. I look up from my place on the bed and gasp.

"Oh, Griffin, you have to see this."

He sets his phone on the bedside table, then lies down beside me. His gaze following my finger to where I point up to the sky above us.

Silence permeates the air, and I glance over to find his eyes wide with wonder and a bright smile lighting up his entire face. "The northern lights," he breathes, with a smidgen of awe in his voice.

I smile back at him. This is a side of him I haven't seen yet. One that is full of admiration for the small things, for nature and beauty. Something about it feels right. Like this is the real Griffin he's been hiding from me.

All I want right now is for him to open himself up to me. For us to be honest with each other.

From the slope of his jaw covered in stubble to the crinkle around his eyes as he smiles, every part of him is insanely handsome.

He turns, catching me staring at him. My cheeks warm with embarrassment, but not enough to stop me from continuing to stare.

"Secret for a secret?" I ask, staring up into his dark eyes.

He nods.

"I'm afraid of stairs."

"Why?"

"Because I have visions of me falling down or up them every time I see them."

"That's crazy."

I scoff. "What's crazy is voluntarily being feet in the air and trusting a stranger's workmanship to keep you safe."

He scoots a little closer to me. "But you were on the third floor at the nonmonogamous motel..."

"Yeah," I whisper. "And I was sweating bullets every time I saw them."

"Is that why you death gripped the rail?"

I laugh. "It is indeed."

We lie in silence, watching the night sky above us as colors swirl, lighting up the world.

"I have a collection of action figures."

"Why is that a secret?"

"Because they are from my mom—every time we would get into a huge fight, she would buy me one as a ceasefire of sorts."

"I like that."

"I did too."

"When was the last time you got one?"

"About six months ago," he says with a chuckle. "She blamed me for not taking the trash to the curb, causing her can to overflow. She swore up and down that she asked me to do it."

"Well, did you forget?"

"Hell no. I happened to be a momma's boy. When she asked me to do it, I did it right then." His hand moves an inch closer to mine. "A week later, she showed up at my house with the action figure and a letter apologizing. It turns out it was Brenden who she asked."

"So, did the toy fix everything?"

"That time, yes. But not every time. It was more or less a way for her to say she missed me and was thinking of me without actually talking to me."

"That's sweet," I say, trying to ignore my raging heart inside my chest.

His arm moves over my side, circling me as he pulls me closer to him.

I gaze up at him to find him looking down at me. A small smile on his lips.

"Secret for a secret," he says. "I really want to kiss you."

"I really want you to."

Without wasting another moment, his lips brush against mine, sending a wave of anticipation and heat through my body. He lingers there, his mouth hovering over mine—our breath intermingling for an excruciating second before I can't handle it.

I wrap my arm around his shoulders and yank him down, closing the distance.

Our lips crash together like a tidal wave against the rocks. All the pent-up emotions from this past week working their way out as he kisses me.

His tongue slides against my lips, and I gasp, opening my mouth to welcome him. The moment our tongues collide, my body thrums with want for him.

He tastes like the spearmint gum he was chewing earlier, and I can't get enough. I moan into his mouth, and he pulls away, beaming down at me with amusement and lust.

"God, you have no idea how long I've wanted to do that," he says, moving his lips across my jaw and down my neck.

"How long?" I ask with a moan.

He pulls back to look me in the eye. "Since the first moment I saw you inside that church."

An overwhelming rush of emotion flows through me for him.

I throw my leg over his hip, tangling my fingers in his soft hair as he returns to kissing me. His hands explore my body. Well, mostly my ass.

He skims over my bare legs, letting his fingers dip under the hem of my shorts before moving back down at a tantalizingly slow pace.

Everything about it feels so good.

Almost too good to be rational.

But I don't care. I can't think about anything other than him.

His lips on mine.

His hands on my skin.

The heat of his body pressing against me.

Every part of it has me close to combusting for better or worse.

Needing more friction, I roll my hips against him, and he must sense what I need, because he pulls me closer.

A breathy moan slips from his lips as I grind against his hard length. The pressure of him beneath his jeans is a perfect form of torture, and I'm dying for more. Griffin rolls on top of me, his hands gliding under my shirt, leaving a trail of goose bumps along my skin.

Desperate to feel more, I lift my arms, allowing him to pull my shirt off. Lust heats his dark gaze, causing my chest to heave with a mixture of nerves and hunger as I reach behind my back, unclasping my bra, and drag the sheer material off my body.

He sucks in a breath, his eyes moving from my bare chest up to my face. "You are so goddamn beautiful," he says, capturing my lips with his again. The kiss is greedy, full of pent-up desire as our tongues clash, lashing against one another as we relish in each other's bodies.

My excited heart races as I splay a hand across his chest, tugging his shirt up with the other until it's completely off. His broad chest is smooth under my touch. Feeling all over him, I move my hands lower until I'm working at the button of his pants. "We need to take these off," I say in between kisses. "Like, right now."

With a laugh, he rolls off me to take his pants and underwear off before helping me pull what's left of my shorts down my legs, dropping them onto the floor.

Heat fills my veins, and I have to bite my bottom lip to stifle the moan that's threatening to slip out as I take in his naked body.

Hot damn.

The man is spectacular. From his toned chest and muscular thighs down to his thick cock that is making my mouth water for him.

Restraint radiates off him as he closes his eyes, letting out a painful groan. "If you don't stop looking at me like that, this will be finished before we even start."

A laugh bubbles from me as I reach down to stroke his hard, silken cock. "Don't tell me you're a two-pump chump?"

"Baby, at this rate, I won't even make it to one," he says as his fingers find my soaking-wet center.

Teasing me, he runs his finger through my wetness over and over again like some form of delicious torture. I gasp as he sinks one finger inside me, his thumb rubbing circles on my clit, working me into a frenzy before he adds another. My grip on his erection slackens while my other hand tangles in the soft sheets, desperate for something to hold on to.

It's perfection. My hips jerk against his hand as he brings me closer and closer to breaking. Eagerly, I run my hands up his toned arms, looping them around the back of his neck to pull his lips back to mine. "Griffin?"

"Yeah?"

"Can you please fuck me already?"

Without another word, he kisses me again, his hand stopping its sweet stroking of my pussy. Frustration boils inside me as the need for more becomes all consuming. I'm about to shout at him in protest when he lines himself up at my entrance and thrusts inside me.

The sweet intensity of his cock stretching me leaves me crying out for more. The cords of his forearms flex as he rises onto his knees so he can watch as he disappears into me over and over again.

It's erotic as hell, watching the lust pour out of him as he focuses on where we're joined.

He lets out a string of incoherent words, and I arch under him, forcing him to fuck me at a deliciously punishing pace.

"You feel like fucking heaven," he pants into my ear between kissing and sucking at the skin on my neck. Sweat glistens over his brows as I begin to shake, my pleasure building at an explosive rate.

"Griffin," I whimper, my orgasm washing over me, causing every part of me to shudder beneath him.

He sucks in a breath through his gritted teeth when my pussy contracts around him, his brow furrowed with concentration. With two more thrusts, he follows me, shuddering as he falls on top of me while his climax rushes through him.

Panting, I run my fingers through his damp hair.

"That was—you were—amazing. This feels amazing," he says, rolling off me, pulling me along with him until I'm lying across his body, my head resting on his chest.

The strong rhythm of his pounding heart beneath my ear helps to ground me back to reality while his fingers draw circles against my hip. "Let's do that again," I say, smiling up at his sleepy face.

"Let's do that a few more times." His voice tapers off into a whisper.

I know by the evenness of his breathing that he's fast asleep beneath me. And I smile to myself as I drift off into a deep sleep with him.

Chapter Thirteen

Griffin

Soft lips pull me from a deep sleep as Audra plants small kisses along my jaw, slowly moving toward my lips. I keep my eyes shut until right after she presses her lips to mine. Audra squeals as I roll us over to have her under me, deepening the kiss.

Her legs wrap around my waist, pulling me flush with her still-naked body. I groan as she grinds against my already hardening dick. My eyes snap open, taking her in underneath me; her hair is fanned out on the pillow, and her arms are linked behind my neck while she circles her hips against me. She smiles up at me, pleased by what her body is doing to me.

"Never stop doing that," I groan, burying my face in her neck. Her skin smells like a combination of roses and sweat. It's fucking intoxicating. The need to kiss and suck her skin fills me, and I let it take over me by doing just that.

She laughs and moans at the same time. "I don't plan on it."

We continue drawing pleasure from grinding against each other until we come in an embarrassingly short amount of time. But fuck, I don't care. A hot woman let me rub my dick against her. Why should I be ashamed by that? Her body is heaven, and I'll take it any way I can get it.

Our breathing finally calms back to a normal rhythm, and we just lie there under the flannel sheets, facing each other like two lovestruck teens with all the time in the world. I push her sweaty strands of dark hair off her face. Her slick skin glowing in the morning light.

"So, we went from zero to one hundred," I say, tangling our hands between us.

She snorts. "You don't say."

"Any regrets?"

"Only one." She moves in closer, her lips hovering over mine.

"Don't leave me in suspense," I say, brushing my mouth over the corner of hers.

"I regret that we didn't do this sooner." She smiles against my lips.

"Sooner?" I laugh. "Any sooner, and we would have been fucking in a church."

"Ooh, just imagine the role-playing we could have done, me as the naughty nun and you as the piping-hot priest who has me kneeling before the altar that is his body."

I groan, unable to control myself any longer. I claim her mouth, devouring her once again as if it's the only thing I was meant for.

She pulls her mouth away from mine, causing me to whine in protest. "Griffin, you know I would *do* you all day if I could."

"Then why aren't you?" I greedily grasp her round ass in my hands and knead the flesh in my palms. Bringing my hips flush to hers, I press my once again hard cock against her.

"Because"—she pushes on my shoulders—"we have to get ready to go to breakfast."

"Go to breakfast? Why would I do that when what I want to eat is right here?"

She groans as my fingers dip into the space between her thighs. "Griff, don't make me say it."

Warmth spreads through my chest, and it's not the horny heat that's been flowing through me since she rubbed her luscious ass against my crotch in the car. Nope, it's from her using my nickname.

It's official. She's nicknamed me. That means this is more than a quick road-trip fling. She and I are a thing.

I want to toss her over my shoulder and jump for joy, but that might be a little much.

Play it cool, Griffin. Play it fucking *cool.*

"Hmm." My fingers inch closer to the sweet spot inside of her that I am dying to feel again.

"We have to see if she is here."

And just like that, the mood is killed.

I huff out a breath, letting go of her as I throw myself onto my back. "You just had to kill the mood."

She sits up, looking over her bare shoulder. "I'm sorry. But this is important."

"And this isn't?" I point at my painfully erect dick.

"I never said that." She jumps up, heading toward the bathroom. I wish I could say that's the end of my hard-on, but no. I watch that beautiful ass of hers sway into the only other room in this place, and memories of the night before and just a few moments ago, of the feel of it against me, has me winding back up.

A few seconds later, the sound of running water fills the room. "Want to—"

"Yes!" I jump up, not giving her a chance to change her mind.

"Take a shower? Want to come take a shower?" She rolls her eyes, stepping back out of the bathroom with a towel wrapped around her body as she digs her toiletries out of her bag.

"With you?" I ask, moving into the bathroom behind her.

"Yes, but there will be no funny business," she says as she drops the towel to the floor, giving me yet another glimpse of that fine ass before she steps into the tiled shower.

I follow her in, my body melting under the spray. "Trust me, baby, nothing about this is funny." I reach out my hand, gesturing to her shampoo. She squirts a dime-sized amount into my palm, and I lather it in my hair without another word or look in her direction.

I try my darndest not to think of her hands moving over her slick breasts, but clearly, I fail, and my dick continues to stand tall like a preening idiot.

You aren't getting touched by anyone but me, buddy, so deflate already.

It takes pretty much the entire duration of the shower, but I finally manage to get my boner to disappear. Though I'm pretty sure the annoying silence hanging between Audra and me is what really did the trick.

All clean and no longer smelling of sex, we dress and head to the main cabin, Audra slipping her hand in mine, giving me a reassuring squeeze. She knows how uneasy this situation is making me feel. But I'm not sure she realizes the extent of it all. That just the thought of Belinda makes my stomach churn and my mouth fill with saliva.

Fuck, if she knew that her best friend makes me sick, would she be holding my hand? Would her eyes still be shining up at me like this?

"Do you want to talk about it?" she asks as we draw close enough to see the large shutters on the main cabin's windows.

Unsure of how to answer, or if I want to talk about it or not, I don't respond.

It's not likely that we are going to find Belinda here, but on the off chance that we do, I know my world will be thrown into chaos once again.

"Whatever happens, it will be okay—I promise."

I stop walking, tugging her to me. "I don't see how it could be."

She wraps herself around me in a hug. "If she isn't in there, we go back to the room, and I show you just how okay this day can be."

That gets a grin out of me. "Oh, I like that plan."

She leans back, looking up at me, her eyebrows wiggling. "I thought you would."

"But what if—"

"What if she is here?"

I nod.

"If we find Bel in there, it will still be okay."

I don't even have to say a thing. My face does it all. Audra lifts herself up, placing a chaste kiss on my lips. "Same plan, baby."

It's so strange just how comfortable and natural it feels with her.

"So, if she is in there, you plan to take me back to the room to fuck me better?" I laugh.

She jumps up, wrapping her legs around my waist as my hand moves to catch her. "You like it?"

I lean in, kissing her. "Love it."

With a pat on my shoulders, she untangles her legs from behind me, hopping down. "Let's do this."

My arms feel empty without her in them.

Almost like it's wrong. It's like our bodies aren't meant to be separated. We belong intertwined and wrapped in each other.

And with that thought, I'm officially obsessed.

I want to pull her back to me. To pick her up and carry her back to our room like a caveman. To possess her every thought and bring her body to the brink of pleasure over and over again until she can't take it anymore.

But I don't.

Instead, I let her thread our fingers together and lead me through the massive wooden doors into the main building.

Rough wood beams cover every inch of the place from floor to ceiling. It is rustic, cozy, and elegant all at once. I glance over the place, taking in the winter wonderland atmosphere that this place has captured damn near perfectly.

Last night, I wasn't focused on looking around as much as I was on watching Audra. After that sex den that we stumbled into, I wasn't taking any chances. Now I'm on the lookout for anyone paying her too much unwanted attention.

Sure, it might have been overkill to give the old man the once-over, but perverts come in all shapes, sizes, and ages. And I refuse to let my guard down, even for a Santa wannabe.

In the end, it all worked out well, if I do say so myself.

Large rustic signs and laughter point us toward the dining room. Rows and rows of tables piled with every type of breakfast food imaginable fill the grand space.

My mouth waters at the scent of bacon wafting through the room just as my stomach growls. Until that moment, I had been able to block out my hunger with my need for Audra. But now that we are here, there is zero denying it. I'm starving.

We split up as we hit the buffet, Audra going straight for the pastries while I go to the bacon and eggs, stacking my plate high, not waiting to get to the table before I pop pieces in my mouth. Behind me, Audra lets out a throaty moan similar to some of the sounds she made last night when I was deep inside her.

I glance behind me to see her eyes closed as she relishes in the flavors of whatever the flaky breaded treat is, and just like that, I'm back to thinking about having her underneath me. About sliding inside her, about how warm and wet she is. Well, shit, my dick just hardened at all of the memories.

She stops, squinting at me as she licks her lips. "You better not be thinking about what I think you're thinking about."

"I'm not the one moaning."

"Keep your dirty thoughts out of my breakfast, Griffin." She walks around me, leading the way to a table while I follow her, admiring her insanely pert, round ass. Who knew I was an ass man?

"Yes ma'am."

I sit beside her, shoveling the remainder of the food into my mouth and not doing the main reason we're here—to look for Belinda.

We're almost done eating when Audra drops the food in her hand. Her head shoots up like a little meerkat in the desert, tilting like she's trying to home in on something.

"What?" I ask.

"I think I heard—" She turns in her chair. "Bel."

I follow her gaze to a table filled with men and women laughing. But immediately, my eyes gravitate to a woman with her back to us. Her long hair sways across her shoulders as her body vibrates with laughter.

It's her.

My stomach drops. My pulse thrums in my head, blocking out all other noises. Everything I've been looking for and avoiding pops up to the surface.

I thought I was ready, but if her back is causing me this much turmoil and inner anguish, I don't think this is going to work. Every ounce of chaos and noise that was quieted from the serene time with Audra comes rushing back in as I stay glued to my chair.

Chapter Fourteen

I t's her. She's here. Bel's here!

I would recognize that laugh and luscious hair anywhere. It's the hair I've been jealous of for the past few years.

I jump up from my chair and rush over to her.

The entire speech I've been planning since Griffin and I set out on this crazy scavenger hunt goes flying out the metaphorical window as I sprint over to her.

She's still laughing at something one of the men at the table has said to her—classic Bel, surrounding herself with people in order to hide—when I stop behind her.

I reach out, tapping her on the shoulder, even though what I want to do is shove her face into a plate of eggs. With a bright smile, she turns her head to look over her shoulder. Her eyes widen as she takes me in, her smile falling.

We stare at each other in silence. My eyes turning into slits as I try to convey everything I'm thinking. I expect her to face me to plead or something, but no. Bel just sits there quietly, not a look of remorse or joy crossing her face, only surprise.

The others at the large table look back and forth between us before one of them interrupts our Mexican standoff. "Mel, who is this?"

"Mel?" I choke out a laugh. Where is the woman who's full of creativity and passion? That woman wouldn't have chosen *Mel* as her alias. She would have chosen something like Fleur or, hell, Geneva. But not Mel. I can't help but be even more disappointed with her because of its unoriginality.

I thought I knew her, knew everything about her, from her toothpaste brand to the first day of her last period. But this boring fake name really has me second-guessing everything. You'd think the fact that she gave a child up for adoption and never told me would upset me the most, but no. It's this stupid, too-similar-to-her-name shit that's pushing me over the edge.

Snapping out of her shock, Bel turns to the man sitting beside her. "De'Montee, this is my best friend and soon-to-be business partner, Audra."

A small wave of relief washes through me at De'Montee's name. At least someone here isn't boring.

"Nice to meet you, Audra." He smiles. "Would you like to join us?" He gets up, offering his seat to me.

I wave at him. "No, it's okay. We just finished breakfast."

"We?" Belinda looks at me with confusion shining through.

"Yeah." I stare straight into her eyes, my anger at her selfish choices boiling my blood. "Griffin and I."

Shivers rake through her as her eyes dart around me to find him.

She swallows, taking a second before turning toward the group. "Please excuse me, everyone. I'm going to catch up with Audra for a few."

Once again, I'm moving without a thought for those around me. I don't look back to see if she is following me. I don't look to see if Griffin is nearby. I just walk and walk until I reach Griffin's and my cabin.

I unlock the door, leaving it open as I step into the room. Spinning on my heels, I find her right behind me, just like I was hoping. And I waste no time laying into her.

"I'm so mad, I could fucking kill you. But I won't. But damn it, I could," I say, shaking her shoulders. "Do you have any idea of the worry you've caused? What in the hell is wrong with you? Have you lost your goddamn mind? Oh, no need to answer that, because it is obvious based on the way you up and vanished.

"You told Jerry. *Jerry*..." I'm practically fuming as I spit word after word out as she rears back, flinching with each one. "Look, I get I wasn't supportive, but friends don't leave friends to wonder if they are dead or not. Understand? God, are you even going to try to explain yourself or just stand there shocked to see me?"

"Um, Audra, she couldn't answer even if she wanted to. You haven't stopped talking..." Griffin says behind me like the voice of reason.

Shit, I forgot about him. Once I set my sights on her, my focus was on Bel and Bel alone. Poor Griffin be damned. I rushed to her, leaving him by himself. I'm the worst lover, maybe ever.

I turn to look at him. His expression reveals nothing. The man has his feelings under lock and key.

I expect his face to be indignant, for him to be seething.

Not for him to seem indifferent.

I purse my lips, wanting to tell him I'm sorry for leaving him in my dust for her—the woman he is struggling to come to terms with, but he shakes his head at me.

"You're right." I spin back to face her. "Bel, want to explain your stupid-ass decisions?"

She swallows, her gaze locked on Griffin, who is looking at me.

"You came looking for me? Both of you?" she asks, almost sounding hopeful. She glances around the room, her gaze snagging on the bed, where the sheets are rumpled in a way that is clear two people slept in it.

When Griffin doesn't respond, I take the lead again.

"Yep, we did, 'cause your dumbass acted like an immature teenage girl who was just told she could be with her loser twenty-something-year-old boyfriend."

"I," she starts to respond, but I don't want to hear it.

"Save it, Bel. I don't want an excuse. I want you to pack up your shit and meet us in the parking lot in thirty minutes, 'cause your little tantrum is over."

She nods before walking around me and Griffin and out the door.

Once we're sure she is gone, Griffin closes and locks the door.

"Are you okay?" he asks, tilting my chin up.

I let out a laugh. "Am I okay? Fuck, Griff, I just left you high and dry to confront my best friend, your birth mother. I'm the one who should be asking you that."

He gives me a small, forced smile. "It's okay."

"No it isn't... You deserve better."

I expect some little quip denying it, but he surprises me by saying nothing, by knowing his own worth.

Reaching up, I wrap my hands around his neck, pulling his lips to mine. "Allow me to show you how sorry I am."

My tongue swipes out against his lips. Griffin responds by opening his mouth for me. His lips taste sweet from breakfast, and I want to lap up his delicious flavor.

Breathless, I break the kiss, walking him backward to the bed. His legs hit the mattress, and he falls onto his back. I lean over him, brushing kiss after kiss down his chest as my hands make quick work of the button and zipper on his jeans.

Lowering to my knees, I press my palm against the rough denim, feeling him twitch beneath me, and it's invigorating. The feeling of power rushing through my veins from knowing I'm causing such a physical response in this man is more than enough to make my year.

I trace the warm skin just under the waist of his jeans, loving the way his breath catches with each swipe of my fingers, before I begin tugging at the edges of the fabric. Griffin lifts his hips, helping me lower the jeans and boxer briefs to the floor.

I don't even wait a full second after getting his pants off before my tongue swipes out and licks him from root to tip.

He lets out a curse that only fuels my need to bring him to the brink of ecstasy.

I slide my hands up his thick, muscular thighs until I reach his hard cock. Grasping him with one hand, I guide him into my mouth, sucking at his engorged head before swirling my tongue around him. I move up and down his length with my mouth, savoring every noise and breath he takes as one hand twists and jerks his shaft in tandem while the other reaches down to cup his balls.

Griffin groans my name as his hips buck, bringing him deeper to the back of my throat. A choking gag sounds from my throat, and he immediately pulls out of me. Sitting up, he clasps his hands around my cheeks. "Shit, baby, I'm sorry. Are you okay?"

With my eyes watering, I smirk up at him while I rotate my hand in circles around his cock. "I'm fine, Griff. I want to make you feel good. And if fucking my face makes you feel good, I am more than willing."

His dick twitches in my hand.

Eyes dark with lust, he asks, "Are you sure?"

I nod. "I want you to fuck my mouth and come down the back of my throat."

His chest rises and falls with his rapid breathing. "Fuck," he groans, leaning down to slam his lips into mine for a hard kiss that steals my breath. "You are fucking perfect."

I smile up at him as he leans onto a forearm before placing one hand on my head, helping to push the hair from my face as I take him back in my mouth.

Griffin wastes no time. His hips drive forward, pushing him deeper down my throat. I place one hand on his thigh and the other on his flexing stomach, bracing myself against his thrusts.

It doesn't take long for my eyes to fill with tears while his movements become erratic.

I can tell he's getting closer by the tightening of his muscles and the sharp inhales of breath, so I wrap his other hand against the back of my head for him to control me however he wants. To hold me in place while he slams into me or for him to push me into him. He wastes no time using my mouth and throat. He finally lets out one last groan, and his cock throbs in my mouth as warmth coats the back of my throat.

I swallow every drop, then lick him clean, all while wearing a wicked smile on my face.

Griffin sits up, wiping the tears from around my eyes. "I'm sorry, I was too rough."

"No, you were perfect."

"Um, did you miss the part where your face is wet from the never-ending stream of tears?"

I climb into his lap. "That's not the only place that got wet."

He lets out a shaky breath, and I guide his hand under the waistband of my jeans until he can feel how much I enjoyed getting him off.

"Fuck, you are soaked," he whispers.

I stare into his deep brown eyes as his fingers slide through the pooling arousal between my legs.

Two fingers slide into me, and I jerk while his thumb finds my clit and presses down. He circles me as his fingers work in and out of my pussy at a leisurely pace until my legs are shaking. Heat builds at the base of my spine, readying me for my release. Griff kisses me, and my pussy clenches. Sensing how close I am, he speeds up his thumb, rubbing me so fast I break with a scream, coming all around his talented hand.

We both collapse on the bed, me splayed across his lap while his hands move from grasping my hips to holding me against him.

"I thought... I hoped we'd have more time," he says after minutes of silence.

"I know, me too."

"Now what?"

I rise from his chest, rolling off him to sit up on the side of the bed. "Now we pack our bags as quick as possible, 'cause we were supposed to meet her, like, a minute ago."

"That's not what I meant."

My eyes soften as I look over my shoulder. He's looking up at the ceiling, one hand rubbing at the base of his neck. "I know." I stand, moving around the room, picking up whatever I can find and shoving it in the nearest bag, not caring if it's his or mine. Not wanting to think about the reality of our situation or what might happen when we make it home.

Chapter Fifteen

Griffin

With no time to clean ourselves up, we pack our belongings and say goodbye to the magical cabin.

I opt to meet her at the car after checking out, not wanting to risk any unnecessary time with she-who-must-not-be-named.

Audra walks off to meet her best friend. Leaving so much unsaid. Maybe it's better that way. But something deep in the pit of my stomach is revolting at the thought of us just ceasing to be.

I only had a few nights with her, and already, I know it wasn't enough. It could never be enough.

She's everything I've been looking for without realizing it.

Hell, in the past few days, the music has returned to my head, filling me with notes and lyrics that all revolve around her and the beautiful person she is.

Mom would have loved her.

That all-too-familiar ache takes root in my chest again as I let grief slip its way back into my veins. I hate that I can't call her and tell her about the crazy woman who is slowly taking over my thoughts. I hate that she isn't here to give me advice.

God, I miss her.

I walk up the winding path to the main lodge one last time. The trees surrounding me no longer making me feel alive; instead, the path feels like it's closing in on me, and soon, I will be stuck with nowhere else to go.

Inside the lodge, I hand over the cabin key to the same man who was there last night and this morning.

He takes the card with the same smile he had given Audra earlier. *Okay, so maybe he isn't a pervert.*

"Looks like you and your wife found who you were looking for."

I nod, warmth filling my chest at the thought of Audra and me being bound together for more than a couple of days.

"That mother of yours is something else. She must keep you on your toes constantly."

Fire licks at my blood. "She's not my mother."

"Oh—I just assumed. You two look so much alike. I'm sorry, sir, my mistake."

"Yeah, it is." I grab the receipt from his hand and storm off.

Gone is the warmth enveloping me from Audra. Now there is nothing but icy darkness seeping into my every cell.

A stranger. A fucking *stranger* could spot us off the bat as mother and son, but I have been oblivious my entire life.

I stalk off toward the parking lot, my teeth grinding together so hard I think I might crack a molar.

I open the back of my Tahoe and throw my bag beside Audra's and a new bright-yellow suitcase, which makes me roll my eyes.

Yeah, she is so shiny and fun, not at all the baggage I would expect from someone who is trying to ruin my life.

Fuck Belinda and her stupid-ass suitcase.

Climbing into the driver's seat, I slam the door. I want to reach over and have Audra hold my hand, reassure me that this will pass, that everything is going to be okay. But she isn't there.

No, instead of offering me her support by sitting in her normal seat, she's sitting in the back, talking with that woman.

As if sensing my thoughts, she meets my gaze in the rearview mirror, her eyes trying to tell me something, but I look away, ignoring whatever it is and her.

I know I'm being an ass, but my feelings matter too. And after what just went down between the two of us in the cabin mere minutes ago, I guess I expected more from her.

Yes, that woman has been her friend for years, while she and I have only been whatever we are for mere hours. But that doesn't stop the sting.

I want to be the one she cares about.

It's selfish, but it's how I feel.

Buckling my seat belt, I don't bother to ask if everyone is ready or buckled. I just pull off, bringing us back to the long, winding road until we reach the desolate highway once again.

Chapter Sixteen

Audra

Our return home has taken three days, all of which have been filled with the most uncomfortable tension known to man. Every moment seems to have an overabundance of silence and stares.

After being apart from my bestie for longer than anyone should have to be, I've been sitting in the back with her, leaving Griffin to be the odd man out. It gives me a small twinge of guilt.

I've tried my best to fill the time by talking, mostly to Bel, since Griffin's been very surly and broody.

I ask her about everything she's been up to in the past few weeks, and she fills me in on her grand adventure of catching a bus, then hitchhiking until she made it to see the northern lights before the season was over. "If it weren't for my new friends you saw at the table, I might have died from the snow."

Crimson heat creeps up my neck as I think about Griffin and me under the night sky, wrapped up in each other. It has only been a few days since, but so much has happened between now and then that it feels like a lifetime ago.

"I still can't believe you not only walked in this weather but got in a van with a group of strangers."

"They had kind faces." She waves off my concerns.

The entire time Belinda talks, Griffin remains quiet and stone-faced as he faces the road. Never once making a peep, no matter how many times I try to include him. I direct question after question his way, hoping he'll let go of at least a bit of what's eating him up or, at the very least, make the situation a tiny bit less uncomfortable for all of us.

But no, he won't indulge me.

Every question goes unanswered.

All of my pointed looks avoided.

Hell, I'm not even sure he's paid any attention to me or Belinda since we climbed into his SUV. With his beanie pulled down to cover his ears, it blocks out most of the beautiful face I'm already missing. The only way I figure out that he's been listening is from the way his fingers turn white, giving the steering wheel a death grip every time Bel speaks, but relax when I talk.

Poor Bel is struggling. With every glance in his direction, she shakes more than a leaf on a windy day, but doesn't say a word to him. After their last interaction, I can't blame her for that either.

But as difficult as this is for her, I know it's worse for Griff. He's pushing the pain this is causing him way deep down, burying it where no one else can see.

I'm torn by the desire to be loyal to both of them while knowing that is impossible. The idea of hurting either of them is becoming more and more like a reality. And I hate it.

It shouldn't be like this. I should think of my best friend. The person I have known for years. The woman who has supported me through every up and down in my life. But it isn't that simple.

The time I've spent with Griffin has caused a part of me I had long forgotten to come alive. I'm falling for him, even though it's beyond ridiculous and way too soon.

But the heart isn't logical, and neither am I.

I haven't gotten to talk with either of them privately since the morning we found her. It's been days of this—me walking around on eggshells, trying to keep the peace, if that's what this is.

Even when we stopped at cheap motels for the night, it was lights out in Bel's and my room the moment we stepped inside. So, zero chance to pick my bestie's brain. And Griff made sure to close his door each night without even a glance in my direction.

With only a couple hours left on our journey, I am becoming more confused about what to do. I don't know how to handle the situation—or either of them—anymore.

We pull over at a small gas station off the highway. Bel is the first to jump out, stretching her arms and legs. "I'm going to use the restroom, then grab some snacks. Either of you want anything?" she asks with hopeful eyes.

Griffin turns his back to her, pushing the gas pump's nozzle into the Tahoe.

I smile. "I'll take a gigantic water and a red Gatorade, please."

"Go it." Her gaze lingers on him for a moment before she turns toward the store.

I wait until she's through the door, then walk the few steps to him. His shoulders are high and his face tight.

"Griffin." I grab his forearm, pulling him to look at me.

His hard eyes soften as they find mine. "Audra, I..." His voice is hoarse and full of pain.

I wrap my arms around him, holding him tight to me until I can feel his heart pounding in his chest. I curl my fingers in the hair at the nape of his neck.

"It's not okay." He leans back to look at me, his hands moving from my back to my face. "How could it ever be okay?"

Caged in each other's arms, I lift on my tiptoes, bringing myself as close to eye level as I can. "I don't know. But I will do whatever I can to make it better for you."

He ducks his head, bringing his lips to mine for a featherlight kiss. I sigh, mouth parting for what's to come next, readying myself to deepen the moment with another kiss.

"Okay, Auds, I have your huge water and red-colored sports drink," Belinda calls from a few yards away.

Griffin jumps back, letting go of me so fast that I nearly topple over as he goes back to pumping the gas as if nothing happened.

The sudden distance is like the icy shock of cold water, leaving me hurt and confused. I understand that he doesn't like or trust Bel, but what does that have to do with her seeing us together? Is it about her? Or does he not want to be seen with me?

Clearing my throat, I plaster on a smile, wiping my sweaty palms on my jeans. I turn, taking the drinks from Bel. "Thanks." I'm climbing into the back when she touches my arm.

"Hey, do you mind sitting up front for a while? I really want to stretch out to get some sleep."

"Sure," I say, backing away so she can climb in. I place the drinks on the passenger side floor. "I'm going to use the restroom before we go."

After finishing my business and leaving the bathroom, I bump into a hard wall of man. Hard muscle flexes beneath my palms as the intoxicating aroma of wood and spearmint hits me, and I'd know that scent anywhere—the one that's uniquely him.

Without a word, he brings his lips crashing against mine. The kiss is fast and full of passion, leaving me stunned when he pulls away. He smiles, moving around me to use the restroom.

Not even the cold wind blowing on my face as I walk back to the car could damper the heat that's still coursing through me from Griffin's kiss. Opening the passenger door, I find Bel fast asleep and the blanket Griffin's mom made sitting in my seat, as if it was placed there just for me. The soft fabric wrapped around my body feels like a consolation prize now that I know what it feels like to be enveloped in Griffin's strong embrace. The seat belt clicks as I buckle up before tucking the blanket under my chin, breathing in his comforting scent.

Griffin climbs in, glancing over to me with a grin, only for the cheerful expression to fade as he catches Bel's sleeping form in the mirror.

I pick up the water bottle by my feet, gesturing it toward him. "Here." Lines form between his eyes as he looks at it questioningly. "I had her get it for you."

"Why?"

"Because I knew you wouldn't ask her for anything." I thrust the bottle at him again, and this time, his hand wraps around it, setting it in the cup holder.

"Thank you—for thinking of me," he says, reaching over to intertwine his fingers with mine.

"Anytime," I whisper, lifting his knuckles to my mouth for a kiss.

A smile tugs at the corner of his lips as his eyes drift from me to the road.

Chapter Seventeen

Griffin

We finally arrive back in town at eleven in the evening. Everyone is silent—well, everyone except for Audra as she directs me to Belinda's place. I'm not sure if she forgot that I already know where Belinda lives or if she's trying to save face for me. Either way, I like her a little more than I did an hour ago.

I pull up in front of Belinda's still perfectly manicured lawn.

"Here we are," I say, talking for the first time in hours.

"Thank you, Griffin," Belinda says, her voice cracking as she opens the door and steps out.

When the door shuts, Audra's eyes bore into me. "Are you kidding me?"

"What?"

"You didn't even respond to her. She was trying."

I gawk at her. "So?"

A coward is what I am. I could just admit that the moment we found Belinda, everything I had planned disappeared and anger filled its place. And that I wasn't sure I could handle the answers I was so desperate for anymore. But no, instead, I play the asshole card.

Her eye twitches as she reaches for her door handle, but I press the lock on my side, trapping her with me.

Her glare sharpens. "So help me, Griffin, if you don't unlock this door in the next second, I will chop your dick off and use it as a curling iron."

I wince at the mental image. "Damn, baby, you have a sick mind."

"Griffin, open the door."

"Just stop for one moment, okay?"

She crosses her arms over her chest, causing her breasts to lift and my dick to misread the moment.

A huff bursts from her nose, and I know that my ogling isn't helping the situation.

"Please don't go," I say, reaching over to pull one of her hands away from her arms.

She looks out the window to where Belinda is standing on the sidewalk, waiting for one of us to get out and unlock the hatch for her to get her bag.

"Please," I plead. "I don't want to be alone with my thoughts tonight."

The scowl on her face softens as she takes me in. "Griffin..."

I shake my head, letting her hand go. "Never mind, go catch up with your friend."

She sits there looking at me before glancing out at Belinda, the conflict clear on her face. "I'm sorry." She leans over, placing a kiss on my cheek as I stare ahead, unlocking the door for her.

The moment she hops out onto the sidewalk, my hands grip the steering wheel so tight, the tendons pop out in my wrists.

I wait until the two of them make it inside the house and shut the brightly colored door before I drive away. With my mind swarming with a fog of confusion that I can't wade through, I drive to my mother's house instead of my own.

My subconscious knew what I needed. Knew where I needed to be. Closer to my mother. Closer to my anchor.

Walking up the stairs, I grab hold of the railing when my vision blurs and my legs weaken. They shake as I lower myself to sit on the steps. My breathing becoming more rapid with every passing second.

I prop my elbows on my knees, lowering my head.

My heart pounds against my chest.

"Fuck," I grumble.

I place one hand on my chest and the other on my stomach. With a deep breath, I close my eyes and exhale. Over and over again until my breaths become normal and my heart has calmed its fucking tits.

Then I reach into my back pocket, pulling out my phone. Instinctively, I click on Bren's contact. He's always been one of my support systems, other than Mom.

"Griff," he answers on the first ring. "Go prepare some ice packs, 'cause when I get my fucking hands on you, I'm going to beat the shit out of your ass for scaring me."

"Good luck keeping your badge," I joke.

"Fuck the badge," he snaps. "The only family I have left just up and disappeared a week ago, and you think I give two fucks about my job? Go screw yourself."

I grind my teeth together. He's right; I'm an asshole, and I deserve his wrath, but at this moment, I can't handle it.

"Bren..."

"No, don't 'Bren' me, you little bitch. You left me in the dark. I understand your life is in tatters, but don't lock me out."

I nod, and somehow, he knows.

"Are you okay?" he asks, his voice calm and soft with concern.

Wetness pools in my eyes as I sniff. "No."

"Are you home?"

"No—I'm at Mom's."

Keys jingle in the background. "I'm on my way."

I stay on the steps until he arrives. The moment he gets to me, he helps me to my feet and guides me inside the house.

"I need booze."

"You want a beer?" he asks, standing on the other side of the dining-room table. I roll my eyes at him.

"So?" His brow furrows.

"If we are going to get deep, I need to get drunk."

He walks away, returning thirty seconds later with two beers. "How deep are we getting?"

When I don't answer, he continues. "Like, balls deep? Or are we talking so deep down that you feel it in every cell?"

I sigh, rubbing at my temples. "Can you not make this sexual?"

His hands fly up. "Fine, I'll stop. I was just trying to bring the somber mood down a peg."

A shit-eating grin crosses his face.

"I cannot stand you. At this point, drinking myself to death is looking better and better by the moment."

His smile drops, all the humor draining from him. "Don't you ever say that again."

I toss my head back with a groan. "Bren, you know I was just—"

"I don't want to hear any of that shit. You might laugh it off like a joke, but it isn't funny."

"Seriously, I was just joking. You know I would never do that."

He takes a long swig of his beer before sitting across from me. "Do I? Because up until last week, I never thought you would run off without so much as a word. So, tell me, is your behavior supporting your declaration?"

I swirl the bottle back and forth between my hands on the table. "You're acting as if you didn't have any idea I was looking for her."

His hand scrubs down his face. "Yeah, I knew you wanted to find her, to talk to her, but I never thought that you would leave me out of the loop. Answering my calls here and there isn't good enough. I know you are going to hate me for saying this, but you just did exactly what she did. Vanished without telling the people who are important what's going on with you. And it scared the shit out of me. You are it. You're all I have, and right now, it doesn't even feel like I have that."

I rest my head in my hands, taking in everything he says, no matter how much it hurts to hear. Because I did this. I put him through hell, and I deserve the shame that's flaming through my skin.

After a minute of quiet, he says, "Look, I understand... Well, actually, I don't. You're going through so much right now that I can't wrap my head around. I might be grieving Mom. But you, you're grieving two mothers."

It's like he's able to smell my bullshit, sniffing out the lies I've been telling myself.

I sniffle, wiping under my nose before bringing the bottle back to my lips. With another drink, I give him a nod. "You're right."

"Damn skippy, I am."

And just like that, I'm laughing again.

"Okay, now that that's out of the way. Tell me what happened with Belinda and the hottie, Audra."

Later that evening, after a few more beers than was smart, I stumble into my bed face-first. My face presses against the pillow, and I inhale the strong scent of the laundry detergent Mom used. A special concoction of hers that she refused to tell anyone the recipe for.

It's like walking into a meadow on a spring day with the sun beaming down on you and a light breeze ruffling your hair. It's bliss and contentment wrapped in one aroma.

It smells like her.

And I never want it to fade.

I'm afraid for that day when the scent is gone and her mixture runs out.

Rolling onto my back, I pull my phone out from my pocket. Not thinking about what consequences might come of this drunk dial, I press call.

"Hello?" she whispers through the phone after three rings.

"Fisher... Do you still like me?"

There's a brief pause before she asks, "Are you drunk?"

"Maybe. But that doesn't answer my question, Miss Avoidy." I curl over onto my side, putting the phone on speaker and setting it on the pillow beside me so I can pretend she's in bed with me.

"Who said I ever liked you?"

I laugh. "Baby, your wet pussy did."

What sounds like a sharp inhale filters through the phone. "Griffin."

"Yes, Audra?"

"Is this a booty call?"

I shake my head. "Nope. Not unless you want it to be. Why? Do you want it to be?"

"You wish."

"God," I groan, "do I ever."

"Your horny ass needs some sleep." Her voice is light and bubbly, and it makes my stomach do flips. Or at least I'm fairly sure that's from her and not the beers.

With a sigh, I admit she's right. "Fine, I'll go to sleep."

"Goodni—"

"But only if you answer my question."

"Really, Griff?"

"I like it when you call me Griff. And yes, I need to know."

"Of course I do. You think I would tolerate just anyone's drunken booty call?"

"I would hope not. I do like the idea of being special. The man breaking through a booty-call wall you've put up."

With one last laugh, she tells me goodnight again before hanging up.

Chapter Eighteen

"So, you and Griffin?" Belinda asks causally while crossing her legs in the chair across from me.

My eyes turn to slits as I stare at her. "What about us?"

"Oh, so you're an *us*. That was rather fast, don't you think?"

I rear back a little, raking my gaze over her at her audacity. "Excuse me?"

She lifts her hands in mock surrender. "I'm just saying."

My jaw tightens as her words have my hackles rising. "First of all, don't you slut shame me, you slut! Second, it's none of your business if he and I are an *us* or not. And lastly, nice fucking try. But you aren't getting off the hook that easily."

Bel groans. "Damn it. It was worth a try."

"Sure."

"For the record, I'm not sure how I feel about you being with my son."

It takes everything in me not to snap back that he isn't hers. She gave away that right long ago when she gave him away. I hate my mind for going there. For instantly snapping against her. It's amazing how much I've changed in just a week. How much Griff has altered my brain chemistry.

Yes, he technically is her son. Her flesh and blood.

But something in me stands with him and his late mother.

So instead of answering, I tilt my head, waiting for her to fill the silence.

After thirty seconds of my silent staring, she breaks. "I'm sorry. I really am. I—I just needed to get away."

"I'm sorry you felt that you couldn't lean on me. That I was part of the push that made you so desperate you would rather run than face it all."

She wipes a falling tear from her cheek. "I was so upset. Not only with you for not automatically having my back at and after the funeral. But also with myself. I don't know what I was thinking."

I stand up from my chair, moving to crouch beside her. "Bel, this question might upset you, and I'm sorry for that, but have you been taking your meds?"

Her chin trembles, and her head shakes back and forth. I already knew the truth, but I needed her to tell me.

She needs to be honest about it.

Hell, I knew from the moment she was fidgeting in that church that something was off. But I didn't want to admit it.

"Why?"

She shrugs. "I thought I could do it without them."

"Babe, you know those meds are to help you, and not taking them can be dangerous. Have you had any... thoughts?"

"No, I'm not going to hurt myself. I know it was dumb, and I can see the stupid mistakes I have made are the result of an episode, but that doesn't stop it from hurting."

Her tears fall rapidly as I gather her in my arms, hugging her as close to me as I can. "What do you need me to do? How can I help you?"

She sucks in a breath. "Just stay with me tonight."

"Like an old-fashioned girls' night?"

A small smile graces her lips, and I take that as a victory. "With cheesy movies and bad pedicures?"

"You got it."

We spend the night curled up on the couch, watching movies with much younger people than us on Netflix, like *To All The Boys I've Loved Before* and *The Kissing Booth*. But Bel crashes before we get around to doing each other's nails.

Exhausted from the past few days, I'm just about to follow her into sleep when I get a drunk call from Griffin that sets my body on fire with desire.

We've only been apart for six hours, and already, I crave him, wondering when I'll see him next.

Bel and I are lying on opposite ends of the couch, nothing unusual for us, but my chest tightens as guilt nags at my conscience.

How can I feel so much for this man who I've just met?

But even more than that, how can I feel anything for someone who is hurting my best friend?

It's not his fault, and maybe that's why I can't get him out of my head. He is going through the motions himself. Grieving and reeling from everything, and yet he still wants me.

I don't know how to handle this situation without hurting someone, unless... They become something like friends themselves.

Maybe I could be that bridge between them. The person who brings them together. Who helps to end the pointless pain they're both inflicting.

It's official. I'm going to be the thing they have in common.

So I devise a plan—well, maybe *plan* is a strong word. Ploy or scheme is probably more appropriate. It's only half thought through, but that doesn't matter. I can figure the rest out as I go.

The only thing that's for sure is that I want both of them in my life.

In the morning, I drive Bel to her psychiatrist's office for an emergency appointment. Bel offered to drive herself, seeing as I'm still unsure about being behind the wheel, but sadly, I don't exactly trust her to go. Can I be blamed, though? She had both a manic and depressive episode very close together and went off her meds. It won't hurt to make sure she takes care of her mental health.

I only tremble for the first five minutes, flashbacks of Griffin's Tahoe spinning on the ice playing on a loop as my foot presses on the accelerator. Around minute ten, my nerves subside, and I'm able to get us both there in one piece.

I wait in the car for her for over an hour before she walks out of the glass doors looking lighter than before.

"You good?" I don't ask for any details. Her appointments are personal, and I respect that.

"I'm getting there."

"That's awesome. Do you think it would help if you had a project?"

"Like what?"

"Like getting serious and finding us a location for our store," I say excitedly. I've been thinking about this ever since my mom fired her. Now that she doesn't have Fisher Floral taking up forty hours of her week, she can devote the time to our dream.

"Do you think we're ready?" Bel asks, and it's like time stops. Does she not believe we're ready? Financially, we are more than ready. Well, I think we are. Mentally… I think pouring ourselves into the business will be good for both of us, Bel especially.

"Hell yeah, I do," I boast.

A bright smile blooms across her face, and she claps her hands together. "Zillow and I are about to get very well acquainted."

Bel pulls her phone out and downloads every real estate app possible, and suddenly, all I hear is ringing as everything becomes real. We are really doing this. And I think I'm going to be sick.

I drop her off at her house, claiming that I need to go straight to work, but that's a lie. I need space to process that I'm taking the next step in following my dreams.

Thankfully, I told my mom that I was still under the weather. The guilt of lying to her is starting to upset my stomach. And unfortunately, the only thing that ever helps when I get emotional cramps is to come clean.

But instead of wallowing or freaking out about what comes next, I take my ass down the street to my favorite bar.

Once inside, I'm hit with a wall of warmth and the stench of liquor. I find a spot near the end of the bar on a stool that has seen better days.

The daytime bartender eyes me with a suspicious look. I guess he isn't used to women like me in bright puffer coats drinking in the middle of the day, but here we are.

He stops in front of me, drying a glass with a white cloth. "What will it be?"

Panicking, I tell him the first drink I can think of. "Cosmo, please."

A bead of sweat trickles down my spine, and I shimmy out of my coat, laying it on the back of the stool as I watch him get to mixing. He hands me the glass without a word, and I pull my phone out, fumbling through Instagram as I drink my worries away.

I'm sipping away on my cosmo when two men around thirty walk in. They take the stools on the opposite end of the bar, facing me.

One of them looks familiar. With his friendly smile, he waves at the bartender. The three share a laugh as two beers are set in front of them.

I look back to my phone, searching through commercial real estate listings, trying to envision Belinda's and business. I wonder which spaces she's going to lean toward.

"Shit, Henderson," one of the men barks out, laughing while clapping the other on the back.

Recognition flares as I look at the man next to him. As stealthily as possible, I snap a picture, praying I'm not wrong. Then send it to Griffin.

> Audra
>
> Does this belong to you?

> Griffin
>
> Audra, darling. Why are you taking pictures of my brother?

> Audra
>
> Maybe I miss you.

> Griffin
>
> I figured. But you don't need his knock-off ass when you could have me.

I don't even have time to reply before he sends another text.

> Griffin
>
> I'll be there in ten minutes. DO NOT MOVE.

Seven minutes later, Griffin strolls through the door, dressed in dark sweats and a backward baseball cap. My mouth waters at the sight of him. I take a long pull of my drink while watching him walk over to where his brother is seated.

Griffin places a hand on his brother's shoulder, and he turns around, gathering him into a big hug before sitting back down. The three men start a conversation that I can't hear, but when three heads turn my way, I know exactly what they are talking about.

Damn hot blabbermouth.

Slinking down in my seat, I shield my face with a hand.

Seconds later, someone grabs my wrist, pulling my hand away. I glance up to find both Griffin and his brother there. Matching smiles filling their entire faces. If I didn't know better, I would have never expected them to be anything other than brothers.

"Audra," Griffin says, "this is Brenden, my older, less attractive and unsuccessful brother."

Brenden elbows him in the stomach, causing Griffin to double over yowling, then offers me his hand. "I think he meant I'm his charming, better-mannered, and much more handsome older brother, Brenden."

I extend my hand, taking his. "Hello, unsuccessful and charming Brenden." I look over to where Griff is swiping my drink to take a sip. Alert my diary: we are at the sharing-drinks level of our relationship. Which somehow seems more intimate than having one another's genitals in our mouths. "I'm Audra, the chick Griffin is now banging."

Said man chokes, coughing down the fruity concoction as Brenden chuckles, patting his brother's back. "I like you, Audra, the banger of my brother."

The choking continues as Griff's eyes widen. In between coughs, he mutters, "Fuck you both."

Brenden leans closer to me. "I bet he will later."

Even with the jokes being about my sex life, I am living for it. Brenden is the quintessential brother. Reminds me of Nate a little. Well, except for the fact that he is hotter than sin, and Nate is... Nate.

I mean, damn, the Henderson genes are something else, because these two are perfection. It's almost as if I manifested them myself.

If I hadn't met and fallen into a deep infatuation with Griffin, I would be all over Brenden. He is just *that* sizzling.

But he isn't Griff. Griff is in a league of his own.

From being a musician to his constant brooding that makes his smile so infatuating it feels like a gift from the gods. And don't get me started on those hands, his mouth, or his—I stop myself before I get sucked into his dicknado, even though, if I'm honest, I'm already spinning inside with the force that is him.

Finally able to speak again, Griffin furrows his brow. "What are you doing here, anyway?"

"Oh, just spiraling about my plans and dreams taking shape," I say on an exhale.

He nods as if my answer makes any sense, then eyes his brother. "And you? Don't detectives have to be, like, sober as a gopher during the day?"

Brenden rolls his eyes. "Yes, little shit, but I'm off today, which you would have known if you ever paid attention to me."

"Pshh, I always pay attention to you. I'm practically your stalker. Besides, you're the one who never listens."

"Sure... That's why last night, after two drinks, you told me all about this one." He gestures at me with his thumb.

My head perks up. "He did?"

"Yep," they both say in unison.

Brenden looks back at him in surprise that he would admit it, but Griff is staring at me with those eyes, conveying everything he wants to do to me and more.

Brenden slowly backs away with his hands in the air. "Well, well, well. It seems I am not needed here." He stalks off toward his friend. "Stay safe, you two."

Griffin slides closer to me.

"Does he mean—" I begin to ask as Brenden shouts across the bar, "I meant sex-wise and in general. Be all the safes."

Not turning around, Griffin raises his thumb in the air. "So, do you have any other plans for the day, or?"

"No plans... Well, other than getting you alone."

A grin flashes across his lips. "Done and done."

Griffin hops into the driver's seat of my Camry, pushing the seat all the way back to fit his long legs. From the passenger seat, I smother a giggle. He is the picture of cramped but content.

Less than five minutes later, we arrive at his house. A small ranch-style home that's everything and nothing like I imagined for him. The version of him that the world sees would never fit here. But the warm, gooey man who holds my hand any time he can fits here perfectly.

The inside is full of dark wood and blues that remind me of the crisp fall evening.

Griffin grabs my hand, not allowing me any time to snoop or gawk at his surroundings as he leads me through the small entryway into the living room.

Instruments fill the room. Guitars, keyboards, and what looks like a pair of bongos are all strung about. Pieces of crumpled paper litter the coffee table.

"Sorry about the mess. I hadn't been home yet when you texted."

I arch a brow. "You didn't go home last night?"

His head quirks to the side as he pulls me into him. "Nope."

"Then where did you sleep?" I raise a brow, waiting for an explanation.

The smile that has been lingering on his lips falls away. "At Mom's. I just needed—her."

My chest aches for him. How could I have forgotten, again, that his mom just passed away?

I wrap him into a tight hug. "Wait—" I pull back. "You just tried to trick me into thinking you were with someone else." *The nerve of this man.* I smack his chest.

"No," he says, catching my hand and holding it to his chest. "You came to that wild idea all on your own."

"Well, your long pause didn't help to clear it up very fast."

He shrugs. "What can I say? I like you jealous. It lets me see how much you like me."

I lean into him, brushing my lips against his. "I like you." I linger over his mouth, waiting.

Griffin wastes zero time kissing me like I'm the air his lungs desperately need. His tongue sweeps inside my mouth, tangling with mine, his hands digging into my hips as he pulls me even tighter against him. Every part of us touching, with no end in sight.

My hands trail up his neck, fisting the silky strands at the base of his neck. A familiar throb starts deep in my core, steadily getting stronger with every second his hands and mouth are on me.

I want him, now.

Just as I'm about to grind myself against his leg for a little relief, he pulls away.

A whine leaves my lips as he does. "No, give me more." I clutch at his shirt.

His chest heaves as he shakes his head. "I didn't bring you here for that."

"You didn't?" My hands release their iron grip on his shirt, falling away from him.

"I just wanted to spend more time with you."

The pout that I'm sure is on my lips fades away as the corners of my lips turn up. "You know you could spend time *in* me."

A groan leaves his mouth as his head falls back. "You can't talk like that when I am trying to be a gentleman."

A mischievous smile graces my lips. "What, you don't think gentlemen fuck?"

"No. It's literally in the word, gentle man, gentleman."

"So, no nakey time?"

"No nakey time."

I snap my fingers in defeat. "Damn, I really thought you would cave."

"Me too," he whispers. "Me too."

Instead of blowing each other's minds in the sheets, Griffin has us propped up on the couch, eating sweets.

I've got to give it to the guy. He's a superb host. There hasn't been one *accidental* boob graze or fondling of any kind.

It's kind of disappointing.

Which is odd in itself.

Since when do I want a man to think with his dick?

I blame Griffin and his gentlemanly ways for making me think with nothing but my vagina.

Somehow, all this respect and distance is doing nothing but making the throbbing in my clit worse. His self-control is apparently the ultimate turn-on.

My hands itch with the need to touch him, to get him to see the light, aka to fuck me.

I caught my horny ass doing just that multiple times while playing a not-so-innocent game of Scrabble.

Did I spell the words *lick* and *thrust*?

Yes, yes I fucking did.

Did he respond with words like *wait* and *savor*?

Yes, yes he *fucking* did, and my pussy clenched.

After an hour or so of games, we ordered Chinese takeout. Shoving noodles and egg rolls into our faces, followed by beer, was the perfect afternoon.

Well, almost.

I excuse myself from the table and head into the bathroom across the hall from his bedroom. After I take care of my business, I wash my hands and go to use Griffin's robe to dry my hands because, like any typical thirty-something-year-old man, he doesn't have any hand towels.

The soft cotton brushes against my skin, and an idea takes root in my brain.

It's either going to end very badly and awkwardly for me, or it's going to be one of the best things I've ever done.

I strip out of my clothes at lightning speed. Then saunter back into the living room, ready to make that man lose his self-control.

He glances from the TV to me, then does a double take and blinks in shock. "What are you doing?"

My hands tremble as I slowly untie the robe, letting it drop to the floor. A thrill races through me. I've never been so bold. "Like what you see?"

"More than anything." His throat bobs as he sets his drink on the table. Everything about him turns me on, from the heat of his gaze on my body to the way his chest has been rising and falling rapidly ever since I walked into the room. With two steps, he's on me, hands moving down my body as he bends, lifting me in his arms.

My legs wrap around his waist as he kisses me. His tongue inside my mouth giving me promises of what's to come. The pads of his rough fingers dig into the naked flesh of my ass as he walks us back to his bedroom and gently sets me on the bed.

"You're playing dirty." He steps away, putting distance between us.

"You love it," I pant, desperate to have him on top of me, inside of me again.

Kneeling on the bed, he grabs ahold of my ankles to pull me to the very edge with a wicked grin on his lips.

He pushes my legs open, his hands running up from my ankles, only stopping at my inner thigh to tease the skin just before he reaches my dripping-wet center.

His dark eyes take in every inch of my open pussy, a feral look washing over him as his fingers dip into me, spreading me open for him.

I gasp at the sensation of his finger entering me, while his thumb rolls my clit in lazy circles.

My breathing quickens as he pulls his hand back, bringing his fingers to his mouth, his tongue darting out to lick each and every one clean.

A groan leaves his throat, and my core throbs, needing more, needing him.

"Lick me," I demand.

"What was that?" He smirks.

"I want you to eat me out, now."

He doesn't waste any time. Before I can dish out another command, his tongue is darting through my slit up to my clit. My hips lift to him, needing more of him on me.

He smiles as his tongue moves in torturous circles, drawing my pleasure out.

I gasp when he applies the slightest pressure to my throbbing nub. His eyes flare with desire.

The moment's so incredibly intimate.

In the past, whenever a man would go down on me, I would close my eyes or look anywhere but at what he was doing. I definitely didn't stare into his eyes as his mouth went to town on my lady bits.

But with Griffin, it's different. It isn't just that I want him to see what he is doing to me, how much pleasure I'm getting from his actions. I also want to see what it does to him.

If it turns him on to coax an orgasm out of me with just his mouth.

His tongue, combined with the intensity of his gaze, pushes me over the edge. My orgasm zaps through me, and I shudder with euphoria.

I'm still riding out the aftershock of my release as Griffin strips off his clothes, then resettles himself on his knees before me.

His heated gaze roams over my body, lingering on my heaving chest before settling between my thighs. Before he can drive into me,

I rub my foot over his straining erection, eliciting a hiss from him. Smirking, I add my other foot to the mix.

He gazes down at where I'm jerking him with my feet and chokes out a laugh. "Are you giving me a foot job?"

I lift a shoulder. "I thought you'd like it."

He grits his teeth, yanking a foot from his bobbing erection. "I told you I don't have a foot fetish," he growls, just as he takes a toe into his mouth and sucks.

My first instinct is to pull back because I'm ticklish as hell, but the way his tongue laps has my body melting. It feels so fucking good, in a weird way that I'm not sure I mind.

I drop my other leg, spreading my hips open for him, inviting him to the sweet spot between them. He releases my foot, setting it on his shoulder before he crawls over me.

He bends to kiss me as he thrusts inside, a groan slipping from his lips.

"You feel," he pants, "like heaven. So wet, so tight."

I push on his shoulder, and he rolls onto his back, taking me with him. My hands brace on his chest, and I lift my hips and slide down his cock with a moan. He raises his head and lavishes my tits in kisses. Sucking and flicking each bud as I ride him.

He lets me control the pace with lazy circles of my hips for a few minutes before he can't take the torture anymore.

The rough calluses on his hands scrape against my hips as he clamps down on them and takes control. Thrusting deeper and harder until he backs off slightly. Both of us are so close to the finish line but don't want the moment to end yet.

I continue to ride him, heat flooding through me as I meet him thrust for thrust. Both of us in tune with the rhythm, knowing exactly how to push the other over the edge.

My release continues to build like a rubber band being stretched to its limit, readying to snap at any moment.

Griffin's hands leave my hips. One pulling my head down to meet him for a rough kiss that takes my breath away, while the other finds my clit.

With just a few swipes of his fingers, I'm coming. Everything inside me snaps as hot pleasure invades my senses. The walls of my pussy spasming as Griffin continues to piston in and out of me.

He groans, eyes snapping shut and muscles tightening as he comes beneath me.

My body is Jell-O against him as I go slack on top of his sweat-slick chest.

"I knew you liked foot stuff, you perv," I pant into the crook of his neck.

"Nope. I still don't have a foot fetish." His heart races beneath me, matching the thrumming inside my chest.

"*Bullshit.*" I sit up, still straddling his hips. "You're feral for these piggies."

"More like I'm feral for you." He chuckles.

"Liar." I smack his arm.

"Ow." He playfully flinches away from me, catching my hand as he rolls us over to pin me beneath his body.

He dips his head, kissing a trail up my neck to my ear. "I've never thought about feet sexually until you brought them into the mix." The brush of his lips, combined with the heat of his breath against my ear, has me ready for round two.

I pull my hands out of his grasp and glide them over his toned back, every muscle rippling beneath my touch. "So, you're horny for my toes?" I tease as my hands move lower and lower. Finding the head of his cock, I move my thumb in a slow circle over his sensitive flesh.

Griffin groans. "I'm horny for every part of you."

Chapter Nineteen

S weat coats my palms as we pull up to the club.

A fucking club.

This is where my wonderful, smart, beautiful girlfriend chose for me to meet her family. Over the past few weeks, Audra and I have become inseparable. Only leaving each other's sides to work and for her to hang out with the soul-sucking witch, Belinda.

Audra pulls me into the line on the side of the building. Music permeates the brick walls, reaching us outside, where it's so cold that steam lifts into the air off our bodies.

Lost in the moment, Audra sways her hips, her short pink dress riding up her thighs. And god*damn*, do I want to slam her against the wall and fuck her in front of everyone on this sidewalk. But I also want to tug it down and hide her so no one gets to see those sexy legs that will hopefully be wrapped around my face tonight.

This is the problem with having a hot girlfriend.

Every thought is conflicting.

We move up a step in line. The cool air nips at my face, causing a chill to run through me. And I wrap my arms around Audra's shoulder, hugging her exposed skin to mine to try to keep my girl warm.

She shakes her ass against me, and my dick jumps.

"Are you sure this is where you want me to meet them? I can barely hear myself think, and we aren't even inside yet," I ask, my lips brushing over her ear.

"Yes, it's perfect."

"How so?"

"You love music."

"I love creating music, not dancing to it."

"Pshh, basically the same thing. It's perfect, trust me." She pats my hands. "Just relax."

"Relax? Have you met me?" I ask, just as the bouncer ushers us inside. He takes a far too quick glance at our IDs for me to be comfortable before moving us along.

The inside is dark and smoky as we enter through a hallway, the music getting closer and closer until we push through deep-purple curtains into a large bar. Tall tables border the dance floor that's centered in the room, and dark, secluded booths line the walls, where you can only see shadows of people.

The scent of cologne and sweat saturates the air as Audra drags me behind her. Every step is determined as she leads me to a large table with three couples already seated. I recognize her mother and father immediately from their age and how Audra is a perfect mixture of the two. Beside them are two younger couples, one of which I know is her brother and his wife, along with their two best friends who are also a couple.

"Family," Audra yells over the music as we stop at the table. "This is Griffin Henderson, my new lover. Griffin, this is my wonderful, yet very annoying, family." She goes around the table, introducing me to everyone personally before she runs off to the bar, abandoning me for drinks.

"So, Griffin, I hear you're a musician," her brother Nate says, and I want to kiss him for bringing up a subject I can go on and on about.

"Yeah, a studio musician."

"Studio? What's that exactly?" his gorgeous redheaded wife asks. *Bless these two kind souls.*

"It means I write music and lyrics for others, as well as record the instrumental parts of songs," I tell her with a closed-lip smile.

"Anything we've heard?" Sutton, the blond woman on her left, asks.

"Maybe," I say, looking around the table as I name off a few of the more well-known musicians I've worked with.

Delia, Audra's mother, gasps, her jaw dropping as she slaps her husband's arm. "Miles, did you hear that?"

"My love, you don't need to repeat everything the poor boy says," he replies with a loving smile at his wife.

"That's pretty badass. Do you ever tour?" the man with glasses next to Sutton asks just as Audra comes back to the table with a beer for me and some fruity mixed drink for her.

"Enough questions, Cooper," Sutton whines. "Let's dance already."

"I only asked one question," Cooper mutters as he's dragged off his stool and onto the dance floor by his girlfriend.

"Come on, Griff," Audra singsongs while rolling her arms in a come-hither motion.

Taking a deep breath, I chug my beer before joining her and her family.

I last five sweaty songs before I need a break. I kiss Audra on the cheek and head back to the table, only to find Vivian, Audra's sister-in-law, already there.

She gives me a shy smile. "Not a big dancing fan?"

I shake my head. "Not even a little."

"Me either, but you better get used to it. These guys like to go every few weeks."

"Oh joy," I say sarcastically.

"So, Griffin, I hope you don't mind, but Audra filled me in on your bio-mom situation," Vivian says, taking a nervous sip of her red drink.

"Not at all. She said you went through something similar a few years back."

She laughs. "It's insane, right? How is it that finding out your mom isn't who you think it is, isn't a completely unique experience?"

"Is it weird to say I find it comforting that I'm not alone in this?"

"Absolutely not. I wish I had someone else who understood when I was still processing."

"Would you mind if I text you sometime? To vent or commiserate?"

"Not at all," she says, pulling out her phone to get my number before texting me. "Text me anytime."

"Thanks," I say, my voice tight with emotion. "I really appreciate it."

"No problem. Have you thought about therapy?"

With a huff of laughter, I say, "Have I thought about therapy? Only every fucking day."

Vivian smiles at that. "I mean with her."

Gnawing on my lip, I glance out to where Audra is shaking her ass, surrounded by her mom, dad, and brother, all attempting to do the same, while Cooper and Sutton attempt some sort of dance-off beside them. They are light and free, everything I wish I could be.

Tipping my beer to my lips, I take a large drink before answering. "I'm not sure I'm ready to humanize her yet."

She nods as if she understands, and I guess she kind of does. Her situation differs from mine, but it's similar enough that she gets where I'm coming from.

"That makes sense. I do highly suggest it, though, whenever you're ready."

The rest of the night goes off without a hitch. I join Audra for more dancing, only stopping after I notice her mother watching her grind her ass into my dick for the third time this evening.

We wave goodbye to everyone outside the club hours later, promising to have dinner the following week, before heading home.

Once at my place, we both strip down to nothing and climb into bed to cuddle together.

"They loved you," she whispers against my chest, one hand clasped in mine as she runs the fingers of her free hand absent-mindedly over my stomach.

"You think so?" I ask, hopeful. I really want them to like me. For her, I want them to like me.

She laughs. "My dad was texting me our entire drive home about how he can't wait to see you again and hopefully jam with you."

That gets a chuckle out of me. "He really said that?"

She tilts her head up to look at me. "Yep. He's in love. Prepare to be love-bombed by my dad in the near future."

"Considered me warned," I tell her, pressing one last kiss to her lips before closing my eyes and falling asleep.

The music pours through my fingertips and into the keys as I work out the melody that's been filling my head for the past few days. Every chord feels right, like I've heard it a million songs before.

It's sweet and sensual. The perfect amount of romance in the notes.

It's her.

Audra.

She's become my muse, filling me with inspiration and music I haven't felt since the months leading up to Mom's death.

It's a symphony of emotions that I've never known before. She's everything and more. It's everything that I ever could have hoped for and wanted for myself and my future, for my career, for my music.

I want to shout it from the rooftops. She's mine, and I am hers.

Every day we spend together is like heaven on earth. With her in my arms, with her in my bed, it sets my soul aflame. She is it for me, and I know it. There's no one else who has ever made me feel so alive, who's ever made my music sing from me.

She's my soul.

My everything.

But I still don't know if it's enough.

Lying in bed with her at night, I've had the urge to tell her I love her. But it isn't time yet, and there's still the problem with Belinda.

Every day is a struggle to get away from her. All Audra wants is for me to befriend her, to let her into my life. But I can't, and I don't want to. This is the woman who gave me away. Who thought I wasn't worth her time, period. Who didn't show up until my mother was dead.

And when she did, she tried to steal what I had grown up with—the person I loved. She thought she could take her place. As if the title of mother was something she could just take on, not something that's earned, not something that you do.

I understand where Audra's coming from. It's a place of love, but it isn't a place of love for me. It's for Belinda and Belinda only. If it were for me, she wouldn't be asking me to do these things. She would understand that I can't. That I won't. My mother means—meant—the world to me, and to bring Belinda into my life is a slap to her face. A dark mark on her memory.

I work on the melody for a little longer before placing the keyboard aside. Picking up my keys and my cell phone, I walk out the door to my studio. I'm meeting Audra in a few minutes, and I can't wait to share this new song I've written. It's all about her and me, but mostly, it's about the love that she inspired in me.

My entire insides are shaking. Will she like it? Will she understand what it means? That she's my muse. That she's my life, my every waking thought, and my dreams. And I want nothing more than to be inside her right at that moment.

In the back of my mind, I have this nagging fear that she won't like it. She might hate it and not feel the same.

But that's horseshit, and I know it.

Audra and I cannot be anything but on the same page about our relationship—at least, that's what I hope.

It's rough. Never in my life had I thought about myself as a horny little bastard. Not until her. It's like she brought out the worst and the best in me. The worst being that I keep thinking with my dick. The best being that my heart is so full of love for her, I can't contain it. That it's pouring out of me and into my music. It's everything I think about.

I chose to walk today instead of driving, so it takes me about fifteen minutes to make it to the café we're meeting at. The winter air, starting to turn warmer with the threat of spring looming closer and closer, whips across my face. Even the trees have begun to come back to life, small bits of green spreading back through the foliage for another cycle of life.

When I get to the café, I stop dead in my tracks. Through the window, I spot Belinda sitting directly across from Audra. The two lost in conversation, laughing as they take bites out of the fries settled on the table between them.

I'm not surprised.

It's typical and hurtful, but sadly, it's classic Audra. At this point, her meddling shouldn't upset me. But my heart constricts in my chest as I take in the setup.

I don't stop to wave. I don't smile at her. I just walk right by. It takes everything I have not to confront her. To not shake her senseless. To not yell or scream at her for her inconsiderate behavior.

Footsteps slapping against the pavement, I speed up as I pass them. Unfortunately, Audra notices. I'm almost to the street corner when she yells my name behind me, but I still don't stop. I keep going, not turning back, not showing her I heard her.

My phone rings, her name lighting up the screen.

Ignore.

I keep going and going until I've circled back to my studio. Opening the door and locking it behind me, I enter my sanctuary, then sit on the couch and string out a sound of melancholy.

I don't know how to handle this. I don't know how much longer I can keep these feelings at bay. To feel so deeply for another, only to have them knowingly hurt you, is a deep cut that I'm not ready to explore.

Not even ten minutes later, there's a pounding so intense on the door that I can hear it through my headphones. I pull them off my head, setting down my guitar.

"Open the fucking door, Griffin," Audra's voice blasts through the door.

Shit.

My neighbors aren't going to be okay with this. I had a hard enough time getting the studio in the first place. Convincing the building manager to sell it to me for that purpose. The other suites were afraid of my noise level affecting them and their work. But my guaranteed soundproofing took care of all that.

But Audra is threatening to disrupt the trust I fought tooth and nail to gain from the accountants and therapists around me.

I throw the door open to her fist coming at the door again.

"Fuck." She stumbles into me. "Goddamn it, what the hell is wrong with you?"

"What's wrong with me?" I look around, as if she must be talking to someone else. "I'm not the one yelling in a place of business, Audra."

She storms into the room, whipping her long hair into my face. "You walked right past me, blowing me off for lunch. Who does that?"

"Who invites someone else to lunch with their boyfriend? Especially someone their said boyfriend isn't comfortable with?"

She pauses, a small smile drawing her lips up. "So, you're my boyfriend?"

My blood boils at her passing right over the most important part of my statement. I close the door behind me, moving around her to take a seat on the couch.

"Griff, are you my boyfriend?"

I let out an exasperated huff. "Did you really not know, or is it not something you want?"

"Neither. I just wanted you to verbally confirm officially."

"You need me to make it official? Fine. It's official. You are mine, and I'm yours. Boyfriend and girlfriend, the whole fucking kit and caboodle. We are in a committed relationship. Now, anything else I need to clear up?"

Her head shakes back and forth as she moves closer to me, pushing my shoulders back into the couch. Her legs part around me until she's straddling me. My hands instinctively reach out to grasp her lower back.

"Boyfriend," she says, pressing a kiss into my lips before whispering it again. "Boyfriend." Her lips find mine again, only this time, she doesn't pull back; instead, she clings to me with everything.

A soft moan leaves her throat as my tongue invades her mouth, finding her tongue with sweet ease.

My body ignites with desire. Every part of me turned on by her.

I don't want to brush what happened today under the table.

But I also don't want this to stop. She's my dream woman. And in this moment, she's fully committed to being mine.

She wants me.

All thoughts of stopping disappear the more she touches me.

I'm hers to do with what she wants. Audra pulls back for a moment, putting some distance between our hungry mouths. My hands glide over her long, silken hair, wanting to yank her lips back to mine.

Her eyes are bright as they shine down at me. Closing them once again, she wraps her fingers in the hair around the nape of my neck, urging my face closer to hers.

"Wait," I say, stopping her a mere inch from my lips. It takes all of my focus not to give in to the heat pouring out of the space between her legs. "We need to talk about this."

Audra's eyes snap open, and a grin rises from her lips to her shining emerald greens. "About this?" She rolls her hips.

I groan, holding her still. "No, not about *that*."

"Then what exactly, boyfriend?"

"About today and what happened."

She raises an eyebrow. "Oh, you mean how you blew me off, walking past me like I didn't exist, then proceeded to ignore me?"

"Fine. Yeah, that was shitty of me. Just like it was shitty of you to invite Belinda on our date." I lift her hips, pulling her up and off me to place her beside me on the couch. The loss of her warmth isn't something I enjoy, but it's what I need to think straight. To have a clear head. And when she's touching me, I can't do that. She consumes my every thought.

"You can't really think that's what happened." She huffs. "I didn't invite her along. We were together because we just had a meeting with the bank about a business loan—it went great. We got it. Thanks for asking. Next thing I knew, it was time to meet you, and she wasn't taking the hint."

"So you just let her stay?"

"No. I told her you were on the way, and she said she would leave right before you got there."

"Do you understand how it looked? How it made me feel?"

She softens. "I'm sorry. I know you are still keeping your distance from her." She pauses, then adds, "But honestly, Griff, you are going to have to face her at some point. She's my best friend, my business partner, and your—you are going to be around her more than you know if we are together."

"If we are together? Already taking back our newly defined relationship."

"No, never. I want this." She gestures between us. "This, us, makes me happier than I have been in—well, ever."

A big grin forms on my face. "Same."

"Okay, so is our little lovers' spat done now? Can we get back to kissing and touching?"

I pounce, laying her flat against the couch as I cover her with my body, kissing and touching her and far beyond that.

Chapter Twenty

"**A**re you ever going to play me something?" I ask, pulling my dress back on.

Griffin peers up from where he's still lying naked on the couch. His skin glistening with sweat from the body-shaking sex we just had. "You want me to play you something?"

I give him a look that must scream "you're an idiot," because he chuckles, grabbing his underwear.

I chastise myself for making him get up. Before, he was blissfully naked, showing me his gorgeous body without hesitation. Now he's covered in black boxer briefs that do little to shield him from my ravishing gaze, but he's still covered more than I want him to be.

"Which instrument?"

I look around the room, noting the full drum kit, keyboard, guitar, bass, and harmonica. Does he have more instruments stashed away, or is this it? Is this the vast extent of his musical playing ability? Either way, it's impressive, and I have no idea what to choose.

"Pick your favorite."

He moves to the keyboard. "What do you want to hear?"

"Play me the song from *Twilight*."

"The song from *Twilight*?" He raises a brow. "You know that gives me nothing."

I rub my temples. "The piano one, obviously."

He tilts his head. "'Bella's Lullaby' or 'Clair de Lune'?"

"'Bella's Lullaby.'"

His fingers flex above the keys for a moment before he dives in with a gentle yet brutal force that I can't take my eyes off. The muscles in his back flex as he plays my song request from memory.

It's mesmerizing.

He's mesmerizing.

From the way his body pours the music into the keyboard to the way he smiles at me every few notes. This man has me ensnared in his trap. And I don't want out.

"How did you know that song? Are you a musical genius?"

He chuckles. "No, not a genius. Just your run-of-the-mill Twi-hard."

I bite my bottom lip to keep myself from laughing. "A Twihard?"

"Yes, and don't play that game with me, Audra." He stops playing to point a finger at me. "You are one too."

"Why do you think that?"

He starts playing again. "Oh, I don't think it, I know it. When we were walking into the lodge that first night, you whispered to yourself a line that every Twihard knows."

"Oh yeah? What was that?"

"Hold on, spider monkey." He laughs. "This right here only confirmed it."

I groan, shielding my face with my hands. "My darkest shame has come to light."

He turns on the stool to face me, nodding as if his ass didn't just admit to loving it too. "Okay, so I have to ask—Team Edward or Jacob? Also, before you answer, you should be aware this is a test that I will judge you on."

I let out a bark of laughter.

His arms wrap around me, pulling me into him. Looking up at me, he rests his chin in the space between my breasts.

"I love the sound of your laugh."

I scoff. "Let me guess, it's music to your ears."

The grin on his face grows. "No, smartass. It reminds me of pureness."

I give him a skeptical look. "Pureness? After what we just did on that couch, you should know I'm anything but pure."

"I don't mean here." His hands trail down my back to cup my ass, gliding over my thighs to my still-wet center. "I mean here." His lips press into the skin just above my heart, and I swear the stupid organ stops.

It's the most erotic and romantic moment, and it's all for me.

He means these things about me, feels them for me.

It's insane to think that this man, this stupidly hot man, could be so damn into a woman like me. I'm a mess.

I want to slap some sense into him. Tell him that he can do so much better than me. That he is in a league so far out of my reach that it must be some cosmic joke that he is with me.

But I don't and I won't.

Because every moment I'm with him is another moment where nothing else matters.

The only thing I care about is him and making him feel as good as he makes me feel.

Call me selfish, I don't care.

When you find gold at the end of a rainbow, you don't leave it. You take it and remind yourself every day that you are the luckiest woman alive.

I press a quick peck on his lips, planning to tell him exactly how much I care about him, but my kiss doesn't stop with a kiss. No, it leads to another full-on bang fest, where I treasure the shit out of Griffin and his controlled fingers.

I always wondered what the big deal about dating a musician was. But now—oh *God*, do I understand.

The dexterity is enough to make me scream, but it's the rhythm and fluidity of his body that could honestly kill me with pleasure. Which is exactly how I want to go out of this world now, with either Griffin's head, hand, or cock between my thighs.

Reclothed and in the best mood of my life, I stroll down the sidewalk, hand in hand with Griffin, to find something to eat. We were both already hungry from skipping lunch earlier, but the said bang fest left us starving for something more than each other.

The walk from his studio is amazing. The trees lining the sidewalk make it almost idyllic. Branches hanging overhead like something out of a movie.

"Are you ever going to answer my question?"

"Huh?" When did he ask me a question? I mean, these trees are pretty and all, but I don't think they are ig-nore-the-hot-boyfriend-worthy.

Nope, I would have paid attention to anything this man said to me.

I think.

"Jacob or Edward. I have to know."

"You tell me."

"What team I am, or what team you're on?"

"Both."

He stops, looking down at me as if he's examining me. "You're a romantic, so I would say Edward."

I smile. "Isn't everyone an Edward?"

He shrugs, and I rear back. "Wait, are you... are you team Jacob?"

All he does is smirk.

"Oh my God, you are." I rip my hand away from his. "Ew."

He pulls my hand back, lacing our fingers. "I'm not team Jacob... In *Twilight* or *Breaking Dawn*. But *New Moon* and *Eclipse* are a different story."

"I'm sorry, hold up. Are you saying you go both ways?" Just as I ask, a group of teenage girls passes us, eyes widening at my words.

Instead of being embarrassed or telling them the context, Griffin just looks me in the eye and says, "There is nothing wrong with liking two different sides of the coin."

My heart races. *Is he referring to more than our* Twilight *debate?* I shiver with excitement.

The girls giggle, and Griffin winks at me before pulling me along the sidewalk again. And once again, my insides are gooey for him.

At Toasted, we grab a booth, sitting beside each other instead of across because Griffin refused to let go of my hand until we were sitting side by side, thighs touching like a couple of lovesick fools. And I, for one, am here for it.

Bring on all the PDA, please!

The fifties-style diner is a family favorite of mine. My parents, my brother, and I have been coming here for years. The old cracked-vinyl booths are like a warm hug every time I sit in them. It's been a while since I've been here, though. When I was dating Nick, he always acted like he was too good for an old-school diner.

Our waitress strolls over, grinning at us like we are the cutest thing she's ever seen, and I agree with her. We order the same thing: pancakes, hash browns, scrambled eggs, and loads of bacon.

The moment the food touches the table, we both fall silent, stuffing our faces as fast as we can, trying to make up for all the calories we burned off earlier.

With my last bite, I throw my napkin on my empty plate, shoving it away with one hand while the other rests on my bloated stomach. "I regret everything and nothing at the same time."

Griffin smirks up at me, still chewing on the last piece of bacon. "I have zero regrets."

I groan, rubbing my food baby. "Yeah, yeah. You're a bottomless pit, I get it. Foodina and I don't you to rub it in our face."

"Foodina?" he asks.

I glance down at my now expanded stomach. "Yeah, it's me and bacon's lovechild. Don't be upset. We didn't mean for any of this to happen."

He places a hand over mine on my stomach. "I will be there for you. Whatever you need. Pepto, Gas-X. I won't abandon you."

"Stop," I laugh and whine. "It hurts to laugh. So full."

He pulls out two twenties, placing them on the table, before standing and dragging me out after him.

The walk back is miserable. The food baby turning on me, making me feel worn down and drowsy. I can only imagine this is the toll a real baby takes on its mother.

When we get back to the studio, I expect to hang out there again, but instead, Griffin leads me to his Tahoe. He opens the door for me, waiting until I'm buckled before closing the door and getting in.

I pass out the moment the vehicle starts, only to be stirred awake by Griffin.

"Hey, babe, we're here."

I open my eyes, looking out the window to see a gorgeous blue house with a white wraparound porch.

"Where are we?" I ask, unbuckling my seat belt.

"My mom's," he says, opening his door and walking around to mine.

The moment I'm out of the Tahoe, Griffin's hands are on me again. It's steadying and sweet, but most of all, it makes my skin tingle with every touch.

He leads me up the stairs and into the house. As we step inside, an air of comfort passes through me. It should feel like I'm trespassing on a dead woman's life. That I'm a traitor to my best friend. But it doesn't.

It feels right.

It feels like Griffin. Like his calmness, his warmth.

And I'm thankful for him bringing me here.

His trust means the world to me.

I let go of his hand, moving into the entryway to stare at picture after picture littering the walls and the tables.

In one, a tall brunette woman stands with two little boys holding her hands, every face full of happiness as they smiled into the camera.

"She was so beautiful."

He smiles. "Yeah, she was."

We move out of the entryway, walking through the boxed-up rooms with items still strung around everywhere... "This place is a mess."

"Yeah," he says, rubbing the back of his neck. "Bren and I aren't the best packers."

"Understandable. I'm shit at deep cleaning. I'll find something, and it will remind me of another thing, and next thing I know, I'm wearing a jacket from 2009 and one random fuzzy sock, dancing to Whitney Houston as I online stalk my high school boyfriend's girlfriend's famous aunt."

He blinks at me. "That was a very specific example."

"Like I said. I get it."

He dips his chin, hiding his smile as he moves me through the entire house, pointing out the spot where he broke his arm trying to pull off some WWE moves on Brenden, the window he used to sneak in and out of, the corner where his nose would go anytime he was in trouble until the age fifteen. It's a walk through his past that I wouldn't trade for anything.

The last place he brings me to is his childhood bedroom. The only room without a single box. It's still intact. Every item still in its place. No sign of moving on.

Beneath my ribs, my heart aches for him.

The walls are covered with posters of bands that I know and some I don't.

"Did they inspire you to be a musician?" I ask, pointing around the room.

He smiles. "Of course. They were my heroes."

"Were?"

"That spot now belongs to my mom." The love for his mother, family, and this house is so evident in everything he says and does.

Damn it, my chest cracks again for him. I don't know what I would do if I lost my mom.

It's official, I'm going to have to either leave this house or get him naked to stop my emotions from welling up. "That's sweet."

"What about you? Did you always want to be a florist?"

I laugh. "Eh, not really. It's what I always knew I would be, family business and all. I always knew I wanted to do something that brought beauty to the world, but I always thought I would do that with dance. It wasn't until a few years ago that I truly fell in love with flowers and preserving their beauty forever."

He comes up behind me, wrapping his arms around my middle. "Are you scared?"

"To come clean with my mom? Or to have my own business?"

"Both."

"I'm terrified." I lean my head back to look into his eyes. "Everything could go wrong. But also, everything could go right. It's worth the risk if my dreams have a chance of coming true."

"I forgot to tell you earlier with the fighting, then the make-up sex and more sex—I'm proud of you. Following your dreams isn't easy, and yet you are still doing it."

He's saying the words I've craved to hear my entire life. I spin in his embrace, wrapping my arms around his middle. This—*he*—means the world to me.

Damn it. There is no letting go of this man. I want him forever.

We stay like that, locked in each other's arms, until the sound of a door shutting and Brenden yelling breaks us apart.

Chapter Twenty-One

Leave it to Bren to ruin the moment. Sometimes it's as if he has a sixth sense for these sorts of things.

Oh, Griffin's having a good time? Time to interrupt.

Griffin's about to get to second base for the first time? Throw a stink bomb into his room.

At this point, I'm eighty percent sure he was put on this earth just to piss me off.

"Gonad Griff, your sulky ass better not be up there going through what I already packed up again," he yells up the stairs. "It was one mistake. Give me a break. How was I supposed to know that Nana's ring was tucked into an old-ass pair of boots that should have been burned the moment they were bought?"

Audra looks up at me with amusement shining in her eyes.

"Come on." I drag her out of the room behind me and down the stairs, making sure I have a tight grip on her to reassure her that she won't be falling down any stairs if I can help it.

"I'm serious, Griff, I will punch you in the dick if you keep hover—" A grin breaks out on his face. "Audra, what a shocking and amazing surprise."

Her head falls to the side in confusion. "Why is it shocking?"

His grin grows even larger. "I figured you two left the bar the other day to play a game of hide the sausage, conquer the pink fortress, wave the white wand."

I groan, but that does nothing to stop him.

"Do two-person push-ups."

"I'm still not understanding," Audra says, looking between us.

"I'm talking about doing the sex with—"

She holds up a hand. "I understand that. I meant why would it be a surprise to see me again after?"

He sucks air through his teeth and looks at me, shaking his head. "Because Griffy is known for being teeny and terrible in that department."

I throw my hands up. "How many times do I have to tell you I never slept with Analise Armentrout? That story isn't true." His ass knows without a doubt she lied. He has seen my dick more than enough to refute it, but being the asshole he is, he taunts me and will continue to until I die.

"I don't know, her story about thirty seconds of lackluster lovemaking was pretty convincing," Bren throws out.

"Lies. Her story had all kinds of holes, and you know it."

Bren and Audra both look at each other and say "holes" in unison, then double over in laughter as they cling to each other for support.

"Laugh it up, assholes. That rumor ruined years of my sex life."

Audra straightens, attempting to rein in her laughter as she grabs my arm, rubbing it up and down. "Oh, poor baby. Did the mean girl keep you from living your sluttiest life?"

I click my tongue. "Why yes, yes she did. And I will always hate her and him for it."

"Me?" Bren straightens. "What did I do?"

"You brought it up... Again."

He wipes under his eyes. "Not my fault you don't measure up." He can't even get the words out before he laughs again, hunching over so hard he falls headfirst into the hardwood floor.

I glance over at Audra, where she's covering her mouth with a hand, struggling to contain her own amusement. "You're just going to let him talk about me like that?"

"What do you want me to do? Dispute it? Tell him you are packing an enormous schlong in those pants, or that you dicked me down so good I died, and you had to do CPR to revive me, but your cock did all the compressions because it is that impressive?"

"Yes. That is exactly what I want you to do."

"Did you hear that, Brenden?" she asks, not taking her eyes off mine. "It's the truth. I'm willing to testify to a court of my peers if need be."

"Fuck," Bren says, sitting up with a goofy proud smile. "You did good, baby bro."

My stomach and chest warm with pride that Bren approves of the woman I'm falling for. I don't need his stamp of approval and would never ask for it, but having him give it so freely means the world to me.

A few hours and beers later, the house is quiet.

In the corner of the living room, Audra is curled up on Mom's old reading chair. She fell asleep watching *Doctor Who*.

Bren and I insisted she watch it after she found our sonic screwdrivers and then proceeded to make fun of us. But joke's on her. She was hooked after only one episode.

She's so peaceful with her eyes closed and little snores. She looks like she belongs here, in that chair, asleep in my family's home.

"You've got it bad." Bren flops his giant ass down beside me on the couch, leaving no space between us.

I shove him away. "And you have zero awareness of personal space."

He doesn't deny it, but neither do I.

"Are you still stressing over the whole 'she loves Belinda' thing?" His eyes are glued to where she's snoozing.

"I want to say no. I want to be okay with it, not let it bother me, but it does. And I can't change that." And fuck, does it bug me. As if today wasn't enough proof of that. I'd almost let it ruin my day with Audra.

He pats my knee. "You know it's okay for you not to be okay? No one would judge you for it."

I let out a small laugh. "They might not judge me for it, but that doesn't mean they have to put up with it."

Audra might not judge me for my less-than-positive feelings that border on hostile toward Belinda, but that doesn't mean she will accept them.

Just like I won't judge her if she walks away because of their relationship. It would crush me, but I would understand. Belinda is a woman she loves and respects. I would never expect her to choose me over that friendship. But that doesn't mean I don't wish and pray she would. I crave to be her number one.

But I know it's nothing but a fool's dream.

It's her fierce loyalty and love that drove me to her in the first place.

He nods, his eyes swimming with understanding and sympathy, and maybe a dash of pain. Clearing his throat, he stands, looking around the room with his hands planted on his hips. "Want to see who can sort the fastest?"

The corner of my lips twitches with the idea of a competition.

And just like that, my gloomy thoughts disappear, being replaced with the need to beat my brother.

The dick knew exactly what he was doing when he said it, and I've never been so grateful to sort out junk before. He's out of his league when it comes to this particular task. He's just like Mom in that way. They both could live and thrive in clutter. While I was like Dad with the need to have everything in the right place.

I stand, cracking my knuckles and my neck. "You think you can beat me at organizing?" I laugh. "You're on."

Chapter Twenty-Two

Audra

After weeks and weeks of searching for the perfect store space, we've finally found it. I thought getting approved by the bank was tough, but finding the space to make Bel's and dream become a reality proved to be a real challenge. We probably walked through ten open storefronts before we found the one.

It was like love at first sight.

The storefront is at the end of a line of brick buildings, nestled right in the corner. It has an old-school charm with its large awnings and exposed-brick walls.

It's perfect. Or it will be once we get started on decorating.

At the door, I stop, turning to Bel. "Are you ready for this?"

She flashes me a huge grin. "Girl, I've been ready for this since the day we started saving."

Today is the day we sign our lease and get our keys, and my heartbeat fills my ears while my palms slick with sweat. But it's all good. I'm good. No biggie... Okay, I might be freaking out just a tiny bit.

"Okay." I wipe my hands on my pants, then grip the handle. "Let's go get ourselves a shop."

The room reeks of the white paint used to cover up the previous store's style, leaving it a blank space where our business can come to life. Stained concrete floors shine so much, I can see my reflection when I look down.

In the back of the space is a large wooden counter. The dark-colored slab with metal pipe legs is massive, but so is the space. My hands itch to touch it, to feel the smooth texture of the grain beneath my skin. It's going to make a perfect cash wrap or workstation.

Beside it stands Ken, our real estate agent. In his usual form-fitting gray suit, he is pretty in a news anchor way. He smiles at us, and I swear the light pings off his perfect white teeth.

"Audra, Belinda." He reaches to shake my hand, then Bel's. "It is so good to see your faces again."

"I would say the same, but we've seen your benches." Bel winks at him in her typical flirty fashion.

He gives her a grin, opening his arms to the space as he slowly turns. "I know you two have already fallen in love with the space. How could you not? I mean, look at those pendant lights. This place is a dream."

"It really is," I say. We are about to embark on a business adventure, and I am in awe of it.

"I won't keep you two. I can see the wheels spinning in your eyes right now," he says, pulling open a blue folder on the counter.

Bel leans into the hard surface across from him. "That obvious?"

"I know an eager beaver when I see one." He leans down, pulling out some paperwork, leaving the innuendo thick in the air between them. "Let's get down to business."

Bel and I skim the documents, not knowing what any of it means anyway. My hand shakes as I flick my wrist, signing my name on document after document with a nervous smile on my face.

"Thank you, ladies," Ken says, smiling as he tucks the paperwork back inside the pocket of his folder. "Okay, now all that's left is the down payment and the first month's rent."

I hand over the check, and he reaches into the breast pocket of his suit, pulling out two sets of keys. "I believe these belong to you two."

Bel reaches out, snatching the keys from his hands before I can blink.

He chuckles. "Like I said, eager beaver." With one last look at Bel, he steps around the counter, walking backward to the door. "Good luck, ladies. Call me if you need anything." His eyes lock on Bel as he steps out onto the sidewalk.

Now alone in our new space, we let the silence wash over us as we stare at our new large open storefront.

"Can you believe it? This is all ours. We have our own store," I practically shout as I jump up and down.

"It is unbelievable," Belinda says, joining me in jumping for joy.

"I can't wait to show Griff. He is going to love it." I spin in a circle with Bel in my arms.

She laughs. "You think so?"

"Oh yeah, he is a sucker for creativity, and this place screams it."

"I'm really glad you two have found each other." She smiles at me, but it isn't bright. It looks a bit sad.

I grab her hand. "Bel, I'm sorry. He'll come around eventually. I know it."

"I hope so." She nods, moving to touch the walls. "I'm thinking a deep, dark purple on this wall and that one." She points behind her.

"And a pale lilac on the others?"

"Yes." She beams. "It will be perfect."

"And I know just the men to enlist to get the job done."

"Men?" she asks.

"Duh, you don't actually want to leave this all for us, do you?"

"Oh, hell no. I just thought we could ask Jerry."

"Don't worry, Bel, your man toy will be enlisted. But I was thinking of also including the Henderson brothers."

"I don't know, Auds. Griffin clearly doesn't feel comfortable around me, and I can't imagine his brother will be any better."

"Well, how is he ever supposed to get comfortable if we don't give him the opportunities?"

"I don't want to push him," she whispers.

"You aren't. I'm just giving him a nudge in the right direction." I wiggle my brows at her. "Besides, I need the two most important people in my life to love each other."

We spend the rest of the day going over all the ideas and dreams we have for our store. With magazines full of ideas and inspiration, we cut out picture after picture of anything we like. From the walls to the counters, we have big plans that will require a lot of help. Luckily, I know the perfect men for the jobs.

I text Griffin picture after picture of the space.

Griffin

Damn, baby, it's huge.

Audra

That's what she said.

I send an eggplant emoji right after.

Audra

Want to come have your way with me in the back storage room?

Griffin

Why stop there, baby? I'd fuck you on the counter, too.

Audra

So, is that a yes?

I bite down on my bottom lip, heat and desire already coursing through my body as I imagine him coming here to do just that.

Griffin

I'm on my way right now.

I chuckle, imagining him in his studio, tossing his guitar aside onto the couch that has been home to a few orgasms.

"What are you smiling at?"

I jump, clutching my chest. I forgot Belinda is still here.

"Shit, you scared me."

She eyes my phone with a questioning look.

"Griffin." My cheeks fill with heat. "He wants to come see the space."

"I'll leave so you two can have some alone time." The smile is still on her face, but her eyes are no longer bright with excitement and joy like they were earlier.

"Bel, you don't have to do that."

"Yes, I really do," she says, picking up her purse. "I saw your face while you two were texting. I know that look. Whatever you two were talking about doesn't involve another person here, let alone me. Besides, I'm going to see what Jerry is up to."

My cheeks burn with embarrassment that I try to cover with my hands. "Oh my God, Bel, stop."

She wiggles her eyebrows as she continues to laugh on her way out the door. "Bye, Auds, have fun."

I've never been embarrassed to talk about sex or relationships with Bel before. But when it comes to Griffin, I am.

I don't want her to know the details of our sex life—or how amazing he is in bed. She probably thinks it's because of the whole she-gave-birth-to-him thing, and maybe it is a little, but in my eyes, I don't see her as his mother. She is still just Bel, my best friend.

The real reason I don't want to discuss my relationship details with her is that I have never felt this way. It's different from my past boyfriends, more intense. It's a deeper connection.

I love him.

And with that, I want to keep every part of him to myself.

It's selfish, really, but I can't help it.

I want him all to myself for as long as possible.

Moments after she leaves, a knock raps on the front door before it opens. Griffin steps inside, his hair hidden under my favorite gray beanie of his. My chest flutters at the sight of him.

His eyes roam around the space, then land on me. "Are you alone?"

I wiggle my brows. "Yes."

"Audra." He huffs, his face tight and serious. "You had the door unlocked."

"Yeah?" I step around the counter, moving to him.

"I walked right in, no problem."

"That was the point."

"What if I hadn't been me? What if a stranger came walking in here and you were alone? They could hurt you." He crosses his arms over his chest.

"You're being dramatic." I sigh, staring up into his eyes. "No strangers walked in. Only you, babe."

"I'm not being dramatic," he says through gritted teeth. "You are being reckless with your life. Did you forget my brother is a cop? I know what could have happened. Someone could have walked right in here." His voice softens. "And—and I can't handle the idea of you being hurt, let alone if it were to actually happen."

I pull him into my arms, hugging him as tight as I can, attempting to soak up every part of him. "I'm sorry. Next time, I will lock myself in here like a princess waiting for my knight in shining armor."

"Thank you. I appreciate it." And just like that, he relaxes in my arms, tipping his head as his mouth closes over mine.

I breathe him in. Everything about him, the kiss, us, just feels right. It's like nothing I've ever felt with another. He and I complement each other in ways I've always wanted.

I force myself to tear away from him and those lips that drive me crazy. "Just so you're aware, I don't need someone to save me. I'm no damsel in distress. I'm my own knight."

He nods. "Never thought differently."

"Just making sure."

He leans down, claiming one more soft and sweet kiss, then swats my ass. "Okay, now tell me all of your plans."

Giddy with excitement, I grab his hand, pulling him around the space to explain my vision.

"Over here will be an array of the vases, candles, and other beautifully preserved flowers we'll offer. And over on that side, we will have a ceiling trellis that will hang over a worktable." I look to see if he is listening. His eyes lock on me as he grins. "What?"

"I think it's going to be amazing, just like you."

And just like that, I melt right there into a puddle of mush for him. "You mean that?"

With one hand still in mine, he gives it a squeeze while his other cups my neck as he stares into my eyes. "Of course I mean it. I would never lie to you." He closes his eyes, pressing his forehead to mine and taking a deep breath. "I love you."

My heart lurches as I let go of his hand to hold his face. Stubble prickles under my palms. A welcome feeling. "You love me?"

He lets out a half laugh, half sigh. "Of course I do."

I press my lips to his, whispering the words that have been dying to come out of my mouth for what feels like forever. "I love you, Griffin."

His lips curl into a smile. "Will it ruin the moment if I tell you that your passion for your business, your future, has me incredibly turned on?"

I throw my head back with a laugh.

"I'm dead serious." He smirks. "I'm super horny for you."

Backing out of his arms, I look him up and down. It's a struggle not to groan at the sight of him. He's dressed for comfort, for a day of making music, in gray sweatpants and an old hoodie, and I am done for.

Sweats shouldn't have that much of an effect on my arousal, but hot damn, Griffin in them is like a light switch to my vagina.

I curl my finger in his direction. "Well then, it's a good thing we have this place all to ourselves."

He's on me in an instant, lifting me as I squeal with delight. Wrapping my legs around his waist, I rip off the beanie that was impeding my fingers from tangling in his hair.

I fist his silky strands, directing his mouth to mine as my hips roll against him. His hands dig into my thighs where he holds me, pushing me into him for more friction.

Even with our mouths joining and bodies churning with desire, Griffin somehow walks us out of the front, where the windows would show anyone what we're doing, and into the back, where more counters like the one up front are being stored.

Still carrying me as I grind against him, he knocks into the solid countertop. He tears his mouth away from the kiss to set me down, my body already missing his touch. Both of our breathing is ragged as I shove my shirt up over my head, his eyes focusing in on the mesh bra that conceals nothing.

Calloused hands find my breasts as he licks my right nipple through the bra from top to bottom before moving to the other side for the same treatment. I gasp, arching into him, loving the way his mouth moves against my body.

"You're so damn beautiful," he says, kissing in between my breasts.

"*Griffin*." My voice is breathy and full of desire. Shivers of anticipation dance down my spine as I run my hands under his shirt to feel the warmth of his skin. He lifts his arms, allowing me to strip him of his shirt, my hands moving lower to the band of his sweats.

The urge and craving to make him feel as desperate for me as I am for him is overwhelming as I tug down the fabric covering his hard cock. Griffin pants when I grasp him, stroking him up and down as his lips continue to shower my nipples in unrelenting attention.

"Griff," I moan. "I need you to move that pretty mouth somewhere else."

Hot breath washes over my skin as he chuckles while his lips trail back up my body to my mouth. The kiss is devouring. I had felt the warmth flowing through me before, but his lips on mine, tongue touching mine, sets me on fire.

I'm burning for him, inside and out.

Talented, eager fingers play with the button on my jeans, snapping them open as my core throbs with the anticipation of him giving me what I need. Raising my hips, I allow him to shimmy the jeans over my ass and down my legs until they are out of sight.

Fingers brush against the fabric of my soaked underwear. "Fuck," he hisses through his teeth as he watches where his fingers slide against the wetness. "Do you want my mouth or my cock? Because I will give you anything. I mean anything, baby, just tell me what you want and where."

And just when I thought I couldn't get any wetter.

Maybe it's the dirty words that fall from his sensual mouth, or maybe it's the intense trust I have in him, but my body feels like it's going into overdrive. Like if I don't have him right now, I might die.

My hips buck upward, searching for more friction. "I want it all."

Smirking, he lowers himself in front of me, wasting no time as he licks up the center of my panties, sending a jolt of pleasure through me. His deft fingers slide the lavender lace to the side, and he groans before his mouth descends on me.

I fall back onto the table with a whimper of pure pleasure. The cool wood pressing into my skin as his tongue tortures me with every lavish flick and lick until I'm squirming from the sensation.

Euphoria is almost in my reach when he pulls away.

"What the hell, Grif—"

With a power thrust, he sends my climax back up to its breaking point.

"Yeah, baby?" he asks, moving in and out of me, his hands wrapped around my thighs, holding me closer with every thrust. "You have something you want to say?"

I'm overwhelmed with pleasure as he manages to hit that sweet spot inside me. My breath comes in shallow pants while I grin at him. "Just keep fucking me."

Leaning up onto my forearms, I watch as he slides in and out of me in a perfect rhythm that sets my orgasm off. Jolts of electricity and pure ecstasy hit me, causing my legs to tremble as I reach up, latching on to his arms.

"You're so fucking pretty when your pussy quakes around my cock."

Dropping my legs, he snakes his arms around my back and pulls me flush against his chest. Crazed lust fills his eyes before he claims my mouth, devouring me in an instant as he continues to fuck me like it's what he was meant to do.

"You want another one, baby?" he asks, grinding his pelvis against my clit with every thrust.

"Please," I beg, matching him thrust for powerful thrust.

My orgasm builds again as he moves in a frenzy. The intense intimacy between us is addictive, and there is nothing that could ever beat the feeling of him driving inside me. I pull my mouth from his so I can watch as his orgasm tears through him. Cords of muscles in his back tightening under my hands and his breath faltering as pleasure crashes through him.

Just the sight of him finding his release causes a chain reaction inside me, and I come again. My eyes fluttering shut, the sensation of it all too intense.

Griffin lowers his head into the crook of my neck, panting while I continue to cling to him, refusing to untangle myself from him.

I love the feel of his body moving against mine with each breath, the small kisses he presses into my skin as he whispers "I love you." A feeling of home fills me at his words, and I'm so thankful to have found him. I brush my hand up and down his spine until our raging heartbeats calm and our breathing evens out.

Lifting his head, Griffin beams at me with a smile that's pure and full of happiness. "Wow. That was—"

"Mind-blowing," I muse. "Earth-shattering?"

He chuckles, running his fingers over my hair. "All of the above."

"And I didn't even have to use my feet."

He groans. "One time, and now I'm being haunted by a fetish I don't even have."

"Sure..." I tease.

"Not to ruin the mood or anything, but have you told your parents yet?" he asks.

And just like that, I'm full of anxiety and not post-orgasmic bliss. "Tonight. She's working late, so I'm going to head over once my legs are working again."

"You want me to go with you?"

I press a soft kiss to his lips. "I think it's best I do this alone."

"Hey, Mom." I knock on her office door.

She's hunched over her desk, staring at her computer, going over the inventory for the week like she does every Monday. Looking up from her screen, she smiles, unknowing that I'm about to rip the rug out from under her feet.

"Hey, baby girl, what are you doing here?" she asks, turning her attention back to her spreadsheets.

"I need to talk to you about something... important." I take a seat in the chair in front of her desk.

"Well, spit it out. You know that holding it in gives you cramps."

I take a deep breath. *Here we go.* "You know the floral preservation idea I talked to you about?"

She sighs. "For the last time, Audra, we aren't doing it."

"I know you aren't... But I am. I got a loan from the bank."

She spins in her chair to face me. "Excuse me?"

My heart thunders in my chest. I can do this. "Bel and I picked up the keys to our storefront today."

"Are you joking? This must be a joke."

"No, Mom, I'm serious."

Her nostrils flare as she stares me down. "You're leaving the family business?"

"Think of it as an extension of Fisher Floral."

"I can't believe this. What about your father and me? You're ruining our plans and for what? A half-thought-out plan with your flaky friend. I thought you were smarter than this, Audra."

It's like a punch to the gut. My mom can be the most supportive person in the world until it comes to the family business. I saw the way she and my father reacted to Nate following his dreams. They iced him out for weeks. I knew she wouldn't be happy, but I never thought she would be this ugly toward me.

I clear my throat, fighting the tears welling up in my eyes as I stand. "I'm sorry you feel this way. But I have a well-thought-out business—"

"You can leave," she says, dismissing me as she returns her attention to her computer.

"Mom." My voice cracks on the single word. "Please."

"I don't want to hear it."

I dip my chin in understanding and turn toward the door.

"Audra," she calls out, and I freeze. "Don't come crawling back to me when you fail."

The tears I've been holding back fall as I leave as quickly as possible. Once in my car, I drive straight to the only person who might make it better. I rap my fist on the door, not stopping until it swings open.

Griffin takes one look at me and tugs me into his arms, closing the door behind us. I bury my face in his chest, letting his clean scent wash over me as I sob.

"Baby, what happened?" he asks, his voice soft with concern.

"My mom," I cry. "I told her."

"It's okay. I've got you." He bends, lifting my legs into his arms and carrying me to his bedroom.

He lays us down in his bed, pulling his comforter over us, and lets me cry until the words tumble out of my mouth.

"She didn't mean it."

"It sure sounded like she did," I say, trying not to cry again.

"I think she was just hurt and reacted badly."

I sniff. "I know, but that doesn't make it okay."

"No, it doesn't," he says, tracing hearts on my back. "What can I do to make it better?"

"You could help paint the store later this week."

He laughs. "Painting? That's what will help?"

I nod. "And maybe enlisting that hunky brother of yours too."

"You got it. And because you're upset, I'm going to let that hunky comment slide."

"Thank you."

Chapter Twenty-Three

"**I**'m going to kill her."

Bren grasps my shoulder. "You can't make statements like that in front of an officer of the law."

"Shut up," I snap, my eyes turning to small slits as I stare into the window at Audra laughing it up with some older man and *her*. Belinda wasn't supposed to be here. In fact, I clarified that far-from-insignificant fact with Audra after agreeing to be her painting labor.

I'm going to kill my girlfriend.

Well, not actually kill her, but the rage is there, along with the twinge of betrayal.

"Just warning you," he says with a laugh.

I glare at him. "We both know you would help me bury a body in an instant and would cover up our tracks like a criminal mastermind."

He pats me on the shoulder. "Let's never find out if that is true, okay?"

"We'll see," I say, storming across the street.

"No." He chases after me. "No 'we'll see.' That isn't good enough."

I pull open the gigantic door, a tad more aggressively than is necessary, but that doesn't matter. I want her to know I'm here and that I'm pissed.

All three of their heads turn in our direction as I scowl at Audra.

She ignores my surliness by wrapping her arms around my neck to pull me down for a kiss. "Hey, foot fucker."

I growl at her, and she waves me off with a wince that tells me she knows she fucked up before moving on to give Bren a quick hug.

Audra drags us both by the hands closer to where the other two stand. With a bright smile, she introduces us. "Guys, this is Jerry, Belinda's... man friend. And Jerry, this is Griffin, my boyfriend, and his brother Brenden."

He offers out a hand to Bren, then me, prolonging the handshake with me for longer than necessary, probably to intimidate me for Belinda in some way.

Jerry clears his throat. "It's nice to meet you both. Let me tell you how glad I am that you're here. My arms are already trembling, and we've only just started."

Bren smiles as he looks around the space, ruining the tough-cop demeanor he was sporting seconds ago. "Happy to be here. Anything for Audra."

Audra takes that as her cue to jump in and save the fucking awkward day. "Okay, so we have paint cans set up over there with trays, brushes, and rollers. And plastic lining the place. Bel and Jerry, why don't you two take the big wall right over there?" She points to the back. "Brenden, you can start right here, and Griff and I will outline the walls and trim."

Bren wiggles his eyebrows at me. "Bossy, just how I like my women."

I punch him in the arm.

"Ow," he says, stalking away. "Jesus, Griff, it's not like I asked you if she's like that in bed... Because I bet she is."

I charge toward him as that big-ass motherfucker giggles before my fist slams into his stomach.

"Fuck," he gasps as he falls to the ground. "I forgot how strong you can be."

"Let that be a reminder to shut the fuck up about Audra."

He reaches up, using my arm to pull himself up, then takes a minute to catch his breath before proceeding as if nothing happened.

"Better?" he asks.

My brow furrows as I take in his meaning. My shoulders are relaxed. The tension has eased since I took everything out on him. Some of my earlier anger that was festering inside me dissipated when it turned on him.

That sneaky trickster directed my anger to himself in order to help me.

I grab the back of his neck, pulling him in for a hug. "Thank you," I whisper, and he pats my back.

The feeling of eyes on us stops me. I give him one more tight squeeze before letting him go and moving to where Audra is staring at us with a mixture of concern and amazement.

"Everything okay?" she asks, as I bend down to pick up one of the angled paintbrushes she had placed beside the two small trays of light-purple paint.

"Yeah. Bren was just being Bren." Always knowing what to say or what to do. And never afraid of a little pain.

Should Bren and I still be hitting each other at our age when we are angry? Probably not.

But it's our love language. It's consistent and hasn't changed since we were children.

She eyes me suspiciously before leaning over to place a kiss on my cheek. "Let's get our Michelangelo on."

Audra and I tackle the outlining like two beasts.

Two vastly differently coordinated beasts.

My steady hands manage straight, even lines and strokes, while Audra's do something else. There are paint drips and strokes everywhere we didn't want.

I finish the section, only to look over at the mess that is my beautiful girlfriend's questionable hand-eye coordination.

"Audra, baby." I bend down next to where she's on her hands and knees on the floor, swiping haphazardly at the wall with a dripping paintbrush. "How's it going?"

"Perfect. I'm almost done if you are needing some help."

A laugh bubbles from my lips. She's so precious with her lack of painting skills. It looks like a two-year-old threw paint on a wall and then tried to blend it all together with their hands.

Her smile falters and a crease forms across her forehead. "What?"

I want to tell her to drop the brush—that she is making more work for the rest of us—but I can't. The pride that was shining off her seconds ago is enough to make me eat my words.

"Nothing." I shake my head. "I just love you."

The smile reappears even brighter than before, lighting up her face. And it's like I can feel the warmth radiating off her. She is my sun, and I'm more than happy to be in her orbit.

"Griffin, you're staring."

"So?"

"So it's a little weird."

I squat beside her. "It's weird to admire your lover's beauty?"

"Lover?" She rolls her eyes. "Ew, Griff."

She turns back to the wall, dipping her paintbrush in an abundance of paint without wiping it off.

Before she can begin again, I grasp her chin in my hand, turning her to look at me. I lean in closer so our mouths are mere inches from each other. "Not ew. We are lovers, baby. Two people who are so in love: body, mind, and soul. I can't help but stare sometimes, because you enchant me." I press a gentle kiss to her lips.

A small sigh comes from her as I let her go. "You can't say stuff like that, Griff."

I'm about to ask her why when she leans closer to me and whispers, "At least not when we aren't alone. 'Cause, God, do I wish I could show you how much I love you right now."

"Later, baby. Later." I back away, wiggling my eyebrows, before moving on to another wall in need of my outlining skills. After another thirty minutes, I have two more walls completely blocked out and ready to be finished. With my job complete, I start filling them in. I grab a roller, coat it in the lighter purple, and roll it up and down and across the drywall.

Out of the corner of my eye, I see Audra chatting it up with Belinda as she continues to butcher the job.

On the other side of the room is Bren, bobbing his head to whatever music is playing through his headphones as he subtly cleans up Audra's shoddy job.

I'm about to move into speed-painting mode because if I don't, this job will go on for days at the rate everyone else is going, when another roller sweeps up the wall next to mine. I look over, expecting Audra, only to find Jerry, Belinda's *man friend*.

We knock out the wall in a matter of minutes before moving on to another, painting side by side in silence.

That is until he opens his mouth. "It's just amazing," he says, getting a little paint on his face as he rubs at his chin. "The resemblance is uncanny."

My entire body tenses. In my periphery, Bren does the same. Always on alert, he must have been listening, observing, pretending to listen to music as he waited for something like this to happen.

"Excuse me?" I say, giving him the chance to backtrack or change his course of thought, to direct him anywhere but where he was about to go.

"It's the gestures and facial expressions."

I glance back at Bren, his eyes still fixed on me. A silent question lingering in them. *"Do you want me to intervene?"*

Sometimes I find it shocking the amount Bren and I can convey with a single look. How the other will just know what it means. At times, it feels like a weird sibling telepathy of sorts. Like somehow our DNA made it all possible. But now that we know what we know about my hidden past, it feels even more special.

Like we built this connection. It has nothing to do with our cells and genes and everything to do with us, our relationship.

I'm grateful for his offer, but I don't want him in the middle of this mess.

At the curt shake of my head, he turns his back on us, raising his roller to the wall again like nothing's happened. But I know he's listening intently to every word I'm about to say.

"Listen, Jerry." I step closer to him, lowering my voice. "I know you think you see obvious signs of relation between me and her, but you don't. And it would be fucking smart if you shut the fuck up about your incorrect observations."

His mouth opens and closes, his face turning a bright red as he stands there floundering like a fish for words.

"Now, I'm going to pretend that this never happened, and you're going to keep your mouth shut about me. Understand?"

He raises his hands in surrender. "Griffin, look. I didn't mean to—"

"I'm sure you didn't. But I'm also sure that either Belinda or Audra told you about our situation, and from that alone, you should've known better. So, either you are dumb or an asshole."

His eyes widen.

"So tell me, Jerry, which is it?"

Chapter Twenty-Four

My gaze keeps darting across the room over to him. Watching him out of the corner of my eye.

His shirt stretches across his back as he moves the roller up and down. I know I should be working, but God, when he is around, I can't even focus on anything but him and being alone with him.

"Earth to Auds." Bel snaps her fingers in front of my face. "Did you listen to a word I said?"

I glance back at her. "Yeah, something about painting." My eyes wander back to the object of my affection as Jerry steps up beside him and paints. I watch them with wary eyes as they work in silence.

My nerves have been eating at me since I told Griff no one else would be here. Yep, I lied, and now I feel like crap about it.

I know he's mad. The moment he walked through the door, I was waiting for him to walk back out and refuse to be here.

The glare he gave me when he got here was a punch in the gut. And sheer panic ran through my veins as I wrapped my arms around him and pulled him into a kiss. I was so nervous that I'd pushed him too far. That this would be the last straw, forcing him to open his eyes to how much better he could do without me.

I don't think I've ever been so terrified as I was in that moment. But he didn't pull away, didn't leave me standing there.

After a few more seconds of taking in his beautiful backside, I let out a breath of relief, turning back to Bel.

"Oh, hi, did you get over your obsessive staring at Griffin and remember me?" She scoffs.

"Don't be mad. If you were me—"

Her face contorts in disgust.

"Never mind."

"No, no, Auds, please tell me more about how I would ogle my son."

I cringe. "Sorry."

She waves me off with one hand. "You're fine. I understand. He's very handsome, and you two seem incredibly happy together."

I can't fight the smile on my face. "We are."

She brushes more paint on the wall before asking, "So it's serious?"

My gaze travels back toward Griffin as my heart swells in my chest. I've been hesitant to share my relationship with her, with everyone. But Bel and Griff are pretty much my social circle, besides my brother and his wife. The two of them make up my everything. And not being able to talk to them about each other has been straight torture on my soul.

The need to share every detail about my day is so overwhelming that I end up sweating while trying to rein in the details that might hurt them. My heart takes a small beating each time I withhold from one of them.

I bite my lip, trying to stop the grin from taking over every part of me. "Yeah. Like a heart attack." 'Cause that's what it feels like. My heart beats for him. Without him, it would stop. And I wouldn't know how to live anymore.

"I'm happy for you—for both of you." She smiles, but it doesn't reach her eyes. "So what are you thinking about for shelves? Metal and wood? Or a mixture?"

I mull it over in my head. "I think I'm going to need to see the shelves before I can make any decision."

"Smart. Shelves are life-changing. We wouldn't want to be *hasty* and *choose* without fully thinking it through."

I peer at her. "Really, Bel?"

"What?" She raises her eyebrows before turning back to the wall to find spots that need more coverage.

"Don't *what* me. You know what. To you, it might seem like we are moving fast, but Bel, when you know, you know. And I know."

She sighs, shaking her head. "I wasn't—"

"Yes, you were. But it's none of your business."

She opens her mouth again, and I cut her off.

"Look, I don't want to fight. I love you, and I love him. It's that simple for me."

With a nod, she swallows whatever protests she had left and gives me a quick hug. "As it should be."

Two more hours pass before the store is as close to finished as it's going to get tonight.

All in all, I would say that tonight was a major success. No one stormed out or threw paint, so it was a good night.

Jerry's the first to head out after being extra quiet for most of the evening. Belinda catches a ride with him, waving goodbye to me and the guys before climbing in the car.

Brenden is nice enough to return the gesture while Griffin averts his gaze, still refusing to even look at her.

The plastic is still covering the floors, but we already washed all the brushes and rollers. Everything is pretty much cleaned up.

Well, practically cleaned up. We left paint cans, roller trays, and rags covered in varying shades of purple everywhere.

Yeah, so we cleaned up... slightly.

Okay, we did the bare minimum. We are tired, and the air's been thick with unspoken tension for hours.

I lock the door, putting my keys in one hand and my phone in the other, when suddenly, the world goes haywire, and I'm thrown over Griffin's shoulder.

One of his large palms lands on my ass with a smack.

I shriek, then press my hands into his back, using what little abdominal muscles I have to help push me up to see something other than my man's fine backside.

Behind us, Brenden shakes his head with a smile playing on his lips.

"Brenden, aren't you bound by duty or something to help a damsel in distress?" I ask.

Griffin lets out a loud laugh.

"What?"

"Oh, honey, he isn't going to save you."

"Well, why the hell not?" I ask with a glare at Brenden.

He tosses his hands up. "Leave me out of your freaky sex games."

"Freaky sex—" My cheeks fill with heat as I stammer, "This isn't—"

"Some form of foreplay?" Griff asks while rubbing his hand a little too close to that special spot between my thighs.

I squeak again, letting my head fall onto his back as my arms circle his waist. "I hate you."

"Sure." His hands move close to the sweet spot again, and thank fucking Christ I'm wearing leggings.

And just when he feels like he's won this round, I take my hands and slap his crotch, successfully hitting his semierect dick.

A grunt escapes his lips as his steps falter, and I fear his knees might buckle.

His breathing comes out a little harder. "Baby, please don't do that when you are in my arms. I could've dropped you."

"Please, you can handle more than a little love tap."

Still behind us, Brenden laughs again. "God, you two are meant for each other."

I smile, but then he says, "Like Dumb and Dumber."

"Excuse me?"

"Or Ren and Stimpy," Griff adds.

"Tom and Jerry."

"Laverne and Shirley," I throw into the mix.

They both stop.

Brenden comes up, patting me on the back. "Oh, you sweet, naive woman. Those two were far too levelheaded to be you and Griff."

"Rude."

They both burst out laughing and then continue to make comparisons of our relationship to outrageous characters until we reach a bar a couple blocks away from the store.

Griff sets me back on my feet, putting my hand in his as Brenden pushes the door open. He drags me to the back of the bar before settling me on his lap.

Butterflies swarm in my stomach as he nuzzles his face against my neck, and I'm so wrapped up in everything that is him, I don't even notice Brenden has left until he returns with three beers.

I take one with a smile, rolling it between my palms.

Brenden eyes me as he sips his beer. "Problem?"

"No, I'm just giving my beer time to settle before drinking."

He smirks. "Settle?"

"Yep." I lift it, inspecting it through the amber glass. "Look at that, it's ready." I take a swig from the bottle. The moment the hoppy flavor hits my tongue, I know my polite ruse is over.

Griff wrenches the bottle away from me as I gag.

"Why didn't you say you don't like beer?"

I wipe my mouth and tongue off with a table napkin. Crumpling it up, I look at him. "I didn't want to be rude and waste your money."

He rolls his eyes. "Don't worry about that. Trust me, Griff or I will drink it. So it's no waste."

Griff presses a kiss to my neck, his smooth lips sending shivers through me as he pauses at my ear. "It's true, we would have."

"Never do something you don't want to do just to be polite, Audra," Brenden says, his tone no longer playful. "I've seen too much wrong shit that happened because someone was trying to be polite."

I silently nod. But jeez, these two are a couple of nervous nellies. First Griff with the unlocked door, and now Brenden with the "it's okay to say no" speech.

"Jesus Christ, Bren," Griff huffs. "Can you not keep the cop shit to a minimum? She is trying to be polite to *you*, dickhole, not a random guy giving her a beer."

I sit up a little straighter at his meaning. He knows me; he has confidence in my ability to stand up for myself.

"It's true," I say, roping my arm around the back of Griffin's shoulders. "I even have my own go-to method of getting men to leave me alone."

"What is it?" Brenden leans in closer.

"I give them the old razzle-dazzle." I wiggle my fingers as a distraction, flipping him off before punching straight at his crotch. He doesn't see the move coming, and I pause mere inches away from dick destruction.

Bren flinches, his hips pushing away from me. "Okay. You win."

"Yes." I pump my fist into the air. "What's my prize?"

Brenden looks around for a moment before his eyes light up. "That." He points to a waitress bringing over a cocktail to our table.

"What is it?" I ask as she sets it down.

"A cosmo, enjoy," the woman says before slinking off back to where she came from.

"It's safe," Griff says. "It's what numbnuts here actually ordered you."

"Why did you hand me a beer if you also got me this?"

He shrugs. "Call it curiosity to learn more about the woman who has captured my sulky brother's heart."

I tilt the cocktail to my lips and let out a moan of satisfaction. Under my ass, Griff shifts his hips while his arm around my waist tightens.

"On that uncomfortable note." Brenden stands, chugging down his beer. "I will see you two pervs later."

I wonder if I should move off Griffin and into the newly vacant seat across from him at the table. But the death hold he has on me tells me that's a big fat no.

"Thank you," I say, taking another larger sip of my drink. "For tonight."

He doesn't respond; he just pulls his beer closer to him on the table.

"I really appreciated both your and Brenden's help."

Still nothing from him.

I let out a sigh, knowing what I need to concede. "I'm sorry for not telling you they—*she* would be there."

"Not telling me?"

"For lying to you. It was wrong, and I understand if you are pissed, I do. I just—"

"No. No 'I just...' It was wrong, and that's it. Please don't do it again."

I nod, turning my body into his. "I won't, I promise."

His lips find mine. Both of our mouths are cool from the alcohol as they move against each other in perfect harmony.

A loud *bang* and then a laugh breaks the spell his kiss had me under, reminding me we are in public.

"Stay at my place?" I ask.

"I'll follow you anywhere, Audra."

Chapter Twenty-Five

Griffin

With my bag slung over my shoulder, I follow Audra into her apartment. The clean and comfortable space is more than welcoming as I walk through. I stop dead in my tracks as the sweet smell of cinnamon fills the air. A smile tugs on my lips at the memory of my mom and dad covered in flour as they attempted to make Bren his favorite cookies, snickerdoodles, to celebrate him graduating from the police academy.

I throw my bag onto the couch, then take off my coat and beanie, hanging them on the rack by the door.

Audra flicks on the lamp closest to the door. The light bouncing off the glass table, illuminating her in its glow. Her soft smile melts me.

"What?" I ask, my lips twitching up to match hers.

Picking up my duffel bag with one hand, she extends the other out to me. "I have something for you."

Her steps are impatient as she leads me to her bedroom. The moment we walk through the doorway, her arms wrap around my hips and she spins us, walking me backward until my knees hit the bed. A look of apprehension contorts her face as she bites the corner of her lip while letting go of my waist so she can hold my hands. Eyes bouncing back and forth from our intertwined hands to my face.

"Baby, what's going on? Why are you acting nervous?"

"Because I'm nervous."

She's so cute as she shuffles from foot to foot, antsy with whatever is eating her up inside. "About?"

"I wanted to give you something."

"If it's your body, I gladly accept."

A huff of a laugh escapes her. "I'm well aware you would. But that isn't it. I wanted to give—well, offer, if you wanted—a drawer."

The corner of my lips quirks up at her obvious nervousness. "A drawer? Where?"

She points behind her, still gnawing on her lip. "There."

"Which one?" I ask, looking over her shoulder.

She turns, pulling open the dresser drawer closest to the door by the dangling handle.

I look down into it. "You already emptied it?"

"Yeah." She beams. "I wanted it to be ready for you—that is, if you want it."

I nod. "I do." Grabbing her hand, I pull her into my chest, hugging her body to mine. "Thank you."

"You're welcome."

"How did you choose this one? What if I wanted this one?" I pull open the drawer beside my cleaned-out one.

"What the fuck is this?" I hold up the small bright-pink, sparkling bag as I stare at her in confusion.

She rolls her eyes, snatching it out of my hands. "It's my fanny pack."

"When you say fanny pack, is that a double entendre?"

A flush creeps up her neck and covers her face as she stuffs the bag back into the dresser drawer and shuts it.

I meant it as a joke, but the way she blushes makes me feel like I'm closer to the truth than I knew.

"It is, isn't it?" I wrap my arms around her waist from behind. "You can tell me, baby. This is a safe space."

"Please stop."

"Stop what? Asking about your ass bag?"

She groans. "I'm not sure I like you very much anymore."

"Stop lying. I happen to know your fanny likes me very much." I roll my hips into her ass to home in on the point.

She forgets herself for a moment and pushes back into me, a small moan escaping her lips.

"That's it, baby. Now open up the bag and show me everything I need to take care of you."

"Griffin."

"Audra."

Her head lulls back against me, and I pull her flush against my front, pinning her to my body with one arm still wrapped around her and the other pulling open the closed dresser drawer to extract the sequined bag.

Once I've successfully slipped it out of the drawer, I whisper into her ear, "Open it for me, or I will."

"Don't laugh," she demands, hands still at her sides as she waits for my response.

"Why would I laugh?"

"That isn't a promise."

"Fine. I won't laugh."

She grabs a hold of the neon-pink zipper, dragging it open to reveal the contents.

I let out a massive bark of laughter, not even bothering to choke it down for her sake. It's everything I expected and more.

Inside is a satin lining holding a bottle of lube, three butt plugs varying in diameter, baby wipes, and something I wouldn't have thought to include in the bag: two mini bottles of vodka. But that isn't what has me bursting with amusement.

No, that's the open notepad inside with dated entries detailing her thoughts and feelings.

Anal Prep Attempt 1: Nope. Dear God, why do people like this?

Anal Prep Attempt 2: It didn't get better. Still horrible.

Anal Prep Attempt 3: How do people put penises up there when I can't even handle the smallest plug?

Last is my personal favorite.

Anal Prep Attempt 4: NEVER FUCKING AGAIN. I QUIT.

"You promised you wouldn't laugh." Her face is crimson with embarrassment.

I try to school my features, but I can't. "I know, baby, I know. But goddamn, I didn't expect that journal."

"It was supposed to track how I moved up in size. But obviously, that didn't work," she mutters while grabbing the bag and stashing it back in her drawer.

"I'm guessing you never worked your way up to full-fledge back-door access?" I tease.

"No, Griff, and it's safe to say I never will." She pushes past me, leaving me in the bedroom by myself.

I finish putting my clothes away in my new drawer with a smile plastered on my face.

Our relationship has been moving along at a great—albeit fast—pace. And we've had a few hiccups in the road, the biggest still being the Belinda issue. And now my free-spirited girlfriend's mortification.

The embarrassment that was plain as day on her face hasn't gone away since she left the room. Nope, her cheeks are stained with it as I walk into the living room and take a seat beside her on the couch.

She turns toward the window that overlooks the city, not bothering to glance my way.

I nudge her with my elbow, causing her to jerk farther into her corner of the couch.

I do it again, and she turns fully away from me.

"Oh, come on, you can't actually be mad at me for finding your *fanny* pack."

She stays silent.

"Baby." I poke her. "Audra." I poke her again in the spot under her ribs that always has her writhing in laughter.

She shoves my hand away, which only gives me more reason to do it again.

But this time, she swats at me. "Stop."

"Nope. Not until you stop the pouting."

This earns me a glare. "I'm not pouting. I'm internalizing."

"Internalizing, pouting. Either way sounds like sulking to me."

She lets out a closed-mouth scream. "You could have left it alone. Not touched it. Let me keep an ounce of my dignity." She tosses her arms up. "But no, you had to make fun of me for trying to prepare for something very traumatic."

My lips quirk. "Traumatic? You think anal will traumatize you?"

"I don't know, probably. I'm feeling pretty traumatized by this conversation, so imagine if I actually did it." She buries her face in her lap.

I choke back the laughter threatening to spill out of me at the sheer mortification she's experiencing over something that's a blip on the radar. If anything, she should be embarrassed by the stuffed teddy bear she keeps on her bed. I'm eighty-six percent sure she snuggles with it every night we aren't together.

But wanting to try to explore her sexual horizons, nope. Nothing about that is remotely embarrassing.

"Baby…" I tug her arm, scooting her over with zero effort, only confirming that she wants my touch, no matter what she's pretending. "Audra, look at me."

She shakes her head. "Nope. I don't think I will."

I chuckle. "Will you please just talk to me?"

"No."

"No?"

"*No*," she growls.

"What if I never bring up anal again?"

She turns her head, eyeing me suspiciously.

"I'm serious. I won't ever talk about it unless you want to."

"Fine." She lifts her chin, rolling her shoulders until her back is flush against the couch. Brushing away a few strands of hair from her face, she says, "Okay, go ahead. Speak."

"Did you start your—preparation before or after you met me?"

Her nostrils flare in annoyance. "Are you kidding me? You want to know if I was readying my… *body*… for you or someone else?"

I nod.

A wicked smile graces her lips. "It wasn't for you."

Well, that didn't go like I thought it would.

At all.

My shoulders drop as the excitement falls away with her words. I thought, I hoped, she wanted to take that sexual leap with me, not with someone else, like that sleazy professor she used to *date*—if you can even call them fucking and fighting dating.

My lips turn down as hers turn up even more.

"What? Not the answer you expected?"

"You know it wasn't."

"Awe, poor baby." She palms my cheek, gently slapping me.

"Who, then? If not me, then who else could have been so special?"

She stares at me, letting out a laugh. "Me, you idiot. I wanted to try it. It was never about anyone other than me."

"Oh."

"Yeah, oh."

My body sighs with relief. She wasn't planning it for him or any man; she was just exploring her sexuality.

"For the record, if I ever decided to do it—" She stops, pointing at me. "Which I never will. But if I did, I would want it to be with someone I trust with my body and soul. And that person is you."

"It would be my honor to take your back-door virginity... if you ever want that." I pull her against my chest, bringing her lips to mine for a gentle kiss.

She relaxes into me, resting her body against mine as we spend the rest of the evening lying on the couch, watching a show about Alaskan bush people that has us laughing until our eyes can't stay open.

Chapter Twenty-Six

Griffin

It's been a month now since the paint party. Which means it's only a few weeks until Audra's store opens. Pride fills every cell as I watch her work around the clock to make the space everything she envisioned.

She's like a machine as she moves from one project to the next. It's inspiring watching her go after what she wants. I've finished all the projects I had lined up for the next four months.

Well, maybe it's not my awe of her that's the cause of me running so far ahead at work. Maybe it's more like I needed something to preoccupy me while my love was busy chasing her dreams.

Tonight's the first night in over a week that she's free. And I plan to take total advantage of that.

I have the evening planned out, from our dinner of steak and potatoes to the wine—an overly sweet red that is her favorite—to the romantic movie we'll watch: *Pride and Prejudice* circa 2005. That damn hand flex is going to set the mood before we head into the bedroom for some music while I worship her body with mine.

In my dark-blue button-up flannel and dark-wash jeans that I know Audra loves my ass in, I wait patiently by the door for her, with only a few minutes left until she said she would be here. I bounce on my toes with anticipation. Seven days is too long to go without her. I miss everything. From her smile to her ridiculously over-the-top loud laugh.

I watch my phone as 7 p.m. hits and she still hasn't walked through the door. Then seven fifteen and seven forty-five. I check my texts religiously every few minutes. Even sending off a few to check in on her that go without a response.

It isn't until eight forty-five that she plows into my place without knocking, as usual. Closing the door with her foot, she stalks over to where I'm now sitting on the couch with a beer in hand. In a long T-shirt-like dress, she climbs into my lap to straddle me, hands wrapping around the back of my neck.

"I'm sorry I'm late. Things at the shop took a little longer than usual deciding which products to display on the front table and which to display on the back. Bel wants the candles to go in the front, but I think the vases and paperweights would be so much better. So it's a nightmare," she says before she presses her mouth to mine. "Forgive me."

My lips form a thin, tight line as I nod.

"You're mad."

"I'm not mad," I tell her, taking another drink of my beer.

Audra leans back, taking a long look at my face. "You are."

"It's fine. Being late isn't a big deal, but I would have liked a text back. I was getting concerned."

Her eyebrows dip as she digs her hand into the pocket of her jean jacket. "Texts?" She pulls out her phone, swiping at the screen. "Griff, I'm sorry. I didn't see them."

"I figured."

A frown pulls at her lips as she takes in my clothes. She climbs off me, looking around the living room and into the kitchen where the food is plated and wine poured.

"Oh, Griff, I fucked this one up, didn't I?"

"It's fine."

"It's not." She shakes her head. "You did all this, and I showed up late—I suck."

"You don't."

"But I can." She smiles down at me with a wink. "If you want."

I chuckle. "Did you just offer to suck me off to make it better?"

"That depends. Will it work?"

I stand, pulling her into me, my arms holding her tight against me. The softness of her dress caressing my palms as I skim them up and down her back. "Baby, there is nothing this mouth couldn't fix."

My lips crash down on hers in a frenzy. She leaps up, wrapping her legs around my waist just as my stomach rumbles.

Audra pulls back, a smile dancing on her lips.

"Rain check?" I ask, glancing over to the table where our cold dinner sits.

She gives me a look that screams "duh" and hops down, heading to the kitchen to reheat our meal.

Audra smiles and dances in her chair as she eats. She's genuinely enjoying what I made her, which only makes me want to cook her every meal of every day, if only to see that satisfied smile on her face.

Once we've finished, I pick up our plates, bringing them over to the sink to wash them. "So, after this, I thought we might watch a movie in bed?"

She places a wine glass in the sink, then turns to me and asks, "By watching a movie, do you mean watch a movie or *watch* a movie?"

"Both?" I wink.

"Ooh, I like—" Her phone chimes, and she pulls it out of her pocket. Excitement dances across her eyes as she taps away at the screen. "Change of plans, Griff. We are going to head out to the bar with Jerry and Bel for a celebratory drink in honor of us finally deciding on a name for the shop."

I gnaw on my bottom lip to stop from spewing my frustrations. Scrubbing at the last fork, I rinse everything off, before placing it in the drying rack. Every muscle in my body is tense as I step away from Audra, pull open the fridge door, and grab a beer off the bottom shelf before sitting back down at the table.

I take two long drags of my Coors Light, watching as she dries the dishes. "What about our plans?"

She laughs. "What plans?"

My teeth grind together. I try not to let it sting. I do. But this entire night was supposed to be about us. I had it all planned out, and she doesn't want it. She doesn't want to spend time alone with me.

Audra spins to look at me. "I—I didn't mean it like that."

"No, I think you did."

"Griff, stop it. We will still spend the evening together while celebrating. Aren't you happy for me?"

My shoulders deflate. Hell, everything in me deflates. She isn't getting it. "Of course I am. But I can be happy for you and not want to spend my time with her. Especially when it's the first opportunity to be alone in over a week."

"You'll be fine." She grabs a plate and wipes it with the towel. "We can have sex when we get back, if that's what you're worried about."

"You're joking?" I stare at her back. She can't possibly believe that's what I'm upset about. "It's more than that, and you know it."

She doesn't respond.

"Are you even listening to me?" I stare at her as she puts away the clean dishes into my cabinets. Her chestnut hair falling in front of her face as she bends over and over.

"Yes, Griff. I'm listening, but I think you're overreacting. One night isn't going to kill you."

My blood boils with rage. I need her to listen. "Audra, please."

"Griffin, it's just a few hours with her, and if you give her a chance, you'll feel better."

"I'm serious. I can't do it. I won't."

"Don't be ridiculous." She grabs for her jacket.

My heart is beating a million miles a minute, but I stay glued to my chair, hands shaking as I realize what I have to do. I've tried to get over it. To ignore the constant pushing and pulling toward Belinda, but I can't do it anymore. She doesn't understand; no, she doesn't *listen* when I tell her no. When I beg her to drop it or leave it alone. Instead, she tries to push me on Belinda as if she can replace the empty space left by my mom. Swallowing down the emotion-filled lump in my throat, I say, "I can't do this."

"Sure you can. Just get up and move."

"No, I mean this." Moisture pools in my eyes as I gesture between us. "Me and you. I can't do this anymore."

She freezes by the door. "That's not funny."

"I wasn't trying to be." My voice is somehow steady despite how every part of me is shaking.

Slowly, she spins to face me, tears well in her eyes. "What?"

"I think we should take a break."

"Griffin." She moves to kneel in front of me, taking hold of my hands. "No. Please don't do this."

"I have to. You won't *listen* to me." My heart hammers so hard that all I can hear is the sound of my blood whooshing in my ears.

"I'll stay home."

"It's too late." The aching hollowness in my chest grows with every passing second. And I wish I could take it all back, every word. I wish I could go back to ten minutes ago, when we were still an *us*.

"After everything, that's it? It's over just like that because of my best friend?"

Her jaw trembles. And I close my eyes, not wanting to see the pain I'm causing us both.

"You know it's more than that. It's bigger than that. She gave me away, then decided she wanted me moments before I put my mother in the ground. You think that's something I can just get over? That you can just make me forget? That I should try for her."

"Not just for her... For *me*. You don't understand how hard it is on me for the two most important people in my life to be at odds."

My voice cracks. "What—what about how *I* feel?"

"I'm sorry," she cries, moving to sit in my lap. She clasps my face in her hands, trying to force me to look at her. "Please, please don't do this. I love you."

I wipe away a tear from under my eye. "I love you too. But I can't do this... at least not right now. I need time. Space."

"I'll do better. I promise," she pleads. "Give me another chance."

"No. You've already shown over and over that I come last. Spending time with me is an afterthought. For weeks, I have shuffled around everything to spend any amount of time I could with you. While you ditch me the first chance you get. I deserve more. To be heard when I tell you how I feel. Hell, we haven't even seen each other in days, and you didn't seem to care then, so what's a little more time apart?"

"Griffin, don't do this."

"This just gives you more time to spend with the person who truly means the most to you."

Audra sucks in a sharp breath, and I know my words hit their target.

My head drops, unable to look at her, at the pain that's visible on her face. "I think you should go."

A tremor passes through her as she vigorously wipes the tears away from under her eyes.

"Please give me time."

She nods, climbing off my lap and picking up her purse from where she dropped it, then continues to walk out the door without looking back.

I press my palms into my eyes, trying to stop myself from letting the heartbreak out.

I didn't plan this.

Hell, I didn't want it at all.

Maybe it's the result of how the night began all wrong. Or maybe it isn't. Maybe it's been building.

It doesn't matter. I can't continue to be with her if she doesn't understand how what she was doing was hurting me.

Talking wasn't getting through to her. This is the last resort. I know she doesn't understand why it's as big of a deal as it is. She acts as if every time I deny hanging out with Belinda, that I'm asking her to choose between us. And maybe I kind of am.

In the end, it doesn't matter. Because I know she'll always choose her over me. The friend to whom she's loyal to the core.

And no matter how much I try to be okay with that, I never will be.

I grab another beer from my fridge and sit down on the sofa with it and my guitar. The strumming of the chords soothing me like it used to before. Reminding me that music was my love before her and will be after her.

Chapter Twenty-Seven

I manage to hold myself together until I step through the door of my apartment. The tears fall rapidly as I gasp for breath. I clutch my chest, sliding down the back of the door until I'm on the floor.

The pain is too much.

And I know this is all my fault. The person I love doesn't want me, and it's all my fault.

I did this. I pushed him. Pushed and pushed until he couldn't take it anymore. Until he couldn't take being with me any longer.

I did to him what my family did to me. I tried to control him. Thought I knew what was best for him. Refused to see his side. His logic, his reasoning, until it was too late.

Left with no choice but to cut out the source of his misery—me.

The tears fall harder with each thought of how I did this. Every one reminding me of how I caused his pain and mine.

Why couldn't I support him the way he deserves? The way he supported me.

I had sent a quick text to Bel before leaving Griffin's.

Can't make it tonight. Not feeling great, I'm going straight to bed.

Bed? You better be blowing me off to sleep and not sleep around with the fruit of my loins.

My chin wobbles.

No loins involved.

Feel better.

Feel better? Better? I laugh. It feels like I will never feel better. This ache in my chest where my heart was ripped out just moments ago only seems to get stronger with every minute.

I fucked up. I fucked up *bad*. And it has cost me the person I love. The most important person in my life.

I made him feel like he was second. And I didn't even care until the moment he stood up for himself and it affected me.

Hell, I had laughed it off or, fuck, even made him feel bad for wanting to be number one. *My* number one. My stupid selfishness is the cause of my own pain.

But he is. He is my sun and stars. The person I want to share every important thing with, as well as the minuscule things that make me happy or mad. He is the first person I think of when I wake up and the person I dream of as I sleep.

But I couldn't, wouldn't, listen to him.

I drove him away. Pushed him to this.

Why?

This doesn't feel like my previous breakups. I dated Nick for longer than I've known Griffin, and somehow, everything he did to me doesn't even compare pain-wise to what I have done to Griff and me.

Our relationship imploded, and I was the goddamn accelerant.

The cool hardwood flooring presses against my cheek as I curl into a ball, clutching my phone. Hoping he'll call.

That this was all a mistake.

That he didn't mean it.

That he still wants me.

But the phone doesn't ring.

And Griffin never calls.

And I stay lying there in a puddle of my tears until my head throbs and my eyes ache from the amount of tears shed.

I can't go on like this. I'm either shoving my face full of candy and Chinese food—but honestly, I would settle for anything I can get my hands on   or I'm crying while reading old text messages and staring at pictures of Griff for hours on end.

I'm not so depressed that I haven't bathed.

No, that hasn't become an issue.

Instead, I spend hours on end soaking in the bath or sitting on the floor of my shower, letting the water roll off my body while I become oblivious to the temperature or anything else around me.

My insides hurt in ways I never knew possible.

Replaying the moment he broke up with me on repeat.

Wondering if I could have changed his mind. If I hadn't been late, would he have been so upset?

But all the different scenarios don't change a thing.

We're still over.

Okay, on a *break*, yeah right.

Everyone knows a break is code for broken up.

He still doesn't want to see or talk to me, so it feels like a breakup.

I need to stop this moping.

I need to get my ass out of my apartment and into the store.

The ending of our relationship doesn't mean the world has stopped turning; it just means the sun stopped shining for *me*.

I have to go on. No matter how dark it gets for me, I still have responsibilities.

Lying in my bed, wrapped up in one of Griff's forgotten shirts, I press ignore on my phone as it rings for the thirteenth time today.

"Give it up, Bel, I'm never going to answer," I grumble to myself.

From my bed, I see my front door swing open.

I roll off my mattress with the stealth of a baby hippo, my heart racing as I search my room for something, anything, to use as a weapon.

Just as I grab my open laptop, prepared to use it to defend my dear life, Bel pops her head into my room.

"Jesus fucking Christ!" I grab my chest, letting my laptop fall to the floor with a *clank*.

"Sorry, did I scare you?" she asks, picking the computer up off the floor and examining it for cracks, which, thank the heavens, aren't there.

"No, Bel, I yelped like a Chihuahua for shits and giggles."

"Well, I'm sorry, but also, I'm not."

"What, why?" I ask, climbing back into my bed and under the fluffy down comforter.

She glares at me in exasperation that soon turns to a look of pure pity. Her gaze softens as she takes in my ratty, wet hair and puffy eyes. "Because you've been ignoring me. And I want to know why."

"I haven't been ignoring you. I text you."

"Once. You texted me once. And all you said was 'I won't be in today.'"

"And I wasn't. So what's your point?"

She lets out a small sigh, coming to sit on the edge of my bed. "The point is, you normally text me at least twenty times a day, and that's on the days we spend together. The days we don't average around fifty times. So something is wrong. And I want to know what."

Shit. She's right. I'm a clingy bitch even on a bad day.

My throat becomes scratchy. "Nothing, it's nothing."

"It's not nothing, I can tell."

I nod. "It's not nothing. It's everything." My composure breaks, and the tears I've kept in for the past few minutes let loose, falling and falling until the neck of my shirt, his shirt, is soaked with them.

"Oh, Auds." She reaches out, gathering me in her arms and hugging me. "What happened?"

I cling to her. Her fingers stroking up and down my back in a light, barely there pattern that's providing me with a steadying, calming force that I have desperately craved.

"Griffin." My voice trembles as I try to speak the words, the truth that's made my heart clench in pain. "He ended things. Well, technically, he said we're on a break. But we both know that's code for Splitsville."

She takes a sharp breath. "Oh, honey. I'm so sorry."

"He doesn't think I respect him."

"What?" she asks, pulling back to look me in the face. "Why would he—"

"You," I whisper. "I kept trying to push you two together, against his wishes." I hadn't planned on telling her that part, ever. But my chest aches at the sight of her. I can't handle the knowledge alone. I need her to share the burden with me, no matter if she deserves it. No matter if it's right.

I don't care.

I just don't want to be the only one who knows. Or the only one it hurts.

Her expression falls as she sighs deeply. "Auds, I—"

"Please don't say it again. I'm begging you."

"Okay." She lies on the bed, pulling me with her. A chime sounds from her phone, and she glances at it with a frown. "It's Jerry. He wants to do dinner tonight."

I expect her to stay until I cry myself to sleep, to be the friend I desperately need. Curling up behind me and wrapping an arm around me, intertwining our fingers.

But instead, she pats my hip and hops out of bed. "I'll talk to you tomorrow."

I'm speechless, the only sound in the room my sniffling and the rhythmic whirl of my ceiling-fan blades spinning round and round as she leaves my apartment. She didn't even hesitate before dropping me for Jerry.

This is the person I put before Griffin.

The person I involve in everything.

Guilt nags at me as cold loneliness sinks bone deep. I drove him away for her, and she couldn't even hold me while my heart is splintering.

In the days following the breakup, my heart hasn't stopped cracking.

I wasn't becoming numb.

No, I was too angry. The sadness that had claimed me has drifted into something else.

Rage.

I am full of it. It's all I can see. Well, that and blame.

It consumes me, and I'm happy to let it. Anything to escape the soul crushing that is losing him.

Griffin dumping me has opened up an entirely new side of me. I'm obsessive more than ever before. I let my work become my everything. Why not? It's not like I have anything or anyone else going for me.

I snap at Bel more and more, quietly blaming her for my mistakes, for my relationship failure.

The resentment continuing to build every day, no matter what she does.

She tries to be there for me.

Tries to comfort me, make me laugh, bring me out of the darkness.

But I can't allow that.

I *won't* allow that.

I don't want to see the light or to let go of the negativity clouding my brain. Because if I do, that will only lead to one place—pain.

At the store, I place a few final touches on the decor and displays before we open in a few days.

The outside of the building is almost complete. It has a new awning, and the window adorns our hours and the store's name in a beautiful curving script. But I still haven't figured out what floral or bush arrangement I want at the door.

The paper covering the windows is still up, blocking the street from seeing what we're up to inside. But on opening day, it will come down, and my little hideaway will be visible and open to all.

My hands tremble a little just thinking about it as I unlock the large wooden door and step inside to find Bel already moving things around.

Her energy used to be something I loved and admired. But now it's eating me alive. I just want her to stop. To let me have complete control over one thing. For her to leave it and me alone.

With candles piled high on one of the brand-new intricate rugs, she walks backward, dragging them with her across the room.

She looks up as I shut the door. "Auds! You're here, thank God. Now grab the other end of the rug and help me set up this candle tower I have been dreaming of."

I drop my purse and stare at her. "Candle tower? Candle. Tower. You want to take our very expensive glass candles and stack them where they could fall and break at any moment?"

"Stop being such a worrywart, I'm not going to break anything." She tugs at the rug hard enough that the crack of two candles breaking fills the room. "Oops."

My jaw snaps closed as I take a deep breath. "Perfect. Just perfect," I grumble, stalking around her to the back room. "Our inventory is shot because you have a stupid whim."

Belinda stands tall, her spine stiffening. "Enough! I'm so sick of your bad attitude. I get it, you blame me for your relationship ending. And that's fine. Go ahead, blame me. I don't care, but this shit needs to end."

My chest heaves with the anger building up. "It can't end. Because when it does, I will be left to feel the pain and agony of my new reality. Is that what you want? For me to be sad. To see me cry?"

"Of course not." She abandons the candles, walking over to me. "I never want to see you sad, but pushing your heartbreak down because it's hard isn't the answer. You need to let the pain in. Feel every ounce. Let it rip you to shreds until you think there is no way you'll ever be okay."

She takes my hands in hers, big brown eyes—Griffin's big brown eyes—staring into mine. "But you will. Day by day, a bit of you will come back together at the seams until you are whole again. Maybe with a few news scars. But whole nonetheless."

My chin trembles as I listen to her.

"Please tell me you will try."

I nod my head once.

"Good. Because I need my best friend and business partner back. Okay?"

I swallow. "Okay."

She leads me over to the table and kneels, picking up the candles and stacking them into the intricate shape she envisioned. Ignoring the ache in my stomach, I join her.

Slowly, my anger melts away. The sadness comes back in trickles. I'm nowhere near happy or fine. But it's a start, and for now, I guess that's as good as it gets.

I don't bother to knock as I let myself into my brother's house. I know he and Viv won't be getting it on, at least not in the living room or anywhere else that isn't behind a locked door.

They've learned their lesson after Sutton has walked in on them playing hide the hot dog not once, not twice, but three times. The most recent time being while Viv was a million weeks pregnant and had heard sex could get labor moving, so she and Nate were going at it without a care in the world, and in came Sutton with a bag of dates and a pineapple, ready to help get labor started in another way.

"Dingdong, Auntie Audra's here," I say, shutting the door behind me.

Nate and Viv look up from their spots on the living-room floor where the three of them are gathered doing tummy time, aka my favorite time.

"Audra, what are you doing here?" Nate asks as I slink down to the carpet beside them until I'm facedown.

"Wallowing," I whine with a mouthful of carpet.

"What's wrong, Auds?" Viv wiggles her way closer to me and pets my hair.

I moan a little, much to my brother's disgust as he gags.

"Hey." I turn my head in his direction. "Don't yuck my yum, you dick."

"Don't say dick in front of my daughter, slag," he snaps back.

I sit up, pushing off the carpet, which is now wet with either my drool or Ev's. Sadly, I think it's mine. "Did you just call me a slut slang, you twat?"

"You're the twat, twat."

"Enough," Viv says, using her new and improved mom voice.

"Ooh, Viv, do it again. I got chills."

"She's right, Cherry. That was hot," Nate practically pants at her.

"That's not what I meant, but also, he isn't wrong. You can be my mommy any day." I wink.

"Ew, that's my wife. Aka your sister-in-law. Stop hitting on her and apologize."

When I don't immediately speak up, he kicks at my shin. "Now, Audra."

"Fine." I hold my hands up. "I'm sorry, Vivian, for sexualizing you for being the MILF that you are."

Nate's eyes narrow. "That was too easy."

I shrug pathetically like the lonely semi-single loser that I am.

"Yeah, where's your usual fire, Auds?" Vivian asks while smiling down at a babbling Evelyn.

My bottom lip juts out. "It got stomped out along with my heart when Griffin dumped me." It takes everything in me not to let my voice crack. To hold back the tears that are so close to breaking through the walls I've built to help hide the crushing agony that is my life without Griff.

"Oh, Audra," Viv says, bringing her attention back to me.

"What happened?" Nate asks.

I spill my guts to them about everything. I wish I could say I keep it together, but I don't. I cry and sob, and at one point, baby Ev joins me, having to be taken out of the room to calm down by Viv. But my little brother remains, listening to me go on and on about how I screwed up. About how my heart has been squashed by the only man I've ever really loved.

"I wish I could say you didn't do anything wrong, Auds, but you did," he tells me after I finish baring my soul to him.

I wipe under my nose with my sleeve. "Thanks, needle dick, that really makes me feel better."

Nate chuckles. "Hey, no need for insults. I am just trying to help you. It seems like all Griffin wanted from you was to acknowledge his feelings, and you kind of walked all over him."

"How is making me feel worse helping me?"

"I'm helping you by reminding you what exactly you can work on. How you can make yourself feel better by being the partner he needs. The partner I know you want to be for him."

"I thought that with a bit of encouragement, he could see how awesome she is."

Nate gives me a sad smile. "Not everyone is going to like the same people, Auds. And we have to learn to be okay with that."

"Ugh, I hate it when you are wiser than me."

"So, you constantly hate me?" he asks, coming to sit beside me.

"One would think, but unfortunately, I love you."

He wraps an arm around my shoulder, tugging me into his side. "I love you too. Now, do you want me to go take over for Viv with Ev so you can have a girls' night pity party like she and Sutton like to throw themselves?"

I nod enthusiastically. "Yes, please."

He pats my knee before standing. "It's going to be okay, Audra. Like he said, it's just a break. You can fix this."

Tears line my eyes. "How can you be sure?"

"Because the love of my life took me back after I screwed up. I have to believe that yours will too."

The rest of the night, Vivian plies me with drink after drink, making me watch cheesy movies for "inspiration." *Inspiration, my ass.* Viv loves to watch people kiss, like the perv I know she secretly is.

After an ungodly amount of booze, two rom-coms, and one Face-Time with Sutton, I'm a little less miserable. So much so that for the first time since that unfortunate night, I fall asleep without crying. Without letting my mind drift to the cold truth that Griff won't be holding me to keep me warm while I sleep.

Chapter Twenty-Eight

Griffin

"I don't get it," Bren says, pressing the button on his controller repeatedly to continue shooting at the group across the clearing in our game. "You love her, right?"

"Yeah." I keep my eyes glued to the screen, moving my character into an attack position.

To take my mind off the gnawing pain inside my chest, I've thrown myself back into packing up Mom and Dad's house.

And by packing it up, I mean living here, crying here, and playing video games with Brenden here. The number of boxes I actually filled before I called it quits? About ten.

I'm not sure why I thought moving from one pain to another was a great idea. It shows that I'm not thinking as clearly as I believe I am, which Bren has continuously told me.

"So why end it?"

"I told you, she kept trying to push me to accept Belinda."

He pauses our game, giving me the concerned-big-brother look. The one with the furrowed brow and questioning eyes.

"What?" I say, throwing the controller down onto the coffee table. "You think I should have let it happen, no matter how I was feeling?"

He rears back. "Fuck no. But I don't think you needed to give up the woman you love to do that."

I drop my head to the back of the couch. "You don't understand."

"I sure as shit don't. If I had a woman I cared about like you care about Auds, I wouldn't let her go for anything."

Closing my eyes, I try to push away the emotions threatening to pour out of me. "You think I wanted this?" My voice cracks. "This—this pain is killing me."

He lays his hand on my shoulder.

"I didn't have a choice. She might have been my everything, but that doesn't mean I was hers, or that she and I want the same things. She couldn't respect my feelings about Belinda because that is her friend and—I deserve better."

Bren watches me with matching sadness swimming in his eyes. "I'm sorry, Griff," he says with a nod. "You deserve better."

I wipe a stray tear from my eye. "Yeah, I do."

"But... I think you are holding on to this hatred for Belinda instead of grieving Mom."

"Bullshit I am," I snap. Fire burning inside me. He knows how much I miss her.

"Griff, calm down and listen. What Belinda did was super shitty and shows that she herself needs some work if she thinks that was okay. But you, my brother, went from burying our mother to hating another. I think that hate is you trying to avoid what really hurts—Mom being gone and the lies." He pauses, glancing my way. "And I hate to say this, but in some ways, I agree with Audra."

Sucking in a sharp breath, I rear back. "*What?*"

"You let your hatred of someone become a problem in your relationship. Yes, again, I agree. Audra didn't listen to your boundaries, and that isn't okay. But it's also not okay for you to let this ugly emotion pull you under."

I rub the heels of my palms into my eyes. He might be right.

"Griff, you fell in love with Audra on a road trip to find Belinda. How can you be shocked, or hell, mad, that she's trying to help you build a relationship with the woman who brought you two together?"

Fuck, he is right, and he knows it. As much as I hate to admit it, maybe it's time for therapy.

Screw his slight knowledge of psychology that he uses on the job to talk people off ledges.

"Okay, that's enough psychoanalyzing, Dr. Phil."

"Dr. Phil? Nah, call me Dr. Drew, the shit-show wrangler."

With my brother's help, we actually manage to finish cleaning out our parents' house. Packing up all the things we want to keep and placing them into storage, and donating or selling the rest.

I hate the idea of selling the house, but it doesn't feel the same anymore, not like home, not without her. The wood floor is clean of all rugs and clutter. Walls bare and repainted for the open house. Every part of this house is empty. Nothing more than a memory.

I thought *I* was taking it hard, using it as a distraction from my rocky relationship status. Replacing one pain with another.

But Bren is a mess. He puts on a brave face as we pack everything away and make the house presentable for the market. But the moment we finish, he breaks down.

"I always thought we would bring our kids here," he says, holding his head in his hands as he sits on the porch steps.

I take my place beside him, wrapping my arm around his shoulder. "Me too."

"Mom would watch over them while we went out on dates with our wives... She would have been a perfect grandmother."

I nod in agreement. "Yeah, she really would have."

His voice is hoarse when he adds, "I'm not sure I can do this."

"Brenden..."

"No, Griff. This place is Mom and Dad. Without it, I feel like we are saying goodbye to them."

"In a way, we are."

"I—I don't want to say goodbye. I'm not ready." Emotion floods his voice.

My nose stings as tears prickle my eyes. "We'll never be ready, Bren. But I really think we need to try."

"Okay." He clears his throat. "Just don't leave me until our kids' children have gray hair, okay, baby brother?"

I chuckle. "Okay."

"Was this therapeutic? It felt cathartic. Right?"

"Can't packing just be packing? Not some part of the grieving process?"

"Sure. But this wasn't just about grief. This was a life process. It might be symbolic that we are sorting and putting things into boxes to move on, but just because you don't want it to mean anything doesn't mean it doesn't."

Chapter Twenty-Nine

Audra

Today is the day.

Opening day.

The shop looks perfect. Everything is set out and displayed in a way that is magazine-worthy. Hell, I've even considered taking some pictures and sending them in to magazines because that's how great I think it looks.

Unfortunately, I am no professional, or even an adequate photographer. So that dream dies quickly. That doesn't stop me from basking in the beauty of what we created. It's a mixture of vintage and glam. Subtle yet eye-catching. It's everything I envisioned.

I spent the morning attempting to relax. But my brain had other plans. From the moment the sun came up and shined through my bedroom windows, my heart was beating a mile a minute.

Nothing I did could calm my spiraling nerves. I tried chamomile tea, a hot bath, meditation, and even masturbation—nothing did the trick.

The opening isn't until tonight, so I have a full day of nothing to do but think about how much I want and need tonight to be a success. My future is riding on this store.

No pressure or anything.

I hate that, at this current moment, my happiness depends on my job, my business.

I'm a business owner.

I own a freaking business.

It still feels surreal to me, making me giddy and nauseous at the same time. I hope after tonight, that will change. And if everything goes according to plan, it should.

Unable to wait any longer, I whip my hair into a braid that forms a wispy crown on my head, then swipe a million coats of mascara over my lashes for good measure. I throw on a little black dress that is the right amount of sexy and casual, and pairing it with a chunky black heel. The look should make me feel confident, like a smart, savvy business owner, but I feel as if I look like a little girl playing around in her mother's closet. Not my mother's, though. Delia Fisher lives for comfort over style.

With only my cell phone and my keys in my hand, I head out, not wasting another minute worrying about what-ifs.

My shoulders begin to loosen and my nerves become a thing of the past as I pound back glass after glass of champagne.

An hour into our grand opening celebration, and it already feels like a success.

I haven't even begun to file through all the emotions pulsing through me. Everyone I love, and even some I don't, show up to support Bel's and my new adventure.

Everyone but him.

But I'm not going to let his lack of support bum me out.

My store is officially open to customers. Eeeek!

Cue the excited screams.

I want to dance and jump up and down, but I don't. Well, not in front of the crowd at our soft opening, I don't. I might have done a little shimmying in the stock room earlier.

My dreams are coming true, and one must shimmy when they do. It's a rule.

From the store knickknacks to the art and furniture I'll create, this space, this business, is something I am extremely proud of, and I hope my parents can see that.

"Baby girl." My dad opens his arms to drag me into one of his over-the-top hugs. "You did good."

A lump lodges in my throat. "You mean it?"

He tips my chin up and beams down at me with a proud smile on his lips. "Of course. This is amazing. You and Belinda have something extraordinary here."

I clear my throat. "Thank you. Do you think Mom agrees?"

"Are you kidding? The woman wouldn't shut up all night about how impressed she was with your preservations."

I look across the room to see her chatting up my brother while Cooper stands beside them, rocking baby Evelyn in his arms while staring lovingly across the room at the very animated Sutton telling Belinda a story.

"Is she still mad?" I ask, unsure if I'm ready to hear anything other than the word *no*.

Dad is silent for a few moments, as if he's mulling over his words carefully. "I don't know how to answer that... She's insanely proud of you, but I don't think that fixes the hurt she is feeling from you leaving."

"I didn't leave... not really. I basically expanded the business. Forever Floral is going to be a great sister company to Fisher Floral. Trust me."

He tsks. "You know she doesn't see it that way, especially since you've partnered up with Belinda." He says her name as if it tastes wrong on his tongue. He and Griffin have that in common.

"Ugh, why does everyone have to have an opinion on my best friend and business partner?"

He gives me a thoughtful look. "Maybe you should be asking yourself why everyone has a different opinion on Belinda than you do?"

"Maybe it's because I see the best in her. I know her better than anyone else."

"You didn't know she had given a baby up thirty years ago."

Shots fired. One to Daddio.

I aim a warning glare at him. It's a sensitive subject for a lot of people. And I hate that he's right, even as I claim otherwise. "That wasn't anyone else's business but hers."

"Really, no one else's... Not even Griffin's?"

That shuts me up real quick.

He's right.

But now I'm fuming.

Not at him for being right, but at him for bringing up the man I can't get my mind off. I swear steam is pouring out of my nostrils as I exhale. "You couldn't help yourself, could you?"

He pats my back. "Sorry, darling, but I'm missing your other half just as much as you are."

"I seriously doubt that. You've only met the man, like, two times total."

"And they were two amazing times. You've always enjoyed music, but your passion manifested in moving your body to the sounds. Not in the art of making it. Talking with Griffin was like a walk down memory lane. I remembered the joy, the feeling of freedom that used to encompass me when I picked up my guitar."

"You could still talk to him. I don't think he would mind. It's me he doesn't want to see or speak with, not you."

"No can do. I'm a loyal man. I've chosen my side."

"Dad, there isn't any side. We aren't at war."

"Aren't you, though?"

He's right again. But not about Griffin and me being on opposing sides. But about the battle raging inside me. The fact that my heart is being torn in opposite directions. One toward my best friend, the woman I've made my dreams come true with. And the other toward the man who makes me feel whole. The person who brings me more joy than I ever knew possible. The man I never want to let go.

I pat him on the back. "Nah, it's okay if you want to be team Griffin instead of team Audra. I'm team Griffin."

"Just be patient, baby girl. These things have a way of working themselves out."

I gnaw on the corner of my bottom lip. "I hope you're right."

Just as my dad saunters back into my scowling mom's arms, a face I could have lived without ever seeing again pops into my line of sight.

"Nick," I squeak out as his arms wrap around me, gluing mine to my sides. The cashmere of his expensive sweater gliding over my skin. "What are you doing here?"

He leans back, arms still encasing me in the world's most awkward hug. "What am I doing here?" he asks incredulously. "I'm here to celebrate my girl's big day."

"I'm not your girl, Nick," I tell him as I twist my way out of his embrace.

"Since when?"

"Since you gave me an STI."

He waves his hand. "It was cured with a simple round of antibiotics. It's hardly anything to ruminate on."

"You gave me chlamydia... of the eye," I snap, balling my hands into fists, readying these puppies to fly into one of his eyes. "I nearly went blind."

"Key word is *nearly*."

I take a deep breath and force a smile on my face. "You know what, it doesn't matter. Water under the fucking bridge. I appreciate you coming out tonight to support Bel and me."

"Of course." He grasps my hand in his, giving it a small squeeze, which I'm sure is meant to be comforting but instead just gives me the ick.

He dips his head closer to my face, and oh dear God, is this man about to kiss me?

I tense up, unsure if I should knee him in the balls and make a scene, thus ruining the perfect night. Or if I should just let it happen and freeze like a statue. Because if I'm frozen, no one else will be able to see me, thus making it look like the bubble-butt bitch is kissing thin air.

Thankfully, I don't have to decide because he stops a few inches in front of my face and asks, "Have you gotten any of my texts?"

I jerk my hand from his and give him a pity smile. "Actually, no. My boyfriend wasn't comfortable with you texting me, so I blocked your number."

It's a lie.

One, I'm not sure if I actually have a boyfriend anymore. And two, said up-in-the-air boyfriend couldn't care less about Nick.

Sure, he wasn't a fan of my ex sending me *I miss you* texts, but he trusted me. Well, he trusted me to be faithful, so he left what I wanted to do about the pestering messages up to me.

So I blocked him.

But guys like Nick don't just let the things they have their sights set on go easily. No, if I told him I blocked him, he might be inclined to try to sway me into unblocking him.

Not that it would work. Nothing that chlamydia-spreading swine could do would ever sway me into unblocking him.

But saying my boyfriend did, that might just be a line he would respect.

"Boyfriend?"

"Yes, boyfriend."

"You don't have a boyfriend," he says with such confidence that I'm circling back to the idea of kneeing him in the balls.

God, I hate his smile. It's weird that there was a time when he would give me that same confident smirk and my panties would melt. And now it's like every cell in my body recoils at the thought of him touching me. At the memories of his skin against mine, as if I was a victim of some cruel torture and not a willing and eager participant.

My jaw drops. "Excuse me, yes I do."

"Where is he, then?" He looks around the room with a raised eyebrow.

"Busy, clearly," I deadpan, wishing he'd drop dead from a sudden heart attack caused by some untreated STI.

"Sure, he is." He smiles in a way that says he thinks I'm lying.

I am, but that doesn't mean this dirty, disease-sharing prick needs to know that.

I plaster on another fake smile. "Are you planning to buy anything tonight?"

He hands me his shopping basket, which is filled with three of the floral-infused candles I made, each of them my favorite scents.

I fight the urge to roll my eyes as I walk him to the register and ring him up. He glances around the store, ogling all the women in his vicinity like the creep he is, while I wrap the candles in a protective paper.

Handing him the bag, I thank him for coming to support us.

"Anything for you, Audra... Anything. Give me a call whenever you're ready to ditch the *boyfriend*."

"Don't hold your breath," I tell him with a sneer. "Or maybe do."

Nick walks away, a bag full of goodies in his hand and a smirk on his face.

Belinda rushes over. From where I know she was pretending not to watch the entire encounter, her arms flailing as if to shoo him away. "Scram, you scoundrel. Nobody wants your contaminated cock."

"Wow, Bel. What would I have done without you running interference for me?" I say in a flat, unamused tone.

"Oh, come on." She smacks my arm. "You didn't need me. You had that situation completely under control."

"I thought about injuring his testicles at least twice during the conversation."

"But you didn't." She raises her fist in victory. "Celebrate the win, Auds."

I rest my hands on my hips as she continues to pump her fists in the air in an alternating motion with so much enthusiasm, one would think she just won gold at the Olympics.

"Come on, Auds. Celebrate with me." She hands me a flute of champagne. "We just opened our store, and you managed not to maul the man who jizzed in your eye. I feel like this has been one for the history books."

I raise my glass. "Ah, yes, the jizz offense that almost blinded a nation of one."

Chapter Thirty

Griffin

My stupid, sensitive heart clenches as she laughs behind the large storefront window, hugging person after person throughout the night. She's magnificent. Mesmerizing, even. With her long legs on display in that black dress, she steals every bit of my attention.

Damn it, I wish she was hugging me.

Those arms should be wrapped around me.

I want to be in there with her. To celebrate her and her amazing accomplishment.

But I can't.

I won't.

I need to work on myself for more than a couple of weeks before walking back into her life. And I need her to do the same. We can't slide back to the way things used to be. Her pushing and me avoiding.

So instead of standing by her side like I long to be, I'm settling for watching her through the grand windows of her store, capturing every moment of it with my eyes.

But the only problem is her.

I miss her so fucking much that the moment I caught sight of her, the rest of the world faded away. She's the only thing I see. And she shines so fucking bright.

With my back leaning against a tree across the street, I can be a part of her night without her knowing.

She was so nervous when the night first began, her posture rigid and her smile weak. It didn't take long for her to guzzle down two glasses of champagne immediately after they touched her hands. But as the hours pass, I watch her come into her own.

The tense shoulders she'd been sporting relaxed. Her smile grew wider with every person she talked to.

Now she's at ease, and I don't think it has anything to do with a few glasses of champagne.

Owning her own business looks good on her.

Every so often, she and Belinda smile at each other from across the room. My gut churns at the sight, my chest aching. Wishing things weren't this way.

I hate how I feel.

Like I'm jealous.

And I'm pretty sure it's of both of them.

I hate even more that I've caught her confidence slipping a few times when she talks to her parents. It's a small shift in her posture. And I don't think anyone else would have noticed if they weren't paying as close attention as I am.

My jaw aches from how tightly I've been grinding my teeth together ever since that prick, Nick, strode in there with this stupid, perfectly coiffed hair and sweater. That fucking sweater rubbed all over my girl as if she would be tempted by what looked like soft fabrics. Pride swelled in my chest for, like, the millionth time tonight as I watched her brush off his advances.

"Stalker much?"

I jump, turning to find Bren looking at me with an amused expression. "Fuck. That's rich coming from a guy who stalks for a living."

He frowns. "It's called a stakeout, not stalking, when you're an officer."

"I see no difference."

"Shut the fuck up." He pushes me. "Seriously though, are you going to go in, or are you just going to stare all night?"

"Stare."

"Suit yourself, but I am going to go in there and congratulate our girl."

"*Our* girl?"

He cringes. "You're right, that was weird. I meant my girl since we both know she isn't yours anymore."

I clench my jaw at his words as white-hot rage simmers beneath my skin. "Oh, fuck off, will you?"

He laughs, walking to the building. "Bren, wait," I call after him. "Here, take this." I push a wad of cash into his hand. "Buy a shit ton for me."

A smile breaks across his face. "Look at you being the best ex-boyfriend that ever lived."

"Yeah, yeah, just don't tell her it's for me."

He rolls his eyes, walking away. "You are such a dumbass."

Chapter Thirty-One

The night is starting to wind down. Guests slowly slinking out the door after mingling for a few hours, buying a trinket or two as they go.

Looking around, I can already tell we're going to have to restock a majority of the items in the morning before opening our doors for the first official full day of service.

As usual, Jerry is plastered to Bel's side. Every time I've looked at her this entire night, he's been right there. But that isn't unusual. Jerry is beyond loyal to her, and it looks like she has finally woken up to the hot, devoted man beside her.

I'm ecstatic about the turnout tonight. Our friends and family really showed out with their support.

Hell, even people we didn't want to show up, showed. Like Nick the prick.

But it's all good. Even though he riled me up while he was here, it doesn't matter. *He* doesn't matter.

Any real feelings, good or bad, I had toward him vanished the moment Griffin walked into my life.

Everything he put me through can never touch me again.

My mood won't be influenced by him.

No, instead, it's crushed by the fact Griffin didn't show.

Yes, we are on the dumb break, but a small—okay, huge—part of me still hoped he would show up to support me.

I'm giving my family quick hugs before they leave, including my mom, which is a tad awkward, but also, I needed it, just as the bell above the door chimes and Brenden walks in.

My heart stops, and I hold my breath, waiting for Griffin to appear behind him. For his tall frame to walk through the door and smile for me. To tell me how proud he is with just one look.

But that doesn't happen.

Brenden walks over, wrapping me up in a bear hug that not only makes it hard to breathe but also makes it impossible for the tears that were threatening to form.

"Audra." He pulls back to look down at me. "This place is—wow. Just wow."

"I know. It's come a long way from the paint-plastered walls." I practically beam with pride. Gathering my family's attention, I say, "Everyone, this is Brenden, Griffin's brother. Bren, this is my family. They were just heading out."

"I heard you're a detective," Nate says.

Bren nods. "It's true. But I'm no Olivia Benson."

Sutton gasps at the SVU reference. "This must be fate. My favorite lipstick vanished two weeks ago. I've looked everywhere. But I'm thinking maybe this is a job for a professional."

"You need professional help," Cooper mutters as he drags her back to his chest.

Bren rolls his lips. "Missing lipstick really isn't in my jurisdiction. Sorry."

"Well, if you ever want to step out of your comfort zone, call me," she says as Cooper drags her out the door, waving.

My family is quick to follow, leaving me and Bren alone.

He wraps his arm around my neck, pulling me into his side. "Okay, show me what to buy to make me irresistible to all the women I am bound to take home."

I chuckle, leading him off into our section of understated and masculine scents. The man picks up every single one I point out, buying two of each.

He's supporting the shit out of me, and it warms my withering heart.

"He's proud of you," Brenden says as we push our way through the crowded door and out onto the sidewalk. The large black paper bag full of items from my store in his hands. "Even with everything that went down, he is."

I scoff. "Sure, he is." I try to push down the ache in my chest by brushing off his comment.

As if being around his brother—and best friend—wasn't enough to remind me of what I'm missing. Talking about him is an entirely worse situation. It sends me into a tailspin of pain and love that I'm not sure I will ever be able to face.

"I'm serious, Audra. It might seem like he doesn't care. But that couldn't be further from the truth."

"It sure as shit doesn't feel that way."

He reaches for my hand, giving it a squeeze before letting go. "He loves you. Trust me on that."

"I've never doubted that. I just—I wish he was here."

"Give it time. I have high hopes for the two of you," he says, backing away from me down the sidewalk. "Just be patient. Or don't." He winks, turning his back toward me, and I watch as he walks off into the night.

"Be patient," I mumble to myself. For him, I would wait fifty years. "Or..."

Chapter Thirty-Two

For the next hour, Audra walks Bren around the store, her face beaming as she shows him all the different ways she preserves flowers, as well as the specialty candles and everything else lining the shelves.

My chest warms as Brenden buys two of every item she shows him. Her face lights up repeatedly as he makes her feel special.

And I hate him a bit for it.

That should be me. But I'm taking the coward's route, lurking in shadows like the love-crazed ex-boyfriend I truly am.

Little does Audra know, he's my unofficial stand in, and if I can't be there for her, at least he can be. It's more than I can ever repay.

The store doors burst open as the two of them walk outside, and I slink further behind the tree.

The joy falls from her face as Bren says something serious before leaving her alone on the sidewalk. She rubs her hands along her arms as a chilly breeze flows through the spring air. Taking a deep breath, she plasters a smile on her face before heading back inside.

I have to jog to catch up to Bren. He's almost to the bike when I grab his arm to stop him. "What the fuck was that?"

"What was what?" he asks.

"Back there. What did you do?"

He exhales. "I gave her something she desperately needed."

"Yeah, and what the fuck was that?"

He shoves the bag into my arms as he climbs on the back of his black Harley. "When are you going to take your head out of your ass?"

"What the fuck does that mean?" I grit my teeth together.

"Shit or get off the pot."

"...Really, Bren."

"Yeah, really. You wanted to know what happened back there with Audra—hope. I gave her hope." His voice is laced with a level of annoyance I haven't heard from him in a long time. He peers up and down the street. "I'll come by later to get my half of this shit." He revs the engine before peeling out, leaving me there to wonder what the fuck just happened.

I should leave like him, but I can't stand the thought of missing another moment of her big night. So I stay and watch as she ushers the last of the guests out the door and, much to my disappointment, Belinda and Jerry leave too. Leaving Audra to clean up the store by herself. I'm not surprised Belinda left her. It's her thing.

Through the window, I can see my girl shaking her hips, dancing along to whatever song she has blasting through the space as she sweeps and spins around the store.

I wish I were in there with her, dancing along beside her as she picks up trash from the night's festivities. I hate that I can't, that I am the reason we are apart.

She spends thirty more minutes taking out the trash and straightening up the store as much as possible before locking the large wooden doors and leaving.

It's time I get my shit together so that, next time, she has someone else to lean on whenever Bel bails.

I don't want to admit it to Brenden, but he was right. The fucker has been right about a lot lately.

He was right about packing.

He was right about me being a dumbass with Audra.

And he was right about me needing to talk to somebody.

So I took the leap and got into therapy. After texting with Vivian, she recommended me to my new therapist, Ms. Tammy, a sixty-something-year-old woman who I know absolutely nothing about other than she loves knitting cardigans, has been having me bare my soul and emotions to her once a week for the past month.

And it seems to help. We've talked about the past few months and all the changes that have brought me to therapy over and over again in extreme detail. But even with my progress in recognizing my unhealthy coping methods, like avoidance, I'm still stalling.

My next step, according to Ms. Tammy, is to reach out to Belinda...

Easier said than done.

Every time I even think about talking to her, my heart races and my palms get all sweaty, and I'm thankful that I don't eat spaghetti often.

Ms. Tammy says that it's my anxiety revving up in the face of the unknown. But I think it's the fact that this woman has ruined two relationships of mine.

The relationship that I thought I had with my mother, and mine and Audra's.

But until I face Belinda, I'll never be able to move on.

So I take the plunge and call her—well, text her, because I am in no way prepared to have an actual conversation with her. Not unless my shrink psychoanalyzes it.

Griffin

> It's Griffin. Would you be willing to join me in a session with my therapist on Thursday to clear the air?

Belinda

> Yes. When and where?

I guess it didn't really hit me that she would actually show until I walk into the muted-gray room to see her already shaking hands with Ms. Tammy. Both of them are full of smiles—Ms. Tammy's her usual welcoming one, and Belinda's a cautious smile that is full of apprehension.

Good. I can't be the only one dreading this next hour.

"Griffin. Come in. Have a seat." Ms. Tammy gestures to the space next to Belinda on the couch.

I give a tight nod and move to the other side of Belinda, sitting as far away as possible, which isn't that far because the couch is pitifully small. Built more for aesthetics than functionality. Definitely not intended for birth mothers to attend therapy with the child they gave up.

"Now, Belinda, as you must be able to tell, I'm aware of your and Griffin's situation. He asked you here today with the intent of—" She waves her hand at me. "Griffin, this is the part where you take over. I'm not here to speak for either of you. I'm only here to help facilitate the conversation."

My insides feel like they're shaking along with my outsides as I take a deep breath for courage. "I wanted to talk about it all. About you and my birth father. Why did you give me away? Why was it kept a secret? But most of all, I want to know why you thought my mother's funeral was the best place to drop the bio bomb." I thought when we finally had this conversation, my words would be laced with anger and disgust. Instead, they are meek and dejected.

"I—I don't know where to start," Belinda says, her hands fidgeting in her lap.

Ms. Tammy gives her a gentle smile. "How about at the beginning?"

"Okay." She nods, gathering herself for a second. "When I was a teenager, I fell madly in love with a boy. It was the type of love that makes you do stupid things. James and I did everything together. We were each other's first kiss, first love, first... lover. It was going to be forever. But then he—died." She sniffs, turning to look at me. "You look so much like him, it's crazy."

"Is that why you gave me away? Because I reminded you of him?" My chest aches. I grip the arm of the couch with one hand, clasping it so hard my skin blanches.

It's all too much. I understand either way. But it's still like some-one is squeezing my heart tight, waiting for it to pop.

"No, that was a part of it. But not the reason." A tear falls from the corner of her eye. "James had been gone a month when I realized I was pregnant. I was distraught and overjoyed at the same time. The family we had always talked about was coming true, but he wasn't here. And I couldn't imagine doing it without him. I was a reckless kid. So I did what I thought was best for both of us. I left you with them. Your family. And even if I might regret it for selfish reasons, I know it was the right choice."

"Did you ever think about keeping me?" Her answer wouldn't affect me either way. I loved my parents, and I couldn't imagine being raised by anyone else. But curiosity is a bitch.

"Yes. And I thought about changing my mind every day."

The pressure behind my eyes grows stronger. "Okay. If you knew it was the right thing, then why tell me after all this time?"

Her shoulders shake, and she presses her face into her hands.

Ms. Tammy passes the box of tissues to me in a not-so-subtle way of telling me to offer them to Belinda.

I grab the box, fighting the urge to deny her this comfort. "Here." I lift the box in front of her. She opens her eyes and takes the tissues from my hand. I've never seen eyes light up at Kleenex before, but hers do. It's as if the box held the secrets of the universe, instead of something I was volunteered to do by my therapist.

Dabbing her eyes with a tissue, she says, "I'm sorry. I know I have no right to be upset—"

"Your feelings are just as valid as Griffin's, Belinda," Ms. Tammy reassures her. "It's okay to be emotional. This is a heavy topic."

Belinda takes a deep breath, and I wait, wondering what in the hell will come out of her mouth next. Will she try to justify her actions, or will she somehow pull a valid, worthy excuse out of her ass?

I'm on the edge of my seat as she turns to look at me while she speaks.

"What I did that day—it's unforgivable. I know that. I wish with all my heart that I wouldn't have made that choice. Maybe if I had been on my meds, I would've handled things differently. It breaks my heart to know that I hurt you. Not only did you lose your momma, you lost a part of yourself that day because of me."

Ms. Tammy and I share a look, and I know she caught the same thing I did.

"I'm sorry, Belinda, but did you say you were off your medication?" Ms. Tammy asks.

She nods.

"Do you mind sharing what the medication was?"

"Lithium." She hangs her head.

"Ah, I see." Ms. Tammy gives her a soft, reassuring smile.

My confusion must be plain to see, because Ms. Tammy asks Belinda, "Do you mind sharing with Griffin what you take lithium for?"

She raises her head, closing her eyes. "Bipolar II."

"Oh," I say, letting everything I know about bipolar disorder run through my mind. "*Oh.*"

"Yeah, I know it's not a good excuse. Nothing ever will be, but it is the reason. I am back on my meds again and seeing someone regularly to help prevent another backslide in my mental health."

I let everything she's said soak in, taking the time to comprehend it.

"Griffin"—Ms. Tammy interrupts the silence—"how does what Belinda revealed about herself make you feel?"

"I—I don't know what to say."

"You don't have to say anything. Just please know that I'm terribly sorry for the pain I've caused you and, well, continue to cause you."

I run my fingers through my hair, unsure of what to do or say next. Bipolar.

She has a mental health condition that explains everything. Every-fucking-thing.

From her erratic behavior at the funeral to running away and even her regret now. It all makes sense. Even the way Audra always describes her adds up now.

That doesn't mean I forgive her. What she did might never be okay with me.

But I understand her a little better now.

"Thank you for telling me."

"You deserve the truth, every part." She exhales, adding, "I hope that we might be able to have a relationship someday."

My eyes widen, but not out of shock.

No, I figured she was going to ask or bring up wanting it.

Nope, they widen out of pure panic. I don't know what to say or do. My heart races again as I try to answer. "I—I." I flounder as silent tears fall down her face while she waits patiently for my response.

Finally, after what feels like a lifetime, she says, "It's okay, Griffin. I understand."

"Can I get back to you on it?" I don't know what possessed me to say that.

She nods, hope lighting up her tear-stained face.

Ms. Tammy clasps her hands together. "Very good job. While I don't know where your relationship will go from here, I'm sure we can all agree today was emotional and left us all with a lot to think about going forward. And with that, I think we should end this session." She stands, signaling us to do the same. "Griffin, I will see you next week at the same time?"

She phrases it as a question, but I know better. The woman runs a tight ship, and she is telling, not asking, me to be here.

I give her a nod and a wave over my shoulder as I walk behind Belinda, out of the office and into the hallway.

We're both silent as we walk side by side to the elevator, climbing in for the short ride down to the bottom floor. Once we make it outside, the awkwardness that was missing from therapy returns.

I turn away, readying myself to leave this and her behind me, when she stops me, grabbing a hold of my wrist. I stare at where her hand is, and she lets go of me.

"Griffin, I just wanted to thank you again for allowing me to explain the best I could. Maybe we can do this again. Continue to work through the trauma together?"

I give a curt nod, not wanting to talk anymore. Even though I hadn't been the one baring my soul today, I am talked out.

"She's miserable."

I stop dead in my tracks. Pinching my eyes closed, I hope I didn't actually hear that. It was a mistake. She said something else, I'm sure of it.

That is, until she continues on that train of thought.

"I've never seen her so emotional. Every day, she attempts to mask the pain of not having you by throwing herself so deeply into the store. It's getting difficult to stand by and watch her work herself to death over the heartbreak."

With my back still facing her, I say, "Belinda, Audra's and relationship isn't any of your business."

"Oh, I know that. But you two don't have a relationship anymore, so."

My skin heats as rage boils under its surface. I'm not sure what's pissing me off more, that Audra and I aren't together or that she is bringing it up.

"With all due respect, Belinda. Just because we had a little heart-to-heart does not mean you get to start *mom-ing* the situation. Now please, back the hell out of my business."

Her eyes turn down as my words hit her. Guilt prickles in my chest. I hate being this much of an asshole, even if I'm not her biggest fan.

"I'm not trying to *mom* anything. I just wanted you to know that she loves you and is having a hard time with the break."

"Me too." I walk away, sticking my shaking hands in my pockets before she can utter another word to me.

Chapter Thirty-Three

And my mother said I'd fail...

In its first week alone, I sold out two classes where I taught people how to make their choice of three things: paper-weights, coasters, or trinket boxes, all with pressed flowers showcased throughout.

I've even been contacted by a few brides about preserving their bouquets. So basically, I'm on cloud nine.

Well, work-wise. Every other part of my life is still on the fritz.

My mom is still giving me the cold shoulder. And Griffin is still icing me out.

I have my work cut out for me.

My to-do list has one thing.

One line.

To do:

- *Win Griffin back.*

Only one problem. I'm not sure what the fuck to do.

Brenden told me to be patient. That Griffin still cared.

But that's been easier said than done.

He left me because of my Bel. That's a lie; he left me because I couldn't stop meddling.

And I'm not sure there's anything I can do to fix that situation. Giving up Bel isn't an option. And bringing them together is never going to happen.

She's the person I want to talk to about this. To ask for help or advice on how to get the love of my life back. But it doesn't feel right to ask that of her.

Also, I'm pretty sure that would ensure Griffin would never want me again if he found out.

So I'm on my own.

Forced to use my own brain to solve the problem I created.

Isn't that some fucked-up shit?

If only schools actually taught how to handle personal and relationship problems instead of how Columbus sailed the ocean blue in 1492, or that the mitochondria is the powerhouse of the cell. I mean, what the fuck even is a mitochondria, anyway?

My one task looks pathetic sitting there by itself on the cream-colored paper. Scratch that, I am the pathetic one, with only one thing I need to accomplish with no finish line in sight.

It's mocking me.

I rip the paper from my notebook, tempted to throw it away. Crumpling it up in my fists, I let out a wail of frustration. I don't know why I feel so much disappointment in myself from just writing what I want down. But the tightness in my chest tells me everything I need to know.

I'm desperate.

And I will be until I put everything I have into winning his trust and love back. Uncrumpling the paper, I try to smooth it out with my palms.

With a tack from my desk drawer, I pin the paper to the wall in front of me. It's a reminder of what I've lost and what I hope to gain back. And it will continue to mock me until I'm able to check that damn line off.

But if I'm going to pull this off, and by this, I mean winning my man back, I'm going to need a dream team.

So I add another line to my to-do list

- *Assemble the troops*

I send out a quick text.

Audra

> Operation Get My Man Back is a go. Meet me at Brew It at 8 p.m. Be there or I will assume you hate me and hope I die alone. XOXO.

I get to Brew It a quarter before eight before anyone else has arrived. Scoring a booth, I order a round of shots because this task is going to require some liquid courage, mostly from me as I fawn at their feet for help.

Vivian and Sutton are the first to walk through the door. I flag them down by waving a white napkin in the air for them to see.

"Are you surrendering?" Viv asks as she sets her purse on the table and slides in on the opposite side of the booth, Sutton right behind her.

"Maybe," I grumble.

"Audra, babe, you aren't giving up. Hence why the girl gang is here." Sutton glances to the open seat beside me. "Well, all but one. Who was the other number in the group chat?"

I open my mouth, but Viv cuts me off.

"It's not Belinda, is it?" She winces just as the fourth and final member of the team slides in beside me.

Brenden raises his hand in a hello as he immediately grabs one of the shots from the middle of the table and slams it back. I follow his lead, shooting back the one closest to me. It burns as it glides down my throat, and I can't help the shiver that shakes my entire body.

Viv and Sutton still look confused by his presence but shrug and drink their shots.

"Fuck, that burns," Bren says with a shudder. "Okay, what's the plan?"

"He's the number?" Viv asks, an alcohol flush already gracing her pale cheeks.

"Duh," I answer. "How am I supposed to win Griffin back without an inside man?"

Sutton nods like she agrees. While Viv rears back. "An inside man? We're trying to get your man back, not rob a bank."

"She's right," Bren chimes in.

Sutton frowns, while Vivian preens at being right.

"Not you," he says, pointing at her. "Audra."

"Ha, suck it, Fisher." I throw my hands up in victory.

Sutton snickers as Viv's face falls.

"Whatever, how can I help," Viv asks.

"Well, I need something to show him that I understand, respect, and love him," I tell them.

"You need a grand gesture," Sutton says.

"A grand gesture?" Bren asks, his gaze flicking around the table as we all nod our agreement.

"Yeah, she needs a Freddie Prinze Jr. moment," Vivian says.

"I understand nothing," Bren says.

Sutton and Viv go off on a long-winded tangent about their favorite actor and all his rom-coms. Which, if you ask me, aren't that romantic, and honestly pretty problematic. But who am I to burst their '90s heartthrob bubble.

"Okay, I think I understand," Bren says. "She needs something big to declare her love and show him she is serious."

"Yes." Sutton slaps her hand on the table. "He's got it. Now tell us the perfect way for Audra to Freddie Prinze Jr. your brother."

"Yeah," I chime in. "Tell me. Please, please, please." I steeple my hands together and push my bottom lip out. I'm not above begging like a child.

"Fuck if I know. All I can do is veto ideas and maybe feed you intel on his whereabouts."

"I hate to even bring this up, but do we think he wants to be wooed?" Vivian asks, and I wince.

"Well, that was a punch to the gut," I say, tossing back another shot. "She's right, though. Finding out where Griffin's head is at before I make a fool of myself is probably a good idea."

All our eyes land on our inside man as we wait for a confirmation or denial.

Bren rolls his eyes. "He's miserable without Audra. Grand gesture your way back into his life. He needs it."

We spend the next two hours brainstorming before Nate and Cooper show up to pick their ladies up and end up vetoing half of our ideas, claiming them to be stupid or too *Suttony*, whatever that means. I happened to love the idea of following him around, learning his routine, and maybe prepaying and ordering his coffee before he walks in to make his life easier. Unfortunately, Bren agreed with them, calling it *illegal* and *creepy*. So that idea died right there.

Going our separate way, we all agree to keep brainstorming in the group chat. Nate and Cooper pout when I refuse to let them in on it. Debbie Downers are terrible schemers, and they know it.

Lying in my bed, I stare up at my ceiling, thinking until I pass out. Hours later, I wake with a jolt. *I've got it.*

I pull out my phone and go straight to the group chat.

Audra

I've got the perfect idea, but it's probably going to take a week or two to set up.

Sutton

Hell yeah.

Audra

Bren, I'm going to need your assistance when the time comes to get Griffin in place.

Brenden

You can count on me.

Vivian

It's 4 a.m. You guys are lucky I'm already up with a baby, or I'd be pissed.

But also, yay!

He's alone.

I spot him at the far corner of the bar, tucked into the darkest booth. Just where Bren said he would be. His favorite gray beanie lying on the table beside an empty glass. It's warm enough outside now that he doesn't need a hat, but I suspected a while ago that the beanie in particular wasn't really about protecting that beautiful head of his.

No, it's a token of some sort. A security blanket.

It's always with him, even when he's wearing a different hat, just hiding in his jacket pocket or somewhere nearby.

I've always wanted to tease him about it but was too afraid that if I did, he would stop bringing it with him everywhere. Or be self-conscious about it.

So I never did. And now I'm left with only my imagination to fill in the blanks.

Unless this works. Then maybe he'll tell me.

I had everything planned out. What to say and how I will plead my case to him. I will beg if I have to. Fuck, I will probably beg either way.

But now, watching him from the doorway is something else.

His gaze focuses on the notebook in front of him as one hand holds a pen, scribbling across the pages, and the other taps away on the table.

From the way his head is bobbling along to the same rhythm as his fingers against the table, I can tell he's in a creative zone.

A smile tugs at my lips as I continue to watch him create music. It's everything and nothing all at once. The simplest of things. His job and his passion. His love and livelihood. And at the moment, it's him, too.

I missed this. Watching him pull sounds and words from his brain and mix them together until something almost magical happens.

It's been almost two months without him now, and the ache in my bones for him hasn't lessened.

It's worsened.

And being in the same room as him only makes it all the worse.

I'm reminded that he isn't mine anymore anywhere but in my heart. That I no longer have the right to touch and love him the way I long to.

Not wanting to interrupt his process, I move through the small crowd to the bar. I order a shot of whiskey, slamming it back before I can think better of it.

Warmth runs through my veins, and I turn to see him closing his notebook and slinking the beanie back on his head.

It's now or never.

With the shot coursing through my body, I gather every ounce of courage in me and rush over to the booth. Despite the familiarity of the bar, of him, I'm nervous.

So much has changed between us.

But also, nothing has changed.

At least not for me.

I still want him with every ounce of my being. And I can only hope that after hearing what I have to say, he will feel the same. That is, if he will even listen.

He's about to step out when his eyes meet mine. The ridges of his throat bob.

A flash of emotion that could have been sadness or surprise crosses his face, only to disappear before I can interpret it.

He doesn't say anything. He just stares at me as I take a seat across from him. I expect him to protest, to say something. But I also hope he won't. So when I'm met with his complete silence, I'm honestly unsure which is worse, his wrath or this soul-crushing silent treatment.

"I'm sorry," I blurt out, forgetting everything I planned to say before jumping straight into it. "I fucked up. Big time. And it's all I've been able to think about since you ended this, us. Well, that and you. I think about you in every way imaginable. I think about how you're doing. How your brother is. I think about those hands and the music they make.

"I think about how much I miss you touching me and holding me. How I destroyed the best thing that ever happened to me just by not listening to you. By thinking I knew what was best for you. And I hate myself for it."

I lean in closer, wanting to reach across the space between us and grab his hand. To feel his skin on mine again.

But I don't.

Instead, I clasp my hands together in front of me. My voice wavers as I continue to talk. "You might not even want to see me. If so, I'm again so sorry. But I couldn't take another day without telling you how I feel."

Griffin looks at me, his expression a mix of confusion and something else I can't read.

I extract the package from my purse and slide it across the table. "I hope you know how sorry I truly am and that, if you'll let me, I will spend the rest of our lives proving it and my love to you."

The silence stretching between us is agonizing as I wait for him to say something. Anything.

He bows his head, not meeting my eye again. My stomach sinks, and I take that as my sign that it's time to leave.

I slip out of the bar without another look back, hoping that it was enough.

Praying that he will accept both my apology and me back into his life.

Fearing that it wasn't enough.

Chapter Thirty-Four

Griffin

My fingers wrap around the silver paper package.

Audra came to win me back. And she got me a gift.

I'm still in shock from seeing her.

Yeah, I have wanted to see her every day since she last walked out of my place. Since I watched her through her shop windows. Fuck, I've even dreamed of her. She fills my head at all moments.

I miss her more than I can explain.

But actually seeing her here. Having her talk to me for the first time in two months—I wasn't prepared for the overwhelming mix of pain and love to slam into me so hard that I was stunned into silence.

I can't speak.

I don't know what I would've said, anyway.

I might have gotten down on my knees and begged for forgiveness without a second thought. Saying fuck it to my plan.

But something in me knew better.

From the second I spotted her in one of those T-shirt dresses with the fabric I used to love to twist between my fingers as we sat together, I was frozen. No longer capable of moving.

I grab my water, wanting something to quench this thirst to chase after her. To demand answers to what the fuck she was thinking by walking back into my life before I was ready.

I had a plan.

A good one.

One that consisted of me doing the right thing. Continuing with my therapy... even with Belinda, selling my parents' house. Also called *getting my shit together*.

I wanted to have all of that accomplished before I attempted to get her back.

But as usual, Audra goes and blows up my plans.

I pull the present closer to me.

My fingers fumble with the taped creases.

If I do this, it will change everything. For better or worse. Maybe I should take it with me and wait to open it with someone else, like Bren or my therapist.

But I can't wait. The itching in my fingers, in my soul, to know takes over, and I rip up the seam of the wrapping.

Peeling away the shiny paper, my hands tremble as I stare down at what she has given me.

My nose burns and my eyes prickle as moisture wells up, threatening tears.

It's an action figure...

The Eleventh Doctor.

I swallow the lump forming in my throat as I pick it up. She got me an action figure from our favorite show.

She remembers. Not only my favorite Doctor from *Doctor Who*, but it's what my mom would do to apologize.

Audra listened, even when I didn't think she would.

She didn't forget.

She remembered how much my mom's apologies always meant to me and how much it hurt that they were gone. That she was gone.

This is more than a toy. This is a way to keep my tradition with my mother alive. To keep *her* alive.

With this, she's showing me she knows me. She honored my mom. And she loves me.

I pinch the bridge of my nose, fighting the emotions racing through me.

Goddamn it, I love that woman.

I need to find her. To tell her I miss her, us, and everything we could be.

With the action figure in my hand, I leave the bar in a hurry, glancing around the street. It's been over five minutes since Audra walked away, but I hope I can still catch up with her.

The sun is setting as I jog up the street in the direction we've walked together in the past, the glare causing me to squint and shield my eyes with my hand. I'm in such a rush, with half of my vision obscured either by my hand or the sun, that I don't even see her as I pass by.

I'm almost at the end of the block when I hear her calling my name.

"Griffin."

I stop, turning around to find her sitting on a bench. Her skin is splotchy as tears streak down her cheeks.

I jog over and drop to my knees in front of her. "Audra, what's wrong?"

"What's wrong?" Her eyes swim with tears as she takes in my face in front of hers with a halfhearted laugh. "What's wrong? You can't be that oblivious."

I search her face and body for some sign of why she's upset. When I make it back to her face, she looks like she wants to strangle me.

"Seriously, Griff, I give you this big speech about how sorry I am and how much I love you, and you just sit there silent. What's wrong? What's wrong is you, you big jerk." She shoves my shoulder.

I stumble back as her words hit deep in my chest, cracking me even further than her apology did.

"Audra."

"No, Griff, I can't handle your pity. I just can't—"

I wrap my hands around the back of her neck, pulling her into me as I slam my lips against hers. She stiffens for a moment before melting into the kiss, pressing herself as close to me as she can.

My body sighs with relief at having her in my arms again. This is right. Every part of her and me together feels like peace—a cozy fall day with spiked apple cider running through my veins, relaxing every limb and cell inside me.

Audra pulls back, resting her head against my chest. "If this is some sort of pity kiss, I don't mind. Just promise me at least one more before you leave."

"Pity kiss?" I laugh. "Never. That was my love."

She peers up at me, eyes wide with tears spilling over and out of them in wave after wave. "This better not be a joke."

"Not a joke."

"You won't change your mind, will you?"

I swipe away at the tears, even though they continue to fall as I fight my own eyes from doing the same. Her fear and apprehension are like a blow to the gut. "I won't."

"You're sure?"

I nod.

"Because if you aren't, this is going to be emotionally crippling as hell." Her voice is so quiet and meek, it makes me want to fall to my knees all over again.

"Audra. I love you. I want to be with you. I have never not wanted us."

"But—"

"No buts. You have zero fucking idea what it's been like for me without you. I've driven past your apartment so many times, wanting to walk up to your door and beg for forgiveness. Hell, I've practically stalked you. Like your grand opening. I was there—"

"You were?" she asks.

"Of course I was. Even when I couldn't deal with my mother's death and having Belinda in our lives, I still wanted you. That never changed. And never will." I grab her hand, moving to sit beside her on the bench. "It's been miserable. I won't lie. But I think it had to happen, our break."

"What? Why?"

"I needed to fix some things within myself. I wasn't coping with all the life changes. Our relationship would have become a crutch for me. And I never want you to be someone I use. I want you to be the person I love and cherish for who they are, not for how they help me cover up the negative feelings. And taking this time apart to heal from everything, with the help of therapy and Belinda—"

"Wait, did you just say—"

"Yeah." I smile. "I'll explain later. Right now, all you need to understand is that I worked on myself. My coping. My alcohol dependency issues that were rearing their head."

Her forehead crinkles as confusion takes over her face. "You just came out of a bar."

"Where all I had was water."

"Then why were you there?"

I shrug. "I needed the noise."

"Okay, so let me get this straight. You are glad we broke up, even though we were both miserable. Because you realized you needed to work on yourself, and Belinda helped, sort of?"

"Yes."

"And you love me?"

"I love you. Audra, I live for you and you alone."

"I live for you too." She wraps her warm arms around my neck as her fingers trail through my hair, massaging my scalp. "Does this mean you liked my apology?"

"More than anything." I hug her closer, wanting her to feel through my touch how much it means to me.

"So, what now?"

"Short term, what now? Or long term?"

"Both," she chuckles.

"Short term, my beautiful Audra, we go back to one of our places and spend the rest of the evening holding each other. We can even whisper declarations of our love into each other's ears as we screw each other's brains out if you want." Her cheeks flush crimson, and I know she's on board with that plan. "As for the long term, we decide whose place we want to live in until we can get a new one that is ours, because I don't want to spend another night without you."

We race across town back to my house. I kick the door closed, never once taking my lips off hers. Having Audra back in my life, in my arms, was all I wanted. And now that I have her again, I won't waste a moment, even if that means having bruises all over my legs from bumping into anything and everything in our horny journey to my bedroom.

"God, I fucking love you so much," she says between kisses, yanking my beanie off my head and raking her fingers through my hair in a desperate attempt to drag me closer.

"Let's never go on a break again," I say as my hip hits my bedroom doorknob.

She hums her agreement as I trail kisses down her jaw, lapping and sucking a path to her neck, inhaling the floral aroma that clings to her skin. She is intoxicating in the best kind of way. The way I never want to stop drinking her in, feeling her skin against mine. I'm addicted to her, and I hope there is never a cure.

Shivers roll over my stomach as she skims her fingers beneath my shirt, dragging the fabric up and over my head, depositing it onto the floor. She groans, "I've missed your body."

I chuckle. "I've missed yours too."

Audra bats her lashes at me as she leans in to plant open-mouth kiss after kiss across my chest. She flicks her tongue over my nipple, and I suck in a breath. "Shit, Audra, do that again."

A grin pulls at her lips as she locks her gaze on mine and moves to my other nipple, flicking it before nipping at it. My cock jerks, and

I'm not sure how much more teasing I can take without coming in my pants.

Audra must notice my ever-growing erection, because she runs her hand down to where my aching cock is straining through my jeans. "Baby, please put me out of my misery already," I beg.

She nods enthusiastically. "Oh, I can do that," she says as she lowers herself to her knees in front of me and unbuttons then hauls my zipper down. My cock springs free, only to have Audra's hot breath caress the underside.

I grit my teeth in anticipation of feeling her mouth on me. Her tongue darts out, wetting her lips while she continues to keep eye contact with me.

"Tell me what you want me to do?" she asks, her breathing turning heavy as she wraps her fingers around my length, gripping me tightly, the way I like it.

"Spit on it."

Her eyes gleam at my command. Then she does it. Her spit dropping right onto my crown. It's the most erotic sight I've ever beheld. I push strands of her chestnut hair out of her face while she uses the extra moisture to increase the friction as she pumps my cock up and down, before sucking me into her mouth.

The teasing seductress is gone. Left in her place is a cock-sucking goddess who takes me as deep as she can, gagging for a moment but continuing on. Swirling her tongue on the underside of my shaft as her one hand twists and jerks, while the other cups my balls, her fingers tracing the seam in a fucking glorious rhythm. It's sloppy as fuck, and I can't get enough.

"You're so goddamn beautiful choking on my cock."

She hums, and the vibrations send a jolt of pleasure straight to my spine. Fuck, she's good at this. I never want it to stop, but at the same time, I want nothing more than to be inside her pussy, having her strangle my cock as she comes.

I fist her hair, tugging her off me. Saliva drips down her chin, and I almost come at the sight.

God, she's fucking perfect.

"What, you didn't like that?" she asks with a knowing naughty smile.

"Baby, two more minutes and I would have been flooding that pretty mouth of yours."

"And?" She stands and rips her shirt off, revealing tiny scraps of pink fabric that in no way should be classified as a bra, but right now, I'm so fucking happy that they are. I pull her body flush against mine, my hands cupping her tits as I slam my mouth down on hers. She instantly opens for me, just as eager as I am to have my tongue tangle and caress hers. Quickly, I peel the rest of her clothes off, then chuck my shoes and pants next to hers. Bending my knees, I grab the back of her thighs and lift, skating her wet center over my cock as I walk us back to the bed, twisting us so I land on my back with her on top of me.

"And I'd much prefer coming inside this flawless cunt." I snake my hand down through her slit, slipping a finger inside her with ease. Audra moans as I thrust and curl my fingers upward. She lifts to straddle me, rolling her hips when my thumb finds her clit. "You're so wet, baby. Practically dripping, all for me."

"All for you, Griffin," she whimpers, and it has me picking up the pace. "Yes, yes, yes. Right there. Don't stop."

"Never."

She's fucking beautiful on a regular day. But on the brink of release, of pleasure, she is something else. She is exquisite. She is everything I've always dreamed of. Everything I've always wanted.

And she is mine.

I won't let her go this time.

No matter what happens. She's it. The one.

And I vow to her and myself never to forget that.

Audra's breaths come in pants as she rides my hand until she's convulsing in ecstasy. I don't give her any time to recover before I replace my fingers with my cock, filling her in one thrust. Warmth envelops me, and we both groan in unison. My hands find her hips, and I lift her up, only to slide her back down my length. Over and over again, I help her ride me until she becomes frantic with the need to come again.

"Play with those perfect tits for me," I practically beg, and she obliges immediately, caressing, tugging, and plucking as she circles her hips seductively.

Heat coils in my lower spine and my balls tighten. I am so damn close, and we just began.

"More, Griff," she pants. "I need more."

I lift up and flip us so she's under me. Her hair fans out around her face, creating a halo effect as I pound into her from above. I press my fingers on her clit, and her legs tremble and the walls of her pussy pulse. "Keep squeezing like that and I'm going to explode."

A perfect pink flush creeps over her silky skin at my words, spurring me on as I drive into her harder.

Gritting my teeth, I push back my own release until I feel her fall over the edge.

It only takes a few more perfectly timed strums of her clit in sync with my thrusts to get her there. Audra's eyes flutter closed, and she sucks in a breath when her orgasm washes over her. A string of moans that sounds like the most beautiful symphony I've ever heard falling from her lips.

I drive into her two more times before the air is sucked out of my lungs and everything inside me tenses. Warm pleasure sweeps through me as my cock throbs, coating her walls in my cum.

Resting my forehead against hers, I try to catch my breath, panting words of love and admiration.

"I love you," Audra says, kissing my neck.

"I love you." I roll us again, holding her tightly to my chest.

Chapter Thirty-Five

Griffin

"I'm sorry," Belinda whines for the millionth time. *Can she give it a rest already?* She repeats that ridiculous phrase as if it's going to change something.

Every session is the same.

Bel cries and claims she's sorry but doesn't actually say anything else.

Every time I walk out the door after our hour's up, I feel the same about her.

I hate her. And I think I always will.

No amount of "sorry" will bring back the memories she destroyed.

I rub at my temples, trying to ease the headache that bloomed the moment she started blubbering. "Do you ever tire of playing the victim? You chose this."

Tears rain down her cheeks, and I'm surprised she isn't dehydrated yet.

Sorry and tears, the Belinda Peterson special. Her signature move.

Clenching my jaw, I stare at the bookshelves that line Ms. Tammy's office walls. I wonder if I should build Audra a bookshelf like this one to display her creations on. She could put all her old dance trophies on it as well. It could be a shrine to her accomplishments. I already plan on building her a worktable for at the house, but maybe I should pivot my energy to building her a custom shelf first.

"Griffin?" Ms. Tammy says, pulling me back to the present.

"I don't know what you want me to say. You're the one who gave up your baby. You're the one who chose the worst fucking moment to drop the most unwanted secret. This is all your fault. You did this." I stand and start slipping my arm into my jacket. "I can't do this anymore today."

"It's not my fault," she whispers.

I turn toward her. "What did you say?"

"Ah, now Griffin, let's not raise our voices," Ms. Tammy chimes in.

Belinda swallows, shuddering. "Nothing. I didn't say anything."

"No, you said it wasn't your fault."

She's silent as she picks at what's left of her nail polish with her thumb.

Ms. Tammy opens her mouth to say something but is silenced when Bel says, "She made me do it."

I freeze, letting one sleeve dangle down my back.

"Who made you, Belinda?" Ms. Tammy asks in her soothing voice.

I swear if she brings Audra into this, I'm going to fucking lose it. I can't handle finding out that she supported this craziness from the beginning.

She gnaws on her bottom lip as she meets my eyes. Taking a deep breath, she wipes under her nose and replies, "Your mother."

"You're a liar," I spit.

She shakes her head with a watery smile. "I wish I was."

"Oh, really, then please explain how my dead mother forced you to drop a bomb at her funeral."

Belinda looks from me to Ms. Tammy, who looks just as shocked as I am by this turn of events, but she still gestures for Belinda to continue.

"It started as letters. She would write to me once a year to update me on you. Always included a picture or two, along with some fun fact about you at the time."

"You're lying."

"I'm not. It's how I know that when you were seven, you crashed your scooter into a ditch and broke your ankle."

"Lucky guess."

"Or how about when you were thirteen, your favorite show was *General Hospital*, and you made your mom record every episode for you to watch after school?"

I sink onto the couch again. No one knew that, not even Bren. It was Mom's and my secret. She pretended to record the show for herself and then would sit in the living room with me as I watched Monday through Friday so my brother would be none the wiser. And to help with the ruse, she always had me fold laundry while I watched to make it look like I was just being forced to do my chores.

"So, she told you about my childhood. How does that mean she forced you to reveal my parentage at her funeral?"

She takes a deep breath, curling her body toward mine. "When she first found out about her kidney failure, she wrote to me saying she thought it was time. Time for me to introduce myself. For you to learn the truth."

"She was diagnosed years ago."

"I know, I refused. I wasn't fit to be a parent in any capacity. It's why I gave you up. So I refused. She asked me time after time. And my answer was always the same. But when the end was drawing near, her letters became more frequent. More demanding. She would send them weekly. She wouldn't take no for an answer."

"I still don't understand. She's gone. She couldn't force you before, and she definitely couldn't after her death."

"But she could. She knew something, a secret that if anyone found out..."

"You're telling me a secret baby isn't your biggest secret?"

She smiles. "No, you are. You are my greatest secret gift. But what she knew wasn't something good. Wasn't a handsome, successful, smart, kind son." She chips yet another flake of nail polish off, and I'm hit with the urge to grab her hands to still them. "No, she threatened to tell something that I had hoped to take to the grave."

"Are you saying my mother blackmailed you from the grave?"

A small huff of laughter falls from her lips. "I really, really wish I wasn't, but..."

"It's a lie. It's a goddamn lie." I stand again, anger surging through my body, making my chest feel like it's going to explode at any moment. So I let my anger detonate in her face. "My mother was the best woman I've ever known. She was kind. She wasn't conniving or crazy like you—"

"Griffin, no using the c-word in therapy," Ms. Tammy scolds in the same soft tone that gives nothing away but, at the same time, makes me feel like a dick.

"It doesn't matter, anyway. I'm done listening to this bullshit." I storm out of the room, slamming the office door behind me. The noise reverberates into the air, feeding my anger as I step out onto the sidewalk.

The spring air kisses my cheeks as I suck in a breath, trying to hold it for four without success.

I can't do this here.

The edges of my vision blur as I force my legs to carry me to my Tahoe, where I jump in, lock the doors, and recline my seat as far as it will go. Shutting my eyes, I start my box breaths all over again. Breathing in and out. In and out, until my body is no longer trembling with the negative emotions ripping through me.

After spending the rest of the day in my studio, attempting to pour my feelings into my work, I head home. Pulling my keys out of my jacket pocket, I stop at my door, finding a shoe box sitting on the mat. Unease pricks at my spine, but I pick the box up and bring it inside with me. I set it on the table before I pull the lid off, only to find a bundle of letters inside.

The yellowing envelopes vary in size and shape. There has to be at least fifty letters in here. All addressed to Belinda Peterson.

Untying the ribbon that binds them together, I take one last steadying breath, then pluck the letter off the top to find my mother's familiar scroll.

Belinda,

Our boy is growing like a weed. He's only one year old but is already as tall as Brenden was at the age of two. I have a feeling he is going to be expensive to keep in shoes.

I thought you might want to know some fun facts about him.

His first word wasn't Mama, much to my disappointment. It wasn't even Dada. It was Bren. Well, more like Beh, but we all know he is saying his big brother's name. The two of them are inseparable. Griffin is always crawling after Brenden. And Brenden snuggles him on the couch, always giving him hugs and kisses. They are going to grow into the bestest of friends and brothers, I just know it.

Favorite food: bananas. The boy is crazy for them. Every meal, he wants his 'nanas. So every meal, he gets his 'nanas. What can I say? I'm a sucker for my baby boy.

Once again, Belinda, thank you for giving me one of the greatest gifts of my life. I love him more than life itself. Thank you for your selflessness. I promise to love him for you every day.

-Leslie

Belinda,

Our boy is a mess. A mess and a little liar.

I wish I could say I was mad, but I'm not. He is ridiculous. The boy crashed his scooter into a ditch this past weekend and didn't say a word about it. I know what you're thinking. What's the big deal? It's just a scooter. Yeah, normally I would think the same, but there was just one minor problem. He broke his ankle. HIS ANKLE, BELINDA. And he didn't say a word... for days. I felt like the worst mother in the world for not noticing his limp or the swelling in his ankle sooner. But he hid it from me well. And don't get me started on the hospital visit. They looked at me like I had done it to him.

They even questioned him without me there to make sure he wasn't being hurt at home. I think the fear of being taken from me and his father was enough to make sure he doesn't pull this kind of stunt again.

Other than lying about wrecking his scooter, he's so smart. You would be so impressed with him. He is a little musical genius. He listens and tries to recreate every song he hears. It's very impressive. So far, he knows how to play the piano and is learning the guitar. Now if only he could sing... It sounds like a cat in heat whenever he tries to belt out a tune, not that I would tell him that. No, I tell him his voice is like an angel's. That I get shivers every time he sings because he is that good. Not that the hair on my arms stands on end because it sounds like a death rattle.

You would love him. I know it. Thank you. Thank you. Thank you.
-Leslie

Belinda,

This year is probably the most challenging year as a parent. Griffin just turned thirteen. And as you can imagine, he's a mess. I'm a mess. Everything is a mess. I had forgotten just how rough these early teen years were with Brenden, but don't worry. Griffin is giving me quite the reminder and more.

He is moody as hell. I swear the boy would win gold if brooding were an Olympic sport. He's just that good. Brenden says he is "emo," whatever that means.

If it weren't for his extreme pouting, I would laugh at the tiny little mustache growing on his upper lip. I can tell he is very proud of it, so it's been a struggle to ensure that his brother and father don't comment on it. No need to hurt his self-esteem when he's already so vulnerable.

His father says he looks exactly like James at this age. He showed me pictures from that time, and it's uncanny. Some pictures had you in them, and I hope you don't mind if I save them to give to Griffin someday.

But other than this self-made emotional distress, he is still doing well in school and excelling with his music... maybe a little too much. He has once again picked a new instrument to conquer. Unfortunately for us all, it's the drums. And unfortunately for everyone around, he has taken quite a liking to the obnoxious instrument.

As usual, thank you for helping to complete my heart and family with the greatest blessing in the world. I'm forever thankful.

-Leslie

Letter after letter, I'm transported back to those memories of my mom watching me and Bren run around the yard while she sat on the porch stairs writing letters. I never questioned what she was writing, and now I wish I had.

My heart stops when I get to the last ten letters. This is it. The last pieces of my mother. Hands shaking, I set them down and pick up the phone, dialing my girl's number.

It only rings once.

"Hey, baby, how was therapy?" Audra asks, her voice already helping to soothe my aching heart.

"Can you come over? I need you."

With no hesitation, she says, "I'll be there in ten minutes."

Chapter Thirty-Six

Audra

"I've got to go," I yell to Bel as I rush out the door, not even bothering to grab my jacket.

I don't give myself any time to overthink the shakiness that was in his voice. I just move. Griffin needs me. And I refuse to let him down by getting in my head.

I don't bother knocking, not since the two of us had moved all of my things into his house a few weekends ago. His home is my home now.

"Griffin, it's me," I announce as I push the door open. Boxes still clutter the floor along the walls, and I have to maneuver my way through them into the living room to find him.

He's sitting on the floor with his back propped against the couch, paper littering the space around him. Throwing my keys on the coffee table, I rush over to him and slide myself down to sit beside him.

He tips his head in my direction, sad defeat marring his beautiful face. "She wrote letters."

"Who did? Belinda?" I ask, hating myself for even saying her name in front of him. We might have made up, but I still feel like I'm toeing the line with him when it comes to her.

His head shakes as he rakes his fingers through his hair. "My mom, she wrote letters to Belinda every year and even more right before the end."

My gaze sweeps over the paper surrounding us. "These were all from your mom to Bel?"

"Yep, apparently my mom wanted to keep my creator informed about me... How could she go this far to write the woman for thirty years but never feel the need to tell me the truth? Why did Belinda get this consideration but not me?" His voice cracks on the last few words.

Wrapping my hand around his, I console him the best I can. "I don't know, baby. I wish I could tell you. I wish I could stop all this hurting for you."

He squeezes my hand, then scoots close enough to rest his head on my shoulder. "Will you read the last few with me?"

"Anything you need. I'm here for you, always."

Belinda,

I have some unfortunate news to share with you. I'm dying. The end is coming for me a lot sooner than we thought.

You're the first person I've told. The boys still think I have months. But I know. You can feel the shift inside when you are getting closer to those final days.

With this change, I thought I'd warn you that my updates on our boy will be coming to an end. I've thought long and hard about this, and I think it's time you got those updates from the source.

He deserves to know the truth before it's buried with me. You deserve to know the amazing man you created. I deserve to have my soul at peace with zero secrets weighing me down in the afterlife.

Please, Belinda. Come see me. Come see him. We can make this right before it's too late.

-Leslie

There are multiple letters with the same tone. The same anguish and hope. My heart aches for Leslie. Her last dying wish was for Griffin to know the truth, and Bel ignored her.

Belinda,

Please. I'm begging you. Call me. Time is not on our side anymore. We can discuss it all. Your fears and hesitations. We can get through this together. I promise.

-Leslie

Belinda,

I'm done begging. You had your chances to do the right thing. Instead, you chose fear. You chose yourself over Griffin, again. I've tried for years to include you in the only way you would allow. Tried to understand how you could do what you did. How you could stay away. But in the end, I've come to the conclusion you're a selfish coward.

The only right thing you've ever done was give Griffin to us. To ensure that he had a family. One good deed isn't enough anymore. He is about to be left parentless. The only family being his brother. They need more support than each other. And if you won't step up of your own accord to be that person, I will have to take matters into my own hands.

I know what happened that night. I know everything. James told us everything. Your secret can die with me or... I'm not above threats. I might be a dying woman, but I have the means to make sure the past doesn't stay in the past, even from the grave. The choice is yours.

-Leslie

Belinda,

I only have days left. You have till I'm in the ground to tell the truth. If you don't, your secret will find its way out into the world. Into the police's hands.

For the last time. Thank you for giving me one of the two greatest gifts. I wish it didn't have to end like this.

-Leslie

"Holy shit, Griff," I whisper, covering my mouth with my free hand.

"She really did it. She's the reason Belinda came forward that day."

"Are you okay?"

"No. And this doesn't change any of the anger I have toward Belinda for dropping that bomb at Mom's funeral. But it makes sense. I didn't believe her. When she said my mom blackmailed her. Why would I? My mom didn't have a cruel bone in her body. She was like you in that regard."

"It's definitely a crazy turn of events."

His chest shakes as a loud laugh bursts from his lips. "My mom blackmailed her."

"She seems like a pretty cool woman."

"She was." He smirks.

"Is it wrong of me to wonder what was so bad Bel would rather come out of the parent closet at a funeral than risk it?"

"No, that's exactly where my head is at too. Honestly, I should be mad at my mom for pretty much causing the most traumatic moment of my life, but I'm not. After reading her letters, it all makes sense."

"How did you even get all these?" I gesture to the letters.

"Belinda left them on my doorstep after I called her a liar." He flinches a little at the word *liar*, looking at me with a sorry expression.

"Since she's being so open and honest, do you think she would tell you what caused her to come forward as your biological mom?"

"I don't know. She went to extreme lengths to keep that secret. It would be weird if she just blurted it out now."

"Do you think your mom was really going to tell whatever Bel didn't want anyone to know? I mean, how could she?"

He rubs his jaw, a mask of confusion flitting over his face. "Yesterday, I would have said no, but now..."

"What do you want to do?"

"I have no fucking idea. Is forgetting an option?"

My nose crinkles. "Unfortunately, unless you want me to smack you over the head with something heavy, resulting in a case of amnesia that could make you not only forget these letters but also, *gasp*, me..."

A hand flies to his chest. "Forget you? More like forget that plan. Let's just get our hands on a Tardis and wiz back in time and ensure that these letters never make it to me."

"Solid plan." I nod a few times before hissing through my teeth. "Shoot, I think there might be a slight flaw in your Tardis time-traveling plan."

"And that is?" He raises a brow.

"It's not real."

"Well, shit. Now what do we do?"

"You tell me?"

Griffin throws his hands up in mock surrender. "Nope, my judgment can't be trusted. Don't you remember how I made the two of us miserable for months because of said judgment?"

I know he's only kidding, sort of. But it has my chest aching as I remember the pain from my days without him.

"Griff, that wasn't all on you. A lot of it was my fault, and we both know it."

"Doesn't matter. I'm leaving you in charge of this one."

"Well, that settles it." I clap my hands and jump to my feet, reaching for his hands.

"Settles what?" he asks with a lopsided smile as he allows me to pull him to his feet until he is towering over me.

I lift onto my tiptoes and press a quick kiss to his lips before tugging him toward the door. "We are going to confront the source."

He stops mid-step, causing my feet to falter, and pulls me back into him. "You want to talk to Belinda about the specifics of my mom's blackmail?"

"Duh, keep up, Griffy. It's not that complicated," I tease, as I drag him out the door with me.

"Audra, I don't think that's a good idea. She clearly wants this secret to stay buried."

And just like that, a light bulb blinks on in my head. "We need a plan. And I know just the schemer to help us."

An hour later, we're at my brother's house, seven of us squeezed in at his tiny kitchen table with all the letters Bel gave Griff spread out before us.

"This is absolutely wild," Bren mutters. His hand still covering his mouth since his jaw dropped thirty minutes ago.

"Do you really think your mom would out whatever this dark secret is?" Cooper asks as he passes out beers to the guys at the table, Sutton behind him, her arms loaded with three margaritas.

"If she did, she was beyond badass," Viv says to Bren and Griff while taking the strawberry margarita Sutton hands her.

Griffin waves his off and I, being the doting, perfect girlfriend I am, pass on my drink as well so he isn't the only one staying sober. With a gleam in her eye, Sutton grabs our booze.

"Baby," Cooper scolds her.

"What? It helps to get my scheming juices flowing."

Vivian gags, spitting some of her margarita back into the cup. "Please don't say juices."

Sutton snickers. "Cooper loves when I talk about juices."

"Not the time or place." He winks at her.

"Okay, now that Sutton has made everyone in the room uncomfortable, what's the plan?" Nate asks, sitting down beside Viv. He was on baby duty until a few moments ago when he laid my favorite family member down for bed.

"That's why we're here," I say. "We need help on how to get Bel to confess to whatever it is she's carrying so deep that she has been acting—"

"Crazier than ever?" Bren supplies.

"Yes." I wince. She might be my best friend, but these people around me are family. And apparently, my best friend has been keeping even more from me.

"I say we ply the woman with enough alcohol to sanitize a public bus and question her while her guard is down," Sutton says, wagging her eyebrows.

"Do we think trickery is the best plan?" Griff asks, his uncertainty shining through.

"No doubt in my mind," Sutton replies.

Vivian drums her fingers on the table. "Well, we all know she isn't going to just spill the beans if we ask her. Not after she went through the trauma of telling Griffin about herself to prevent whatever it is from coming out."

She's right. Bel went through hell to keep this secret. It almost makes me wonder if we should let sleeping dogs lie. But then I think about the tortured look on Griffin's face when she told him she was his bio mom at his mother's funeral, and my sympathy wanes. She would rather hurt him like that than let whatever it is be known...

At the very least, Griffin deserves to know what was so important that she would rather hurt him after thirty years than face it.

"Brenden, couldn't you just whip out the ole lie detector and end this charade, pronto?" Sutton asks with a raised brow.

All eyes find Brenden as he shakes his head. "No can do, scheme-a-roos. Police resources cannot be involved."

"Lame," Nate and I say at the same time, just like we would as children. Sometimes I forget how much the two of us think alike. Maybe it's because he somehow seems to have his shit together while I'm still floundering most days.

Bren raises his hands in a placating gesture. "That doesn't mean I can't do some old-fashioned detective work. It's clear whatever she's hiding is from over thirty years ago, based on what we know from the letters."

We all look at him with matching confused expressions.

He sighs, rubbing his forehead as if he's frustrated that he even has to explain it to us. "In the letters, Mom mentions James spilling the beans. So, what does that tell us?" he asks us in a tone that I can only assume is meant for five-year-olds.

When none of us answer, he rolls his eyes but says, "It means whatever she wants to stay hidden happened before James died. So we are most likely looking at the years 1990–1993. My guess is it is probably somewhere in '91 or early '92, before Bel was pregnant."

"Well, that settles it." Sutton takes a long drink of her margarita. "Brenden is going to dig into the past while the rest of us come up with a plan to sweat the truth out of her in the meantime."

Frown lines form on Vivian's forehead. "How does one sweat the truth out of someone when they themselves don't know what they are looking for?"

Chapter Thirty-Seven

Griffin

"Any progress this week?" I ask as Audra finishes straightening the shelves while I sweep the floors of Forever Floral. The schemes we concocted with our friends have so far been unsuccessful. I know I've tried to get her to be honest in therapy, but she shuts down the moment I ask for details. Audra tried a different approach. With the help of Vivian and Sutton, she orchestrated a girls' night, where they plied an unsuspecting Belinda with booze while playing games like never have I ever. But that was a bust. And Bren's been looking into the past with no real leads.

Even though we spend hours together each night and morning, the two of us have struck a "no scheming or Belinda talk" rule at home.

I know it's hard for Audra, seeing as, until I came into her life, she considered Belinda to be her person. But the more that's come out, the more she's realized how much she doesn't actually know about her supposed best friend.

I can tell she's having mixed feelings, and I don't want to taint her friendship or sway her in either direction.

Whenever she's ready to talk, I'll be there for her. I won't let anyone, even Belinda, come between us again.

"None," she grumbles, pushing a floral nameplate half an inch over. "It's like the woman is a steel trap, which is insane because she once told me all about the time she bled through her pants while sitting on a guy's lap, only to then pee his bed later that night."

"What kind of person shares those kinds of mortifying stories?"

"Bel. That's who. So, what on earth could be so bad that she hasn't even let it slip a tiny bit?"

"That makes her seem even more suspicious at this point."

"Right! This is driving me to the brink of insanity, Griff. Insanity," she yells, spinning to face me.

"I can tell."

She rolls her eyes. "Pshh. As if you had any idea. I am the epitome of calm and collected on the outside."

"Babe, you literally throw your phone while yelling 'tell me your damn secret' anytime she texts you."

She huffs a laugh, moving around me to the worktable in the back, where she has multiple bouquets drying and prepping for preservation. "That proves nothing."

"You've also yelled 'cracking this secret is driving me mad' in the shower," I say, following her like the lovesick puppy I am.

"Damn," she mutters under her breath. "I'm far too transparent."

I wrap my arms around her waist and tug her until she is flush with my chest. "Baby, you are basically clear at this point."

She glances over her shoulder. "Does that mean I've broken our 'no Belinda talk in the house' rule?"

"Not intentionally." I kiss her neck. She shivers and spins in my arms.

I lean down, ready to make her forget all about cleaning by using my lips to distract her, just as the bell above the door chimes. The door was locked, I made sure of it, which means it can only be one person.

I groan at the interruption and bury my head in Audra's neck as she lifts on her tiptoes to say hi to Belinda.

"Good, you're both here," she says, which has my head popping up from where I was hiding in Audra's sweet-smelling skin.

"And why is that a good thing?" I ask, not bothering to hide my dislike for her and her interruption. Audra smacks my shoulder as she mouths, *Be nice,* before moving out of my embrace.

Belinda didn't even flinch at my tone, but Jerry did. She's probably used to it by now after weeks of our dysfunctional therapy. They both look uncomfortable, though.

"Can we sit?" She gestures to the deep-purple couch and two armchairs in the corner of the store.

Audra and I share an apprehensive look, but I nod and move over to one of the chairs while Jerry and Belinda take a seat on the couch across from me. Instead of sitting in the chair beside me, Audra perches herself on the arm of mine.

We all sit there in awkward silence until Jerry nudges Belinda with his foot and nods in our direction.

She clears her throat. "This might come as a shock to you both, but I've been keeping more secrets."

I turn to Audra. "Baby, she thinks we're idiots."

Audra gives Belinda a tight-lipped smile. "It appears so."

Jerry shifts in his seat. "Now, there's no reason to be rude, you two."

"And there is no reason to treat us like idiots," Audra snaps back.

"You two have to promise that anything I say stays between us. That no one else ever finds out the truth," Belinda demands, her eyes shifting like a wild woman between us.

This is ridiculous. If she harmed another human being, I would report it. My moral compass wouldn't allow for anything else.

"Yeah, yeah, just get on with it." I wave her on.

"The night James died. Not everything happened as I told the police."

Oh shit. A million different possibilities flash through my brain.

Was she the one driving?

Did they hit someone?

Is this an *I Know What You Did Last Summer* moment?

My mind races as I wait for her to explain further. Audra, sensing my unease, places her hand in mine.

"Bel, what really happened then?"

She swallows, looking at Jerry for confirmation.

Audra tracks the look, a hint of hurt flashing across her face that she quickly tries to mask with the interest of hearing more. I squeeze her hand, giving her my support as she gives me hers.

"As you might already know, James and I were a rebellious pair. Constantly pushing boundaries and getting in trouble. Shocker, I know." She laughs, trying to lighten the mood. Only Jerry gives her a reassuring smile.

Audra, like me, remains the picture of impatience.

"Tough crowd," she mutters to Jerry.

"Please just continue," I say, not hiding my irritation.

She folds her hands back into her lap. "So, being the troublemaker that he was, James's parents got fed up and told him he had to enlist, or he was kicked out."

Audra curses beside me. "That's harsh."

I can't help but agree. I knew my grandparents were strict, but putting your child on the streets seems extreme.

"It was, but James did it anyway, and he was miserable about it. He was terrified of what would happen to him. The night before he was set to leave for basic training, he wanted to have one last hurrah. We met up with some people we knew, and some we didn't, to party."

I cross my arms. "Let me guess, everyone was less than sober on the ride home."

"Bingo." Belinda winces. "James and I were so far gone that a guy named Henry, who we had met that night, who was just passing through, offered to drive us home in James's car as long as we dropped him off at the bus station in the morning because he was off to Mexico to start a new life. We took him up on the offer and passed out in the back seat. I don't know what exactly happened, or if Henry wasn't as sober as he said, but the next thing I knew, we were flying through the air. I had never been so scared in my life. When we finally landed, there was smoke everywhere, and it was clear that Henry hadn't made it. He was halfway through the windshield and his eyes were open and unblinking. I think I threw up the moment I saw him."

Belinda trembles as she continues to relay what really happened that night. "We panicked. We screwed up again. No one was going to believe that we were trying to do the right thing. They would only see two teenage screw-ups drunk with a wrecked car and a dead stranger. So, amid our freak-out, we did something that has haunted me every single day. We chose to pretend Henry never existed."

"Excuse me? Do not tell me you buried that poor man's body and acted like it never happened." I grit my teeth, waiting for her to fucking verify my claim.

Tears cascade down her cheeks as Jerry takes her shaking hands in his. Her voice is wobbly as she says, "No, we didn't bury him. What we did was so much worse... We pretended he was James."

"What?" Audra gasps. "How?"

My stomach plummets.

"I can't remember whose idea it was exactly, but with Henry dead and the car already on fire, we took advantage of the fact that he was the same height and build as James. We crafted a plan within minutes. I ran for help, claiming that James and I had gotten into a car wreck. He wouldn't wake up and the car was on fire. Poor Henry was unrecognizable."

"They didn't check dental records?" I ask in pure and utter shock at the acts of these... these *people* who are my biological parents.

"Why would they? They had an eyewitness to the crash. There was no reason anyone would think he was anyone other than James."

Audra raises her hand. "If James didn't die that night, what happened to him?"

Again, Jerry and Belinda share a silent conversation before Jerry nods and Belinda carries on spilling more secrets than I ever thought possible.

"James ran, catching the Greyhound bus Henry had planned on taking and not stopping until he reached Mexico."

"He... he's alive?" I ask.

"He is," Jerry says with an expression I know all too well. It's the same one my father would wear when he was about to tell Bren and me something we weren't going to like.

"No." I shake my head. I must be confused. There is no fucking way. My body sways as the implication, no, the *reality* sets in. *They're insane.*

I look into Jerry's eyes, my fucking eyes. The same eyes I share with my brother. My mouth dries as if I have been licking sandpaper.

Jerry nods solemnly. "Once I got to Mexico, I started a new life. Changed my name. Hell, I even changed my face. One nose job and chin implant later, and the James Henderson everyone knew was gone."

Audra pales beside me, clasping a hand over her mouth.

"I waited months before contacting Bel once I felt it was safe, and that's when I found out about you." He smiles sadly. "We were desperate to be together, and a baby would make Bel moving to Mexico impossible. So I called the only other person I could trust, my big brother. I told him everything. He was so silent at one point, I thought he had hung up on me. But I convinced him to take our baby. To keep him safe because we weren't fit to. Then I called Bel and talked her into contacting my brother and his wife."

Belinda chimes in, "I had no idea your parents knew about James until your mother told me in that letter that he told them everything. I thought... Well, I thought it had all just worked out perfectly for us. You were going to be raised by your family that loved you, and we would get to be together."

"I'm confused," Audra says. "You two only began seeing each other a year or so ago, and it's been on and off."

"It turns out love is difficult when one of you isn't the same person anymore, let alone both of you. After I had you, I went straight to Mexico. We tried for a while. But it wasn't right. Maybe it was the fact that I was a foreigner who spoke no Spanish and felt extremely isolated because of it, or maybe it was because I was still dealing with the trauma of not only faking James's death but giving you up. But it just became too much, and I left after six months."

"We continued to have this push and pull that would resurface every few years, bringing us back together. But we always got hung up on the fact that Bel was the one who always had to leave everything, not me. I had a life in Mexico, and it was good, so I was selfish. I had a fake identity and documents where I could come to the US anytime, but I chose not to. I chose to be a coward and hide."

"What changed?" Audra asks.

"Bel stopped calling. Stopped checking in. The love of my life was letting me go. And I couldn't handle that. We might be on and off, but we've always been friends. After two months of radio silence, I packed up my shit and moved back. It was surreal. Not a soul recognized me. It was freeing. All my fears had been for nothing. Once I got settled, I began trying to win back the woman who is my world."

"This entire story might be romantic if it weren't for the fact that you guys used a dead man's burned body to fake your death. What about his family?"

"Bel found out that Henry's only living relative was his estranged father. We did what we could by sending postcards every few years from Henry to his dad until he passed fifteen years ago."

"Wow, postcards. You guys sure are saints."

These are the people I share DNA with. Lying criminals.

Thank fucking God they left me with my parents, or imagine who I might have been.

"We know we aren't perfect or anything close, but we were scared teenagers who did what we thought was best."

"We are so, so, so sorry for what happened not only that night but for not being able to be parents to you," Belinda sobs, her eyes already rimmed with redness.

"Did my mom or dad know you came back?" I ask, wondering how far the secret flows in my family.

James/Jerry shakes his head. "No, they never knew. Sometimes, though, I would pass them at the gas station or be behind them at the grocery store, but they never recognized me."

"You never thought to just tell them?" Audra voices my next question.

He shakes his head. "When I told my brother the truth, he wasn't supportive. In fact, he was livid. I had never felt that level of shame and disappointment in myself as he instilled in me that day. He agreed to be your parent because he knew neither of us were cut out for it. That you deserved more and to be with family. It breaks my heart to know that I was so close to him and never reached out before his death. That I'll never talk to my brother again, all because of my dumb pride."

"This is a lot to process," I tell them both, and it's the truth. Finding out that my parents weren't my parents was one thing, but to find out my biological parents faked my father's death so he could avoid the military is another.

I focus my sights on a clear floral vase. Homing in on it, I wonder how Audra created it. The flowers aren't scrunched; they appear perfectly pressed. She would've had to create some kind of mold, right? Then slowly add her resin and flowers in. Damn, my girl is a mastermind.

"Griffin, did you hear me?" Audra squats in front of me.

"Huh?" It takes me a moment to reel myself in, but I focus back in on her.

"They're gone. They said they'll wait for you to reach out."

"Good." And it is, because I'm not sure when or if I'll ever be ready to face them again.

"Are you okay?" she asks, sitting in my lap. My arms instinctively wrap around her waist.

"No, it turns out I come from crazy." I had thought maybe I just had to deal with Bel's mental health issues. Which was fine. The more I learned, the more I understood. Not that it made her actions okay, but it made them make sense. But now, hearing that James, or should I say Jerry, faked his own death, I think they are both certifiable. Which now has me questioning my own mental health and sanity. Fingers crossed it's not hereditary.

She laughs, smooshing my face into her chest. "Does this help?"

"Your boobs?"

"Mm-hmm."

"Yeah, actually it does." I relax against her plush chest pillows, taking a deep breath.

"Good," she says, as she strokes my hair. "You can stay here as long as you need."

We sit like that for minutes, my head on her bountiful bosom, while we talk about the shit show that was everything we just learned.

"Audra?"

"Yeah?"

"This is making me a little horny, which is confusing." My dick apparently didn't get the memo that her boobs are for comfort right now, not for fondling.

She snickers, and the jiggle of her breasts doesn't help a thing. In fact, it gives me a raging hard-on.

"I don't think I can keep this from my brother."

"That makes sense. You two don't strike me as the type to keep big secrets, let alone life-changing ones."

"Babe, did you forget what my brother does for a living?" I ask, pulling away from her glorious chest to look into her eyes.

"He is the law."

"I'm pretty sure that makes him a mandated reporter of any crime-like activity."

Her nose crinkles. "I just thought maybe he would throw caution to the wind."

"Bren would never. The man loves his job."

"But one could argue he loves you more, and if you asked him not to say anything, I bet he wouldn't."

"That would eat at his law-abiding soul. I couldn't."

"Couldn't you?" She raises an eyebrow.

"Nope. Sorry, sweet breasts, I wouldn't do that to him," I tell her, my mind made up about that as I lie my head back on her ample bust.

"Did you just call me sweet breasts?"

"Would you prefer tasty tits?"

She mulls it over for a minute. "Actually, yes."

"Tasty tits, it is."

Chapter Thirty-Eight

Audra

Vivian

Blasphemy! I once had a palm reading done that was so accurate, I peed my pants in excitement.

Sutton

Viv, babe, it wasn't that kind of excitement that had your panties wet.

Nate

Ay-oh.

Vivian

Nathaniel, I suggest retracting that reaction right now if you ever want any type of wetness from me.

Audra

Ew, you're all pervs.

Cooper

I didn't do anything. Blame the horn dogs you call family.

Sutton

Awe, am I officially a member of the Fisher clan?

Nate

No.

Audra

I can make you one. All we need is a minister.

Griffin

Or a judge.

Audra

What about a captain?

Griffin

Bren, how far away are you from becoming a police captain? A day or so?

Brenden

Try ten to twenty years.

Vivian

Damn it! It would have been perfect.

Cooper

Can we all stop trying to marry Sutton and Audra?

Sutton

NEVER!

Nate

I know a great florist who can hook you ladies up with a discount.

Cooper

Come on, Griff, you have to be on my side. Right?

Griffin-

Shrug Who am I to tell a woman what she can and cannot do?

Vivian

Feminist king alert.

Sutton

Stop your worrying, our marriage will be in name only… after we consummate it, of course.

Cooper

Oh really?

Sutton

Cooper

Okay.

Sutton

What do you mean, okay?

Cooper

I mean okay.

Vivian

Uh-oh.

Audra

Should we call off the wedding?

"What if we say they were both concussed, and that's why they acted irrationally," I toss out while chucking my shirt on the bathroom floor. Steam fills the air as I tug aside the shower curtain and join Griff under the cascade of hot water.

It's been two days since we learned the truth and lies that Bel and Jerry/James have been carrying around for years.

Griff and I were no closer to figuring out what to do about the secret they dropped.

We had given up on the "no Bel talk in the house" rule.

Every time one of us came around to the idea of telling Bren and the police, the other would argue against it, even though Griff knew in his heart that he couldn't keep something of this magnitude from his brother, but he still tried to come up with alternatives to the truth.

Our outlandish ideas ranged from Jerry/James witnessing a mob-related crime to him secretly being part of the CIA, and faking his death was all part of a government scheme that Bel had to corroborate or her life was in danger.

Griff tilts his head to the side while massaging shampoo into his glorious locks of hair. "That won't work because currently, they are technically of sound mind and have still reported their crime."

I reach around him for the shampoo, brushing the peaks of my breasts against his arm. I squirt a quarter amount into my palm before replacing the bottle on the built-in ledge.

"Audra," Griff groans. "This was just supposed to be a joint idea shower, nothing more than that."

I smirk to myself. He is too easy to trick. "I'm not sure I understand what you mean."

I told him that my best brainstorming happens in the shower, and the man fell straight into my horny trap by admitting he, too, works out issues under the spray of water. So naturally, I then said two heads were better than one, and we should try to work out our little Bel problem together... in the shower.

And that, folks, is how you get a man naked without letting him know you want to ogle his impressive junk.

I mean, really, can he even blame me? No, he should honestly blame himself.

I didn't tell him to look this good soaking wet.

Nope, he did that all on his own. He even went so far as to drench my nether regions, and not just with water.

So really, I'm the innocent party here.

He glances down at his half-erect dick that looks like it's getting ready to strike at me.

God, I hope it does.

"You're doing this on purpose."

"Whoa"—I throw my sudsy hands up—"don't go blaming me for your penis's reaction. I said I wanted to connect on a mental level, not a physical one."

"Oh, and I'm supposed to believe that those sharp-as-knives nipples weren't meant to arouse me?"

"Ignore the nips. They have a mind of their own when it comes to temperature changes," I tell him as I press my body against his, rubbing my pointy nips on him once again as I slide behind him to wash my hair out.

"Audra," he warns.

Ignoring him, I say, "What if we claim aliens abducted them and didn't think anyone would believe them, and that's why they kept hush-hush about it all these years?"

"Ah yes, a classic alien-abduction story. Those are always well received."

"Hey, anything is possible, even a little extraterrestrial visit."

He exhales as if he's annoyed with me, but his gaze tells another story as it roams over my body to where my hands are massaging soap into my skin while I let my conditioner set in my hair.

Licking my lips, I glance down to see his cock bobbing, and I know my plan is working perfectly.

Should I actually be trying to find a solution where my best friend doesn't potentially get in trouble with the law for something she lied about thirty years ago? Well, yes. But I'm strung so tight with stress right now that I can't think, and the only person who can help is my sexy-as-hell boyfriend who just so happens to have a fat cock that he loves to share with me.

"Fuck, you look so sexy with water cascading over those luscious tits like that," he groans.

"What, like this?" I ask, pushing my breasts together, putting on a little show for him.

"Fuck," he says, his voice full of need as he strokes his cock.

I look up at him through my wet lashes. "Do you want to fuck them?"

"God, yes." He steps forward, pulling my face to his for a searing kiss that has my pussy pulsing before he pushes me onto my knees.

He pours some body wash into my cleavage as I continue to hold my boobs snuggly against each other.

Bending his knees, Griffin slides his cock between my tits and thrusts.

It's so fucking hot. *He's* so fucking hot as he uses my body to get himself off. My core throbs while I watch his face flush with pleasure.

I love this, making him wild with lust. All I want to do is push him even closer to the finish line.

He fucks himself with my tits, over and over. And just when he gets used to the rhythm, I tuck my chin and open my mouth, letting the tip of his cock slip into my mouth.

"Fucking hell, Audra."

I suck on his tip for a second in response.

"I'm going to fucking blow, baby," he warns me. "Where do you want it?"

"Anywhere you want."

"Anywhere?" he pants.

I nod as I look up into his eyes, letting him know I'm serious.

"Fuck," he whimpers, pulling back to stoke his cock. "Close your eyes, baby."

And I do, just before he comes all over my face.

Wiping my eyes, I bring my fingers to my mouth, moaning as I lick his jizz off.

He throws his head back, biting down on his bottom lip as he guides me to my feet. He dips my head under the water, helping to clean my face and hair.

Once my eyes are clear, I open them to see Griffin beaming down at me.

"What?" I ask, my grin now matching his.

"You let me come on your face."

"I'm aware," I tell him. "Did that orgasm fry your brain?"

"Maybe," he says, pulling me in for a kiss. He wastes no time delving his tongue into my mouth, causing the throb between my legs to grow into an ache that only he can fix.

I grab his hand from where it's tangled in my hair and lower it to my pussy, pressing his fingers between my folds to my needy, sensitive clit.

"You want me to finger fuck you?" he asks against my lips, pressing one finger inside me while his thumb rubs tight circles on my clit.

My knees buckle as a wave of pleasure flows through me, and if it weren't for Griffin's arm wrapped around my waist, I would have fallen straight to the floor.

"Fuck, baby, did me titty-fucking you drive this pussy crazy?" he asks as he adds a second finger inside me, pumping them at a deliciously fast pace that has heat coiling tighter and tighter in my lower belly. The man knows my body better than I do. Always giving me exactly what I need, when I need it.

"Keep going," I demand as he sucks the skin around my neck, helping to pull my body to the brink. I'm so close as Griffin pulls his fingers out of my pussy and slaps my clit.

I erupt. My release shoots through my veins, heating every inch of my skin as bliss rolls out of me. I throw my head back, moaning his name as he slips his finger back inside my spasming pussy. He continues to fuck me through wave after wave until my legs are shaking so much, I can no longer stand.

Still holding me, Griffin sits me on the edge of the bench at the back of the shower and spreads my legs wide open, exposing my sensitive pussy to the stream of water.

"What are you doing?" I ask as he grabs the showerhead and points it directly at my clit. I yelp at the sensation and instinctively snap my legs closed, but he stops me.

"Ah, ah, ah," he tsks. "I'm not done with this pussy yet."

He lowers his head, and I think he is going to move the nozzle away from my clit and give me his delicious mouth. But he doesn't do that.

Nope. Instead, he keeps it right on my clit while he brings his tongue to my entrance and fucks me with it.

He thrusts in and out, plunging and flicking me as he sprays my clit until I'm screaming his name repeatedly, tears streaming down my face as my body goes boneless. Stars fill the shower as my vision flashes in and out. But Griffin doesn't stop. He drinks the water that slides down from my clit as he eats me so thoroughly that I think I might never recover.

Satisfied with himself, he finally moves the water off me and licks me from my entrance to my clit, causing me to cry out at the sensitivity before he pulls back and licks his lips clean. "Have I ever told you how much I fucking love devouring this pussy?"

I huff out a sleepy laugh. "I don't think you ever have to say it. You prove it when you feast on it like a starved man."

Proud of himself for eating me into a coma, he turns off the water and wraps us both in towels before leading me into our bedroom to hopefully sleep for days.

I flop down on the mattress, not caring about clothes, just as the doorbell rings. "Go away," I groan.

"I'll get it," Griff says with a chuckle, pulling on a pair of sweats over his still-wet skin.

I quickly dry off my body and throw on one of Griffin's shirts before finding him in the kitchen with a manilla envelope in his hands.

"What's that?" I ask, stepping up beside him.

"I don't know. It's addressed to you." He hands it to me.

I twist the envelope over in my hands, searching for a sender with no luck. The only thing written on it is my name. Not even our address.

"This is weird," I tell him as I go to open it.

Griffin smacks my hand, knocking the envelope to the ground.

"What the hell?" I yell, shocked that my sweet, loving boyfriend just did that.

"What if it's anthrax?" His eyes grow wide with worry.

"Anthrax?" I scoff, bending to pick up the envelope, which is definitely not filled with a dangerous substance. "And you thought alien abduction was a crazy idea..."

"How about I open it just in case," he offers, as if that will stop the potential chemical threat from reaching me.

I toss it at him. "Have at it, my knight in shining sweatpants."

Griff tears open the top, slowly peeking inside, only to lose a breath of relief. "It's just a piece of paper," he tells me as he hands it over.

"Oh, is it now?" I say in a mocking tone that has the corner of his lips pulling up. I glance down at the paper, and my heart stops.

What the fuck?

What the *actual* fuck?

I read the page over and over again, still not understanding.

The shock of what I'm reading must be evident on my face because Griff asks, "What's wrong?"

"She signed it all over. Everything. It's all mine."

"Who signed what?"

"Bel, she signed over her share of the business to me." Tears fill my eyes, and I can't stop them as they flow down my cheeks. "Why? Why would she do this? I don't understand."

Griff shakes his head before wrapping his arms around me. "I—I don't know."

Both our phones go off from across the room.

We move to the couch, grabbing them to find we have a new group text with Bel.

Bel

> I'm sorry to do this to you both after causing so much pain. But Jerry and I have decided to leave now that our secret is out. We know we asked too much of you by asking you to carry the burden of keeping our secret. If you feel the need to share our story, your story, please do so with our blessing. Know that we love you both very much. And think this, us leaving, is best for you.

> I hope you one day find it in your hearts to forgive me. I know I made wrong decision after wrong decision, but it was all in the name of love, something I know you both can understand.

> I will reach out once we are settled.

I immediately call her, only to get her voicemail. I call her repeatedly until finally I get a different result.

"We're sorry, but the number you have dialed is not a working number."

My heart drops. "She's gone. Just like that," I whisper to Griffin, who is still staring down at his phone.

"She transferred her ownership to me, then left. How could she do this?" I ask, my voice shaking with sadness and rage. She left me. My supposed best friend just left me.

Griffin's mouth opens and closes as if he's going to say something, but then stops himself. He scoots closer to me and pulls me to sit in his lap. "I'm sorry."

"Why are you sorry? It's Bel who should be sorry." I lean back to look him in the eyes.

He swallows. "You don't blame me for running her off?"

"What? Of course not. Everything that has happened is all on her and Jerry or James, whatever the hell his name is."

"Really?"

"Really." And I mean every word. Everything that has happened is all on Bel. "I think she was my best friend, but I wasn't hers. Does that make sense?"

He nods. "Yeah, it does."

"Are you okay?" I ask him. Bel had turned his life upside down, only to leave when things got tough.

"I'm not sure," he says honestly. "I'll let you know when I figure it out."

"Thank you." I brush my lips against his. "It hurts."

"I know it does." He holds me closer, tucking my head under his chin.

He doesn't try to fix it or tell me how much she sucks. He just holds me while I cry, supporting me through my pain. And I love him for it.

Chapter Thirty-Nine

It's been one week since Bel and Jerry/James skipped town, and tonight is the night we plan to spill the beans to everyone, and by everyone, I mean my brother, Viv, Sutton, Cooper, and Brenden.

Our ragtag scheming gang, as well as my parents and my favorite niece, Ev, are all gathered in the backyard of Bren and Griff's childhood home. In the morning, the sale on the house closes. So we are having a farewell party of sorts. A celebration of all the love that was shared here one last time. The men all congregate around the grill, arms folded and wearing serious expressions as if they are performing brain surgery and not flipping some meat. Lying in the grass a few feet away, Sutton blows raspberries on Ev's tummy, to her absolute delight, causing baby giggles to fill the yard.

Inside the house, Vivian is making her now-Fisher famous margaritas for us all. My mom carries two bowls of food across the yard, placing them on one of the foldable tables we brought. She places her hands on her hips, examining the food placement, before moving things around with a triumphant nod.

Our relationship hasn't been bad since I quit the family business, but it hasn't been great either.

She's still been standoffish anytime I mention Forever Floral, which hurts, but I remember her doing the same thing to Nate when he pursued his passion.

That doesn't mean it doesn't hurt to not have her blessing.

She spins, finding me staring at her, and smiles as she moves to my side, where I'm tidying up some of the mess we've already made.

"Hey, Mom."

"Hey, baby girl." She pulls me into a quick hug before releasing me. We stand in silence for a moment before she says, "I'm sorry."

"For what?"

"Not supporting your dreams with Forever Floral immediately. For waiting this long to tell you how in awe I am of what you've done. The store—your products are amazing. I've gotten so many customers telling me how amazed they are by the work you are doing with preservation."

Tears clog my throat. "Thank you, Mom."

It's everything I wanted to hear. All I've wanted from her for months—hell, probably years—was to be seen and heard. And now that I've got it, I want to weep with tears of joy.

"And I'm sorry about Bel. I know how much she meant to you. Do you think she will be back?"

Rocking back on my feet, I say, "I don't know. I hope so. Our relationship will never be the same, but that doesn't mean I don't care for her, you know."

"You have always been such a loving girl with a big, tender heart."

"There is nothing wrong with seeing the best in everyone."

"No, there isn't." She pats my hand and walks away just as Griffin approaches.

"You okay, baby?" he asks, bending his knees so he's at eye level with me. "You look like you're about to cry."

"You're about to cry," I say defensively as a tear slides down my cheek.

"Do I need to beat your mom up? Because I will."

I wipe under my eyes with a laugh. "No, these are tears of joy."

"Oh, thank God." He straightens, pulling me into his arms. "I was really nervous about fighting Delia."

"As you should be, she's a hair puller."

"Noted for future reference."

"I thought all you men folk were grilling?"

"We were, but the food is ready, so I came to escort my lady love to her seat."

He walks over to the foldable table circled with camping chairs and deposits me into a large purple one before making me a plate, then one for himself.

In a matter of minutes, the table is full and so are everyone's mouths as they stuff them with delicious kebabs.

Soon after we all finish eating, my parents leave, taking baby Ev for the night, while the rest of us congregate around the table with half-finished margaritas.

"Are you two ever going to woman up and share what happened with Belinda?" Sutton blurts out. Cooper slaps his hand over her mouth.

"I think what my lovely other half was trying to say was, inquiring minds would like to know."

Sutton yanks his hand down. "Nah, I meant you two are being little dicks by keeping us on the edge of our seats."

Nate raises a hand. "I second the tiny-dick comment."

"Hey, that's my man you're talking about." I point to Griffin with my thumb. "And he has a massive dick hiding in those pants."

Brenden scoffs. "Doubtful, or you guys would have told us everything by now."

Griffin's jaw drops. "Can we stop talking about my penis, please? And you"—he pokes his finger into his brother's chest—"know my dick is average."

I hold my hand up in shock. "Average? No, good sir. You have a hog hidden in there, and I'm going to prove it." I pull my phone from my back pocket and go straight to my pictures.

Griffin slaps my phone to the ground, shouting "No!" before I can pull up the dick pic I took last week that might have involved my feet.

To my surprise, everyone but Brenden frowns at him.

"Belinda was covering up the crime of her high school sweetheart faking his own death," Griffin admits when everyone begins to bitch and moan about the dick pic they missed out on.

"Wait, wasn't her high school sweetheart your dad?" Nate asks, pure confusion crumpling the doofus's faces.

"Yes," Griff answers while staring straight into Bren's eyes. Bren raises a brow, and Griffin's lips purse, the two of them having an entire silent conversation before us.

I relay everything to them, spilling the beans on who Jerry really was and how they had fled, running off into the sunset together.

Jaws are on the floor by the time I'm finished.

"Griff, can I talk to you in the kitchen, please?" Bren asks, already walking away. Griffin squeezes my hand, then gets up to follow. Ignoring all the questions being shouted across the table at me, I watch the two of them stand face-to-face and have what looks like a very intense conversation.

After a few seconds of them giving micro-expressions to each other, Bren's shoulders sag in relief. And I know Griffin has soothed his brother's worries about having to keep this secret.

"So, she just left without a word?" Nate asks, his jaw grinding back and forth with irritation.

I lift my hand to give him a sort-of gesture. "She sent a text, and she signed over her share of the business to me."

"What?" Cooper coughs, chips and guac flying out of his mouth and hitting Nate in the face.

Nate flicks away the soggy tortilla chip from his cheek with a glare.

"Yep, I'm the sole owner of Forever Floral now. Yay." I lift my fists in a sad victory.

It's not a bad thing. At least I don't think it will be. I was already handling the majority of the store's business and creative sides my-self. It just means I'm officially alone in this journey. There is no one to cover the store if I need to leave. To lead classes while I preserve bouquets for brides.

"Are you okay?" Viv asks.

"Eh." I shrug. "I just kind of always thought I would have help. And now I'm going to have to figure everything out for myself."

"You're not alone," Sutton says, standing from her chair as if she's about to make a loud declaration. "You have me."

"And me," Vivian says, joining her in an awkward power-pose stance.

"Us too," Nate and Cooper say, joining them.

"What in *the Fellowship of the Ring* of idiots is going on here?" Griffin asks as he and Bren gape at us from the stairs.

"They all just offered to help me on my quest of solo ownership of Forever Floral. Isn't that sweet?"

"Well, clearly, you can add us to the group." Bren gestures at him and Griffin.

My heart practically doubles in size at the amount of love I feel from their offers to be there for me. It makes me realize how wrong I was before. I used to assume that all I had was Bel. That she was my person. My ride or die. Now I see I was wrong. Nate, Vivian, Cooper, and Sutton have been here for years. I was just too dumb to see it. And now I have Griffin and Brenden too.

For the first time since I got that damn envelope, I feel lighter. Like I can do this. This group, this family we've created, won't walk away or let me down.

We spend hours pouring drinks and discussing the utter shock and awe of the secret and length Bel and Jerry/James went through to keep the truth buried. As well as who is going to help what days this week in the store.

It's almost midnight by the time we all sober up and finish cleaning up the last remnants of our BBQ.

Sutton, Cooper, Nate, and Viv all hop into Nate's truck, waving goodbye as they pull away.

"Thank you. For tonight." Brenden's voice cracks as he stares up at the big, empty house that, in a few hours, will no longer be theirs.

Griff nods, clearing his throat. "I think Mom and Dad would have really loved this send-off for the house."

Even though I didn't know their parents, I have to agree.

The two men wrap their arms around each other's shoulders and take one last moment to admire the home that helped raise them.

Bren pats Griffin on the back. "Love you, man."

"Love you too," Griffin says, giving him a hug. We watch Bren pull away, then walk back to the porch to sit on the stairs.

"How do you feel?" I ask, scared that his world might be falling apart while mine feels like it's coming together.

"Is it wrong to say relieved?"

"Not at all. You've been through so much over the past few months. Letting go of this house is just another stop in your journey to healing."

"I'm ready to move on. Ready to let go of the past and live for the future. A future with you."

Swoon. This man knows how to make my knees weak with love.

I angle my face upward, pressing a kiss to his lips. "I'm ready for that too."

"I love you, Audra."

"I love you too, Griffin."

"You know I'm not mad at her anymore."

"Who?"

"My mom. She sent Belinda into my life so Brenden and I would have someone other than just each other. So we would have a family. And in a twisted sort of way, she succeeded. She brought you into my life."

"Awe, Griff, you're going to make me cry."

"You are the best thing to ever happen to me, and I will forever be grateful to both my mom and Belinda for setting you in my path."

"And there go the waterworks." I laugh as tears stream down my cheeks.

He kisses me one more time on the steps, and I say a silent thank-you to Leslie for being such a badass and blackmailing my best friend, because she brought me to him. The love of my life. My future. My home.

Chapter Forty

Six months later

Trees and snow are the only things visible for mile after mile. I've tried to keep my curiosity at bay as long as possible, but my patience and willpower are running low, along with the room in my bladder.

"Can you please, please, please tell me where we are going?" I steeple my hands together as I beg Griffin for the first time.

Okay, not the first time, but the first time this hour.

Okay, fine. The first time in the past thirty minutes.

"Nope." A tinge of annoyance colors his voice, but his body shows zero signs of tension. In fact, his muscles are looking a little too relaxed in that tight, long-sleeved shirt that hugs his body oh so perfectly.

I glare at it, realizing it's my favorite shirt of his. It's one of the first ones I ever saw him in. He knows I'm a sucker for it. And don't get me started on how the man has a backward baseball cap on, making the ends of his hair curl at the nape of his neck in the most delicious way.

"Are you trying to seduce me?" Because it's working. Watching his forearms flex as he turns the wheel has my skin heating.

He glances toward me, wagging his eyebrows. "That was not the plan, but it's a pleasant bonus."

"Ugh," I whine, crossing my arms over my chest. "Then what in the seven circles of hell are you up to?"

"Patience, my love, and all will be clear soon." Griff pats my thigh as I huff my annoyance.

"This annoyingness better be worth it."

"It will be. I promise."

Two hours later, the sun has set, and I'm dozing off when Griffin gently calls my name.

"We're here."

I open my eyes to find the cab light on and my passenger door open. Griffin has my suitcase in one hand and his duffle bag slung over a shoulder as he holds out a hand for me to take.

As he helps me out of the Tahoe, I finally see our destination.

Upside-down pineapples are scattered around the yard, and small pineapple string lights illuminate the path to the gazebo on the side of the massive house.

"Oh my God, you brought me to the swingers' shack of sin."

"Shack of sin feels very judgmental but also correct." He snorts, nudging me with his shoulder before walking ahead of me.

Griffin holds the door open, and it's like a blast from the past. Everything is just as I remember it—even pervy Mr. Front Desk with the slicked-back hair. What was his name again?

Tucker?

Taylor?

Talen?

Screw it, it doesn't matter. He will always be pervy Mr. Front Desk to me.

He smiles as we place our bags down before the counter. "Back for a second year in a row."

Griffin grunts as he reaches into his back pocket for his wallet.

"I'm surprised you remembered us," I offer with a polite smile.

"Like I could forget two newbies."

Griffin side-eyes me as he slides his credit card across the desk.

"Do you guys hold many open-minded themed weekends like this?" I ask, rocking back on my heels.

"Sounds like someone has caught the pleasure-seeking bug and can't get enough." He licks his lips before taking Griffin's card.

Griffin steps in front of me, blocking the creep's view. But I'm not so sure that he minds.

"Your room, as requested." He hands the key and card to Griffin, who takes them both without a word. "I hope to see you both at tonight's festivities."

He hands the key to me as he slips his card back into his wallet before grabbing our bags. With one hand on my lower back, he leads me away from the front desk and up the stairs.

Griffin stops me at the same room we shared last year. The first time we shared a bed.

He tilts his head to the door.

"You got us the same room? Griff, this is so romantic." The shock and awe must be written all over my face, because he smiles and leans down to kiss me.

"Happy anniversary, Audra," he says against my lips.

"Happy anniversary, Griff."

Unlocking the door, we find the grandmother floral theme hasn't changed a bit in the last year, every doily still in the same place.

I flop back onto the bed. "Drop the bags and ravage me already, lover boy."

Our bags clunk against the hardwood floors as he throws them down and pounces on top of me.

Laughter fills the room as he rubs his face into the crook of my neck.

"Stop, Griff, or I'm going to pee. And we both know if we have to call downstairs for more sheets because of piss in the bed, that creep is going to assume we like water sports, and things are bound to get disturbingly messy from there."

At that, he rolls off me onto his back, dragging me on top of him. "Can the ravaging wait until later?"

"Did you have something else in mind?"

"Actually, I was thinking we could go downstairs—"

I slap my hand over his mouth. "If you are about to offer that we join in on the swinging, I fear you have greatly misunderstood our relationship and my insane jealousy."

His tongue darts out to lick my hand, but I keep it in place as he glares.

"I swear, Griffin, I will chop your balls off and give them to this fine establishment to use as a bell above their door if you tell me you even thought about sleeping with another woman."

He pushes up to a sitting position, forcing me to brace my arms on his shoulders. Looking into my eyes, he says, "Audra, I'd rather have my balls chopped off than ever touch another woman. And I'd rather have them used as a door chime than have you fuck another man for funsies."

"Okay, so what was your grand plan, then, mister monogamous?"

He grins. "I thought we could go down there and see how many of them proposition us and how many free drinks we can score."

I light up, clapping my hands together with excitement. "Oh, I love being hit on."

"I'm well aware."

He knows me so well, it's crazy. We are a perfect match in that way. Always finding ways to show the other that we love them and listen to them. It's moments like these that make me so happy I took the risk of embarking on a crazy quest with a stranger.

Neither of us bother to change into anything more appealing, instead sticking with our wrinkled sweats we've been wearing for a day of driving. It just means it will be an even bigger compliment when someone chooses us to be their swinging partners. Not that we would ever, but the thought is very flattering.

The bar is packed, and I mean bodies writhing everywhere. It takes a solid ten minutes to find an opening at the counter to order drinks.

"There is no way they all have rooms here tonight," I say, attempting to count the number of people in the room without success.

"I don't think it's one couple to a room." Griffin scoots closer to me as the couple next to him moans in unison.

"Do you think there will be an orgy?" I ponder, unsure how many it takes to count as an orgy, but it must be four or more... maybe. I'm going to have to google that when we get back to the room.

"Oh, honey, there are going to be two orgies tonight. One in Paul and Francine's room on the second floor. And the other taking place right where we are standing in a few more hours after all the less adventurous couples sneak off," a gorgeous blond woman next to us supplies.

"That has to be a health code violation." Griffin's nose scrunches.

"Don't worry, sugar, we might get dirty, but we sure know how to clean up after ourselves." She drags her tongue along the top row of her teeth as she assesses him.

To his credit, Griffin stands there giving her nothing. No disgust or interest shows on his face. Zero expression as she leans into him. "No nonsense, I see. I like a good spanking when I'm naughty."

"Oh boy, does she," the bartender says, as he stops in front of us. "What will it be, folks? Maybe a slippery nipple or sex on the beach?"

The woman speaks up just as I open my mouth. "Get them my favorite, Hal, on me."

He nods. "Two screaming orgasms, coming right up."

We both thank her for the drinks just as she slips away into the crowd, calling back at us, "Come find me later if you want more than just the drink."

Two milky-looking drinks are placed in front of us with a wink from Hal. "Just so you both know, I already have two other drinks ordered for the both of you from the two gentlemen at the far end of the bar."

We look down toward where he nods to find two distinguished men raising their glasses at us.

I raise my own at them before taking a sip. "Oh, hot damn, this is good."

Glancing at Griff, I find his glass almost empty. "I hope they also ordered us screaming orgasms, because I'm dying for another."

It turns out they did not. Instead, we received two blow jobs and two leg spreaders. We're on our fourth drink and seventh proposition when we decide to call it a night.

Walking hand in hand, we silently watch other couples go at it.

"Does this make us voyeurs?" Griffin asks when we stop in our tracks as three people undress not ten feet in front of us.

My skin prickles with an uncomfortable heat that I only want Griffin to soothe as the three of them engage in acts that should not be performed in an open bar.

"Eh, I wouldn't give it a hard yes or no."

"Fair," he says, his words slurred enough that I know the special celebration drinks we had are hitting him just right.

Ever since Griff started therapy, and especially after he learned the truth about Bel and James, he's watched his alcohol intake. Not drinking on weeknights, and only ever indulging whenever he knows we have a safe place to stay or a way home. It's understandable, and I've adopted some of those habits too. Well, except on Margarita Monday—my weekly tradition with Vivian and Sutton, where we bitch about how Mondays should be outlawed.

With the alcohol filling my belly and veins, I'm feeling a little reckless as I push Griffin into a wall and attack his face with my lips. I nip, suck, and lick every inch of lips, cheeks, and down his neck. His thick erection pushes against me as his hands find my waist, dragging my body against his until we are forced to break apart by the throat clearing beside us.

"May I cut in?" an attractive woman with honey-blond hair asks.

Griffin straightens and smiles down at me. "Sorry, I'm a one-woman man tonight."

The woman drops her gaze to mine. "I was actually asking about her."

I sputter out a laugh at the way his eyes narrow on her and how his arm wraps a little tighter around my waist.

"Flattered. I really am, but I'm giving this one all my attention tonight."

The woman's lips pull into a pout for a quick moment before a seductive smile replaces it. "Maybe tomorrow night, then."

I swallow. "Yeah, maybe."

She brushes her hands across my arm as she passes by us.

"Holy shit, my woman is so damn irresistible. Everyone wants a piece of you, baby."

"But I'm only for you."

"Mine," he says, leaning forward to capture my lips in a kiss that is anything but PG as he squeezes my ass. "Come on, let's get back to our room before we attract another willing participant."

By the time we get up to the room, my body aches for him.

I flip the lock on the door, and in seconds, we are tearing off each other's clothes with a sense of urgency that feels like if he doesn't get inside me in the next few seconds, I might die.

Griffin must feel the same way because he lifts me, pressing my back against the cool wood, and slams into me. I feel like I might explode from the first thrust.

Moaning and panting fills the air as Griffin drives himself in and out of me in a punishing pace that is sure to have us both crossing that finish line in mere minutes.

"Play with that perfect clit for me," he demands, staring down at where we are connected.

I follow his order immediately, swiping quick circles over the sensitive spot until I shatter into a million pieces.

Seconds later, Griffin groans, his head dipping to the nape of my neck as he spills himself inside me.

He lifts his head to kiss me. It's a lazy kiss full of love. And just when I think it might be the start of round two, screams of pleasure echo from the hallway.

"You would think that might be a turn-on, but just knowing randos are fucking all around us kind of has my dick deflating." He laughs, pushing my sweaty hair out of my face.

"Same, man, the vagina would be a dry desert if it weren't for you watering it just a few minutes ago."

"What do you say to a bath?"

"Followed by sleep?"

He nods.

"Sounds perfect." I disengage myself from his body, and we stroll into the bathroom with a tub that isn't meant for two, but we make it work.

In the morning, we have breakfast in bed before hitting the road to his next stop on our anniversary getaway.

I'm not at all surprised when Griffin pulls up to the coziest place in the north. But that doesn't make it any less exciting. Once again, he manages to get us into the same cabin as we had last year. Every part of this trip was planned out perfectly. The perfect walk down a romantic memory lane.

After dinner at the main lodge, Griffin orders champagne to our cabin. He pops the cork, and bubbly liquid shoots from the bottle, spilling on the counter. I wipe up the mess as Griffin pours us each a glass before we sit outside on a bench with a flawless view of the night sky.

The chilled night air nips at my face, but I don't care as I stare in awe at the natural phenomena lighting up the darkness with its beautiful colors. "Griffin, I think it's even more amazing seeing it the second time around."

"A truly stunning sight."

I can't help but smile in agreement. This entire trip has been spectacular. The most romantic thing he could have ever done.

Griffin's warm hand tugs mine, turning me to face him. "Audra, I've loved you since our first trip here. I think even then, I knew you were the one for me."

"It was the deep-throating skills, wasn't it?" I ask as I stare into his bright, shining eyes.

"It didn't hurt. But no, it was your steadfast loyalty, your kind heart, and your ability to make the best out of a shitty situation. You've kept me in awe this entire time we've been together. You're the light on my dark night. I love you more than words could ever express, but I hope that this will convey the seriousness and depth of it."

With a speech like that, he is definitely getting a repeat of said throat skills.

I don't know what I did to deserve this romantic, loving man, but God, am I glad he's mine.

With shaking hands, he reaches into his coat pocket and produces a small box.

My heart skips a beat, and I gasp, covering my mouth. "Griff, is that what I think it is?"

"Open it up and find out."

With the box still in his hand, I flip the lid open to reveal a beautiful oval-cut diamond ring. My hands tremble as I touch the gorgeous gem. "Really?" I ask, tears filling my eyes.

"Really," he replies with a watery laugh. "Audra, I want to marry you. I want to be tied to you in every way imaginable."

"I want that too."

"Good." He kisses me once, twice, and a third time before taking the ring out of the box and slipping it on my finger.

Engaged. Griffin and I are going to get married, and I already know the perfect place to celebrate our love.

Epilogue

Audra

Two years later

I reach over to find Griffin's side of the bed cold and empty. Sitting up, I climb out of my blanket burrito and rub my eyes. I hate waking up without him. And lately, it's been happening more and more.

The coolness of the hardwood beneath my feet sends a chill through my bones that has me wide awake as I walk to where I know I will find him.

I stop at the open door at the end of the hallway, watching Griffin's big body sway back and forth, side to side, in the soft glow of the lamplight. His arms are full with a light-pink blanket as he holds our daughter, Reese, while she sleeps.

The man has been rocking her to sleep for the past month since she was born. It should be normal now. I should be used to this, to watching him hold our baby.

But the warmth and joy that fills me every time is something I hope I never get used to. And the love that washes over me just from seeing his love for her is more than I ever thought possible.

When we exchanged our vows a year ago at the place where it all started, the coziest place in the north, I never would've expected that anything could make me love him more.

He's faced his fears. Even accepting Belinda into his life, sort of. It's been easier since she and Jerry/James ran back to Mexico. We all talk on the phone every few weeks. I've even caught Griffin asking both her and Jerry questions about their days. It's a win in my book.

It hasn't been easy, any of it. But neither of us cared, as long as we were together.

He hugs Reese tighter to his chest, and my vagina practically sighs.

The man is a total DILF.

Like, I almost want to throw caution to the wind and mount him like the stud he is before my doctor gives the okay... Almost.

I won't. But God, is he temping.

Not that Griff would ever allow it.

On top of being the best father, the man is the perfect partner. He takes care of me like no other. From ensuring that I'm sleeping and eating enough to taking on more of the household duties that we used to split fifty-fifty.

He's the husband of every woman's dreams.

And damn, am I glad that I get to call him mine.

Neither of us expected to add on to our family as soon as we did. Hell, we thought we had years before we were even going to consider kids. But the moment that test came back positive, we knew it was meant to be, and we wouldn't change a thing. Even if the timing wasn't ideal.

Forever Floral just celebrated its three-year anniversary by officially partnering with Fisher Floral to add bouquet preservation to their floral packages. It's been an on-and-off-again battle to make my mother understand that I wasn't abandoning the family business. That neither of her children had abandoned her and my father's dreams. That we just wanted to add more. To have something that was mine but that could add to her wishes and goals.

I lean against the doorframe. A small smile plays at my lips as he whispers "Daddy loves you" to her repeatedly.

"You can put her down now," I say in a hushed tone, walking into the room. The lavender walls sparkle as Griff presses the projector, letting twinkling music notes appear everywhere around us.

It's peaceful and breathtaking. But that unfortunately makes it all the harder to get him to leave the room.

Don't get me wrong, I'm beyond grateful to have a smoking-hot husband who takes his role as a father seriously, taking part in night feedings and diaper changing no matter how tired he is. Most would give their left boob for a man like him. I know I'm lucky. Nothing could ever make me think differently.

He shakes his head, smirking at me with his tired eyes and clean-shaven face. He has been meticulous about shaving ever since Reese was born, never wanting to scratch her while holding her close to him. "Nah, she's still awake."

"Baby, she's out." I lift her tiny hand without causing her to flinch, pressing a kiss to each of her tiny fingers. "Put her down, you need sleep."

"I'll sleep later. You go back to bed."

"No, I refuse to sleep without you." It was the same thing every night. Griff would let me sleep all night every night if he could. But not on my watch. He deserves for someone to look after him as he wears himself to the bone being the best damn dad and husband possible.

His head tilts to the side and a sleepy smile forms on his lips. "Fine. But if she wakes up, it's your fault."

"It's a risk I'm willing to take." I lean down, inhaling her precious baby scent. "Sweet dreams, baby girl."

I wait until Griffin places her back in her crib before grabbing a hold of his hand and dragging him back to our bed. We have about three hours, if we're lucky, before she will be wailing, and I plan on ensuring that we both use the time appropriately.

There will be no middle-of-the-night talks or secret spilling. There sure as shit won't be any sex happening. Even if my body was ready, the exhaustion wouldn't allow it.

The only thing we need to be doing is sleeping.

Rest has become such a rarity that I refuse to waste any opportunity for it.

I pull the soft gray duvet until it covers everything but our heads as I snuggle into him, wrapping my legs in his and my arm around his stomach.

I sigh at his warmth, thankful for my heater of a man on chilly nights like this.

He pulls me even closer to him, running his hands through my hair as I kiss his chest before closing my eyes.

"I love you, Audra," he whispers into my hair.

I melt into him. "I love you too," I murmur, letting myself drift off to sleep, excited to wake up to my two loves again.

Acknowledgements

We've done it again. Whew.

Truths and Lies was such a fun and emotional book to write and truly hope it comes across that way to everyone who reads it.

Special thanks to Twilight. I wish I knew how to quit you.

Brooklynn- My editor extraordinaire, thanks for putting up with my continuous use of the wrong tense and my use of some foot action. I promise to never do it again...maybe. Who knows when some foot hanky-panky might be necessary. It's a promise I cannot guarantee. But I will try. I can't wait to get to work on the next one with you. Your kind/funny comments always make my day!

To my bestie, Tori, thanks for watching my millions of videos of me complaining over and over again about this book. Be prepared to be overwhelmed with new videos and frustrations with the next one.

To my amazing co-workers, you guys are so supportive, and I am forever grateful for that. Also thank for not opening judging me for acting out a certain foot gesture. *Haley, I promise to write a secret nod to you in the next one*

Soy Sauce, thanks for supporting me all the time and thanks for keeping your nosy eyes off of my computer while I write highly inapacopriate stuff that you can't read for many, many, many more years to come. And sorry, not sorry, I won't be writing a book about you romancing the KarJenner clan.

Rae thank you for taking on a nervous, antisocial authors ARC management. You have been so kind and helpful I cannot thank you enough for making this process easier.

Jess @booksarebetterjess and Cassie @cassiecreative_ you both are amazing! Thank you so much for creating amazing graphics so my brain wouldn't explode from staring into the dark pit of despair that is Canva.

And to my ARC readers. Thank you sooooo much. It means so much that you go out of your way to read my books. I'm giving each one you a warm hug through the page.

Lastly, thank you, thank you, thank you to everyone who read this book. You are helping a slightly delusional woman follow her dreams. It means the world to me.

Dick-tionary

To find or skip the spice.

About Author

Registered Nurse by day romance writer by night. Bretta dreamed of becoming a writer since she was a little girl but finally wrote her first novel during the pandemic-imposed social isolation.

A self-proclaimed triple threat, Bretta loves to read smutty books and has an unabashed addiction to Coca-Cola. When she's not writing or caring for patients, you can find her daydreaming about her next book, making sarcastic comments, or being a mediocre crafter. She lives in Oklahoma with her hot mess son and a few furry babies.

www.ingramcontent.com/pod-product-compliance
Lightning Source LLC
Chambersburg PA
CBHW020226010826
48973CB00006B/1399